COPYRIGHT

DEDICATION

To those who supported me to make this journey possible. You know who you are, and those who stood in the way? Have fun watching from the sidelines.

Special shout out to m good friend and fellow author, Melinda Harris, who spent tons of time away from her Big Girl Job to help me in my struggle to make Killer perfect.

QUOTES

I'm not sure what I am. I just know there's something dark in me. I hide it. I certainly don't talk about it, but it's there always, this Dark Passenger. And when he's driving, I feel alive, half sick with the thrill of complete wrongness. I don't fight him, I don't want to. He's all I've got. Nothing else could love me, not even... especially not me.

Or is that just a lie the Dark Passenger tells me? Because lately there are these moments when I feel connected to something else... someone. It's like the mask is slipping and things... people... who never mattered before are suddenly starting to matter. It scares the hell out of me.

—Dexter Morgan (Jeff Lindsay) *Darkly Dreaming Dexter*

We often allow guilt to consume us but we must realize that we can start over.

—Unknown

We'd stared into the face of Death, and Death blinked first. You'd think that would make us feel brave and invincible. It didn't.

—Rick Yancey

CHAPTER 1

Keller

Have you ever wished for death? Hoped it would strike you down and end your pathetic existence? No? I have. I've thought of a hundred different ways I should die. None of them are painful enough for what I deserve, so I continue to live.

"Come on, guys! Quit being a bunch of pussies! I can't believe I had to twist your damn arms to get you to skip school." I push my key fob and unlock the doors to my brand new Shelby GT500 convertible. Slinging my arm around Rory Vanderbilt, my current girlfriend—for the weekend at least—I razz my friends.

"We're here, aren't we, Keating?"

Craning my neck, I peek over my shoulder at Logan Sanders, one of the guys in the group I run with. Me, Logan, and our other pal Silas rule our exclusive private school. Whatever we do or say is accepted as cool, no questions asked. Now we've started our senior year, and pretty much everyone at North Atlanta Prep treats us like we're gods.

I laugh. "Surprisingly, you *are* here, Logan. But the question is, are we going to have fun?"

Rory slides her hand around my waist and down over my ass, squeezing. "We're going to have fun, Keller," she whispers in my ear right before she sticks her tongue inside.

"Fuck yeah we are."

Rory climbs into the passenger side of the Shelby, and I shut her door. She winds her hands around my neck and yanks me down for a hot, wet kiss through the open convertible top.

"Go Keating!"

"Woo-hoo!"

Smiling, I walk around the car to the driver's side and slide in. It's a gorgeous September day in Atlanta, so I left the top down. North Prep is so elite, the students so wealthy, I never worry about leaving the car open. There's nothing to steal that everyone here doesn't already own for themselves.

Logan, Silas, and two girls climb into Logan's Range Rover, giggling and shouting while I rev the Shelby's powerful engine. Rory slips her hand up my thigh, letting her fingers trail over my hardening cock.

I flip down my sunglasses and grin. Fuck it's good to be me.

* * *

"I'm gonna go back out by the pool." I climb out of the bed in Logan's guest room and pull on my shorts.

"M'kay, Keller," Rory murmurs as she falls asleep.

I laugh to myself, glancing back at Rory's naked body before leaving the room. I fucked her good. The bright red handprints across her perky ass stand out against her tan skin.

"Grab a beer, Keating!" Logan shouts from across the huge patio in his backyard.

I walk over to his outdoor kitchen and swipe a bottle from the fridge. Silas is in the pool with the two girls they brought, getting all handsy and grabbing their tits. The girls squeal, pretending to be offended, but come on, if they're going to swim topless, guys are gonna grab. Logan is watching our friend fondle his date with a heated intensity in his eyes. Logan and Silas have been known to share girls, so I know Logan's not pissed or anything. Hell, to them this is probably just foreplay before their girl-swapping orgy.

I flip off the cap and collapse into the chair next to Logan's. "How long are your parents out of town, Sanders?"

Logan takes a long swig of his beer while I wait. "Let me think." His blond eyebrows rise as he counts in his head. "Today's the fourteenth, and they're coming back on the twentieth, so six more days."

"Cool." I nod. Logan's parents are never home. They're both big time movie producers. A lot of their stuff is filmed right here in Atlanta, but tons of their movies are done in other states or countries, or lots of times his parents are in LA for meetings and shit.

"I wish my mom and dad would take a fucking vacation," I grumble, picking at the soggy label on my beer. My own parents are the exact opposite of Logan's. First, if my mom and dad worked together, they'd have killed each other by now. They fight *a lot*. About stupid shit, like my dad working too much or my mom's drinking or prescription drug use, or the other doped-up, rich bitches my mom hangs out with.

"Yeah, well, if your dad ever sells his company, he'll have plenty of time to do whatever the fuck he wants. And plenty of money," Logan points out. He holds his bottle up for a toast. I tap mine against his with a clink and roll my eyes.

"The old man's talked about selling. Some crap about missing our entire childhood and wanting to make up for lost time. Screw him. He's too fucking late. I'm eighteen in two months."

"Your sister is still young. What is she, fourteen?"

I nod. "Yeah, she's a freshman this year."

"So… maybe he'll at least put some effort in and show up in her life before she graduates," Logan says. He puts his empty bottle on the ground. "It's hot as hell out here and there's naked chicks ten feet away. I'm going in." Logan stands up, shedding his shirt and shorts before doing a cannonball into the pool wearing only his briefs.

The girls screech in delight and Silas laughs his ass off. I'm buzzing from the satisfying filthy, rough sex with Rory and the multiple beers. I finish the one in my hand and grab another, downing half of the cold drink before stopping to take a breath.

That would be the day my dad would ever stop working. I'd bet everything in my enormous trust fund he'll eventually drop dead of stress or old age while sitting at his desk. Dad's company is his life. My dad started and runs Hybrid Technologies, one of the largest software companies in the world. My mom, my sister, me… we always come second to Hybrid.

Six beers later, I wake up to Rory's hot mouth around my dick. I squint in the bright sunlight. The pool is empty, which means Logan and Silas went in the house with their girls. My mouth is dry and I would love a drink of water, but there's no way I'm going to stop a blow job. Instead, I lie back and let Rory work her magic mouth up and down my cock.

Britton

Have you ever looked death in the eye? Felt the icy chill of it crawling over your skin until you taste it? No? I have, and sometimes I think death would be preferable to living with that knowledge. Thankfully, I can't remember.

I glance at the clock… again. Ugh! Only two minutes have passed since the last time I checked. Today is the slowest day in the history of school. It's as if time stopped and is on a constant loop of the most boring ten minutes in the history of my existence. When the bell finally rings, I waste no time leaping from my chair and darting for the hall.

"Britt! Wait!"

Darn it!

My best friend, Reece, catches me the second I my shoe hits the ground. Whatever, I'm in too much of a hurry to stop and talk, so I continue down the hall. If she has something to say, she can do it while I head to my locker to get my stuff.

"What is your hurry, Britt? Pants on fire or something?" she huffs, increasing her pace to keep up with me.

I dodge the other students, all of whom are eager to start the weekend. It takes forever to weave through them to get to my locker all the way on the opposite side of the school.

My face heats up and I duck my head to keep Reece from seeing. "Nothing. I, uh, just really need to get home on time today. No big deal." My casual shrug ends up more like a stilted jerk of my head.

Reece's hand darts out, gripping my upper arm, yanking me to a stop. "Hold up, Britton. I want to talk about tonight. Are you coming out with us?"

I'm so frustrated I want to scream. Friday is the only day of the week I get my fill of my favorite eye candy. Those few, meager minutes have to last seven whole days before I get another hit. And now my, used-to-be best friend is going to make me miss my weekly dose.

Agitated, I agree to going out later so she'll let me go. "Call me, okay? I'll talk to my mom about getting dropped off at your house."

Reece grins and gives me a hug. "See? I'm easy? All you needed to do was say yes!" She releases me and flounces down the hall, flipping her long hair over her shoulder. As I stuff my books in my locker and grab my bag, Reece turns around, walking backwards as she calls out, "Don't forget, Britton!"

I can't help but laugh at my friend. Spunky, redheaded, and gorgeous, Reece Fielding and I have been inseparable since the second grade. Our dads are both executives at the same Fortune 500 company in Atlanta, so we've known each other practically forever.

I pull my phone out of my bag and check the time. *Shoot!* With a gasp, I hustle out the front door of the school, down the steps. If I'm really lucky, Keller will still be in the parking lot and I'll be able to get a glimpse of his perfect, gorgeous face before he hops in his car and leaves.

I snort behind my hand, holding back a giggle. A freshman crushing on a senior—a super hot, super popular senior. I'm a walking 80s movie cliché.

But the heart wants what the heart wants, and mine wants Keller Keating. Badly. I giggle again and this time, my cheeks burn as my mind wanders to my now familiar fantasy of Keller and me together, kissing as he pulls me into his strong arms. How ridiculous! Like that would ever happen.

As long as I only look, no harm can come of it. Besides, Keller Keating would never notice a girl like me. I'm not ugly by a long shot, but I'm no supermodel. The girls I see Keller leave with every Friday since school started three weeks ago are taller, thinner, and older than me. In other words, they're women, whereas I'm stuck in half-girl, half-woman territory. Not exactly Keller Keating girlfriend material.

My feet hit the pavement and I whirl around, scanning the remaining cars. Already, the lot is nearly empty. On Fridays, people clear out fast, staff and students alike, the administration usually the only ones left. I don't see Keller's very conspicuous blue sports car among the few vehicles left in front of the school and sag in disappointment. My bag slides off my shoulder to land on the ground with a thud.

"Damn," I mutter.

"Hey."

I startle at the unexpected voice. When I turn around, a girl I recognize from around school but have never actually met is standing about a foot away.

"Hey," I respond.

The girl squints, her perfect little nose wrinkling up as she shades the sun from her face with a hand. Her eyes immediately catch my attention. They're the most shocking shade of silver I've ever seen. *Literally* silver.

"You okay?" the girl asks. "Are you looking for someone?"

I stare at this unknown, silver-eyed girl. I've seen her here and there in the hallways since school started three weeks ago. I think we're both freshmen, but we don't run in the same circles and we're not in any of the same classes. North Atlanta Prep is exclusive, but not exactly small.

"Ummmm, my ride," I stammer, not wanting to admit I'm out here stalking a guy who doesn't even know I exist. "I'm waiting for my driver, I mean. He's not here."

Come to think of it, my ride *isn't* here yet. Where is he? Charlie is never late. I hope he's okay, though he's probably just stuck in hideous Atlanta traffic.

"My ride isn't here either," she says. "We can wait together."

Her face is so hopeful I can't say no. Besides, where am I going to go without a ride?

I sit on the steps next to her and pull out my phone. "I should call Charlie. Ummmm, my driver."

She nods, her dark ponytail bobbing behind her.

"Is there anyone you can call for you?" I ask.

The girl shrugs. "My brother was supposed to give me a ride. He probably forgot since I usually have cheerleading practice after school on Fridays. Our captain is going to some big gala tonight with her boyfriend so practice was cancelled." The girl rolls those intriguing eyes and her mouth curls into a mischievous smirk. "I don't mind though. I know he loves me. He's just a free spirit kind of guy." She shrugs, accepting the fact that her brother left her stranded.

My gaze drops to her cheerleading squad T-shirt, sporting the black and red colors of the school.

"Oh. Well…I'm sure my driver can give you a ride."

The girl smiles, two dimples framing her perfect teeth. "Thanks. I'm Kinsey." She holds out her hand.

Befuddled, I clasp my hand around hers. What ninth grader shakes hands? It's weird, but she's so genuine in her actions I can't help but smile back.

"I'm Britton."

Finger swiping on my phone, I pull up my contacts and scroll through for Charlie's number. While I'm searching, the loud squeal of tires on the driveway leading up to the school catches my attention. Along with the noise, the acrid scent of burnt rubber stings my nostrils. I glance up from my phone to watch as a black car fishtails into the parking lot, swinging widely to the left and screeching to a stop about a hundred yards away.

"Who's that?" Kinsey asks.

I squint to block out the bright September sun. "No clue, but he probably shouldn't be behind the wheel if that's how he drives." We watch as the driver's door of the car is thrown open and a tall boy a few years older than us steps out. Despite the oppressive Atlanta heat, a chill goes down my spine. Something is very, very wrong.

"Britton," Kinsey whispers, her voice shaking.

My eyes scan the boy, trying to make sense of what's happening, to piece together the images, but my mind can't rationalize what it sees—simply can't process the horror. Fear chokes me, tightening around my throat, squeezing the air from my lungs. Kinsey tugs on my sleeve, but I'm frozen. Unable to move.

Too late, the pieces begin to drop into place—camouflage, greasepaint on his face, and guns…lots of them, in the boy's hands and hanging from straps on his arms. Everything around me slows to a stop as my heart thunders in my chest, reaching a pace so rapid, it can't possibly be sustainable. A bizarre lightheadedness separates my mind from my body, surely a protective instinct to keep my psyche from fracturing. It's as if I'm watching the scene play out as a casual observer. Life is merely a movie on a screen.

The boy circles around the car and raises a large, black weapon, lining it up with his eye—at us. Kinsey's voice breaks through the fog, hysterical and sobbing. "Britton, run!"

Kinsey grabs my hand, pulling me up the steps of the school. I twist my body to run, but not before locking eyes with the boy. They're dead, cold, shut down—the eyes of a killer. Adrenaline propels me up the stairs and through the doors, where we burst through into an empty hall.

"In here," Kinsey cries.

I follow her into the main office where only a few staff members remain. We dive under the long front counter just as popping sounds split the silence, cracking the air like fireworks.

Then the screaming begins.

Kinsey wraps her arms around me, using my shoulder to stifle her sobs. I hold her tight, clinging to the faint threads of reality as they loosen in front of me.

Will school be canceled Monday? I nearly laugh out loud at the thought. A single long thread works its way free.

More screams fill the small office. Another thread pulls loose, allowing more of my mind to slip away.

I cover my ears with my hands, vaguely aware of Kinsey clinging to me. The fabric of my world unravels to one single thought.

Survive.

I stare into her damp, silver eyes, seeing my own fear reflected back at me. And when black boots scuff across the floor and stop next to us, I know without a doubt I'm about to die.

Keller

My eyes are blurry as I attempt to focus. *Fuck*, my head is killing me. After rubbing the sleep from my eyes and adjusting to the dark room, I realize I'm in Logan's guest room with Rory sleeping next to me on one side, another naked girl I don't recognize on the other.

Despite the headache and general all-around shitty feeling, I smile. Yesterday was fucking epic. When word spread that Logan's parents were gone, a bunch of our friends showed up to party. And man, did we party.

I slide out of the bed without disturbing either of the girls and grab my shorts. After tugging them on, I use the bathroom and catch a glimpse of myself in the mirror. The satisfied look on my face is enough to bring a smile to my lips. I used both of those girls until my dick ran dry and I collapsed in exhaustion.

Wetting my hands, I run them through my dark, matted hair, letting it stick up randomly on top of my head. I make sure my keys are in my pocket and shove my shoes on my feet, headed for the front door. People are passed out all over the living room in different states of undress. I have to carefully step around them to get out of here.

The glow of the clock in the kitchen says 5:45 a.m. Fuck, it's earlier than I thought, but I don't want to be here when everyone wakes up. Listening to people bitch about hangovers and dealing with clingy girls are not my things. Fucking and fun? Those are my things. The next morning? Hell no.

I start my car and pull out of the driveway before lowering the top on the Shelby. Going slow so I don't get pulled over, I travel the deserted early morning streets of our affluent suburb at a leisurely pace. When I get home, I drive around back, turn the car off, and pull a joint out of my wallet. Lighting up the blunt, I sit back in my seat, taking several long drags. Chemical bliss floods my system, relaxing me enough to go inside and deal with my parents.

Fuck, I hate this house. The only thing that makes it worth coming home to every day is my sister Kinsey, and half the time, even knowing she's inside isn't enough to make me want to leave the safety of my car.

I pray my mom isn't already high, then giggle at the hypocrisy, pulling another long drag from the joint. Me having to get high in order to deal with my prescription drug abusing, alcoholic mother? I snort in sick, twisted delight.

Later, when I look back on this moment, I realize it sucked that I never saw the police car parked out front or noticed the thirty-seven missed calls on my phone. Maybe I wouldn't have smoked that joint. Maybe I would have been better prepared for the worst moment of my life. Maybe I wouldn't have laughed like a hyena when I found out I was a killer.

But that's exactly what I am.

CHAPTER 2

Killer

Darkness. And pain. Definitely pain. A dull, throbbing, nauseating pain that radiates from my head all the way down my entire body to my toes. A long, violent tremor shakes me, stripping away the last vestiges of unconsciousness and thrusting me into the horrors of being awake to live another day.

Fuck.

With one hand, I rub my sore head as I throw my feet over the edge of my bed. I use the other hand to snatch the bottle of whiskey off my nightstand, chugging down a few big gulps. Hair of the dog. I huff, unamused as I wipe my mouth with the back of my hand, wondering why they don't just call it what it is—the *need to go back to fucked-up oblivion.*

One more swallow and I cap the bottle, shoving it in my back pocket after tugging on a pair of jeans that have somehow become two sizes too big. Tired and groggy, I shuffle down the hall to the enormous kitchen that no one cooks in, my stomach protesting the lack of food by growling loudly. Even though I feel sick and the last thing I want to do is eat, I put a slice of bread in the toaster and wait.

The eerie silence of the massive mansion I call home sends chills down my spine. I fucking despise this house. It's a house of death, sinister and black, as if a dark shroud covers it from top to bottom. Every inch is filled with morbid ghosts of the past, threatening to tear free from the walls and smother me until I join them in the next life.

The pop of the toaster sends me two feet in the air. *Jesus, my head hurts.* I snag the piece of bread and eat it dry, each tasteless bite scraping its way down my throat to land in a lump at the bottom. Food is merely a necessity. I could care less what or even *if* I eat.

Bored, I wander to the back windows, staring at the glistening water of the pool and greenery of the lush lawn. Doesn't matter where I look, I'm not really seeing anything through my hazy vision.

Goddamn, the sun is bright. What time is it?

I remove my phone from my pocket and grunt. Two in the afternoon. Another wasted day, just like every other day in the six weeks since I killed Kinsey and my life disappeared along with her. My entire existence is a waste of fucking air and space.

The agony of overwhelming guilt punches my gut like a wrecking ball. It's so powerful I hunch over from the pain, clutching my stomach. My other hand reaches out blindly, gripping the window frame to keep from falling over. I claw at the edges, my nails digging into the wood to stay on my feet.

Fuck!

The pain is devastating. I squeeze my eyes shut, holding back the tears that burn behind my eyelids. It's my fucking fault she's dead. My beautiful little sister, gone because I'm a selfish asshole. I inhale a ragged breath, choking down the sob trying to wrack my body.

Once I get my sorry ass under control, I slowly stand up,

glancing one last time at the backyard and stop breathing.

Oh fuck no. She wouldn't. No, no, no…

In a panic, I dash into the great room, yanking at the patio doors. My hands are shaking so hard it takes several frustrating tries to unlock the latch and fling the doors open. Ignoring the loud crash of one of the windowpanes shattering from the impact, I dart outside only to trip on the paved stones and land hard on the uneven ground.

Shit! I scrabble to my feet, heedless of the blood dripping from my scraped palms, and dial 911.

Fully clothed, I jump into the pool and swim over to the lifeless form. When my arms go around her waist, I know I'm too late. But I still spend an agonizing twenty minutes administering CPR until one of the paramedics pulls me away.

Soaked through, I collapse on the ground and shiver. Violent convulsions wracking my body. It's fitting, how cold and numb my skin is, because that's exactly how I feel inside.

Britt

"Heel, toe. Heel, toe. Heel, toe. Wonderful, Britt! That's the most you've done without using the parallel bars."

I grin. The achievement seems small in the wide scope of things, but at one time was an impossibly huge hurdle for me to overcome.

"Thanks, Nina." My left foot wobbles. "Ummmm, I may need help getting back to the chair."

Nina laughs. "Sure." She hooks her arm around my waist. "I should make you go back on your own just to prove you can do it," she teases.

I fake a look of horror as she eases me down into my wheelchair. "You wouldn't!"

Nina smiles, her pretty face crinkling up with humor. "I would."

"Yeah, I know." Nina Petrov is my rehab specialist and she is my favorite person in the world. Only a few years out of school, Nina is spunky and fun, from the top of her sleek, dark bob to the soles of her neon athletic shoes.

"Friday, you're going to go the length of the room and back on your own, Britt. I hope you're ready." Nina points at me and grins.

"I'm ready, I swear."

No I'm not.

"All right, your ride is here. See you in a couple days?" Nina waves to my mom as she enters the huge room. Even with her haughty appearance, Mom manages to hide her disgust, gracefully dodging gym equipment and various patients doing exercises with their therapists to reach my tiny corner in the midst of chaos.

I don't get to answer Nina, because my mom barges in, inserting herself between the therapist and my chair.

"Britton. Ready to go? We have a meeting scheduled with the woman over at Students Speak—"

"Mom, I told you I'm not going," I snap, feeling petulant.

"Ummmm, another client is waiting on me, Britt." Nina turns to my mom. "Nice to see you, Mrs. Shelton-Reeves." I might love Nina, but right now I hate her. Nina knows my mom well enough to vacate the area when she goes on one of her rants, leaving me to deal with her alone.

"You too, Nina. Thank you." My mom's voice is tight and clipped. Once Nina is gone, Mom scowls. "I will not argue with you about this, Britton. Especially not in front of other people." Her voice is quiet, but laced with irritation.

I press my lips together, knowing if I say anything else right now, she'll push even harder. Mom wheels me out to the car, trying to coddle me into the front seat.

"I can do it!" I shake off her hand and ignore the hurt look on her face.

After "the incident," as it's called in my house, my mom went into full-blown overprotective mode. Helicopter parents have nothing on Rose Shelton-Reeves. Since I woke up from a coma six months ago, she has one goal and one goal only—to fix me up so she can turn me into a walking, talking billboard for school-related shootings.

Mom starts going on her usual diatribe as she pulls out of the lot at the Blake Atkins Center, the premiere brain injury and spinal cord rehab center in the Southeast. I spent four months here as an inpatient after having two surgeries, and now come three times a week for outpatient rehab.

I only catch bits and pieces of her monologue listing all of the good things I can do for students everywhere if I just act reasonably and do what she says.

"So, Britt, then we would go to schools and…"

I let her go on, pretending to listen. Whatever. She's on my left side, so I can't hear ninety percent of what she says. According to her it's *so* important for me to speak out about the shooting, even though I can't recall a single thing from that day or the weeks leading up to it. How ironic that my mom can't be bothered to remember a tiny little thing like the fact I lost all hearing in my left ear when a bullet tore through my skull.

"…and then we would travel… many states…"

I gaze out the window, rolling my eyes. All I want to do is move on, something my parents—my mother in particular—can't seem to do. I mean, yeah I feel bad for what my parents went through—a daughter shot at school, brain surgeries, rehab, homeschool—but I didn't ask Mom to quit her job to do all those things. She's the one who said I couldn't go back to regular school with all those "dangerous killers" out there.

More important, I don't *want* to remember the shooting. I'm glad I can't. I don't think I could live with the memories of that day. Mom either refuses to acknowledge my wishes or isn't listening, because the last thing I want to do is discuss the worst day of my life in front of students across the country over and over and over. I just want to be Britt again, not *Britton Reeves, school shooting victim and activist*.

Mom's hand touches my knee and I flinch. "Sorry honey, I was calling your name and you didn't hear me. We're here."

In front of us is the tall, gleaming glass high-rise where the offices of Students Against School Shootings are located. What a dumb name. Are any students *for* school shootings? A laugh escapes before I can squelch it.

I feel the heat of my mom's glare as she exits the car.

"Great," I murmur while Mom gets my chair out of the back of the SUV. Just how I wanted to spend my day.

Killer

"Maybe you've had enough, Kell."

I glare at Logan and hold up my hand to signal for another round of drinks.

"Maybe it's none of your fucking business," I snarl.

"Fuck, Kell. I never should have got you that fake ID. last year." Logan slouches back in the booth, crossing his arms over his chest. "In the eight months since the shooting, you've turned into a fucking drunk. Dropped out of school to do what? Feel sorry for yourself all day?"

The waitress places another whiskey in front of me. "Shut up, Sanders. You're not my goddamn mother." I cringe, realizing what I just said. Then a weird sort of hysteria takes over and I begin to laugh maniacally. "Fuck," I snort, "I don't even *have* a mother anymore!" Slamming back half the whiskey, I laugh louder. "Hell, I hardly have a father. My mom got fucked up on pills and booze and fell into the pool, or maybe she just fucking threw herself in!" I wheeze, tears of laughter streaming down my cheeks.

As if a switch flips, the laughter stops and an icy calm slithers down my spine, oozing like a living thing slipping into every crack and crevice of my body. "No mother, no father, no sister…" My voice hitches. "Fuck." I down the rest of the drink, praying for the blessed numbness to take over.

"Kell—"

My best friend gapes as I stare at him. Hell, not just my best friend, Logan is the *only* friend left since my sister died and my soul was buried six feet under along with her. Once more, my mood changes in the blink of an eye, uncontrolled rage replacing the frigid emptiness. Fury suddenly burns hot over the ache of loss.

Anger is so much goddamn easier to deal with than guilt.

Lurching to my feet, I stagger over to Logan's side of the table. "You wanna say that bullshit to my face? Huh, Lo? That I should just get over it?" My fist twists in his shirt, wrapping the fabric around my hand. I lean down, almost tumbling face-first into his lap. "Fuck you. You don't know what it's like to be a *killer*. I fucking killed them, Lo. Me!"

Letting go of his shirt, I wobble as I stand up straight, hammering my chest with my fist on each sharp word. "I. Did. It!" I roar, heedless of the crowd in the bar. I turn to face the stunned patrons. "I fucking killed my family!"

Logan puts his hands on my shoulders behind me and I freak the fuck out. Spinning around, I shove him into the booth, landing hard on top of him, fists flying. Someone grabs me around my waist, trying to yank me off of my best friend.

"Don't fucking touch me!" I can't squirm out of the man's strong grasp. Panic overwhelms me in my drunken state. My hands scramble for anything to hold on to, not finding any purchase on the slick table or fake leather bench seat. When my fingers finally grasp something I *can* hold, I pick up the heavy glass and smash it into the person's head.

The next thing I know, my face is pressed into the filthy linoleum floor, the strong stench of stale beer in my nostrils.

"You have the right to remain silent…"

My hands are jerked behind my back while a knee digs in between my shoulder blades.

"…right to an attorney…"

Laughter and tears pour out of me, loud, inhuman sobs ripping through my chest. When the metal cuffs clink around my wrists, the sound marks the exact second my mind snaps.

CHAPTER 3

Ten years later

Britt

"Britt, can you double time it downstairs to cage four? Jack just pulled something in his back."

I glance up at one of the coaches at Souza MMA, the elite athletic complex where I work as a sports therapist. "Sure thing, Max."

"Thanks, Britt. He's waiting for you."

Once I finish restocking my backup freezer with disposable ice packs, I trot down the flight of stairs to the main level. Roxie, who works the front desk and is an all around awesome chick, grabs my arm when I pass by.

My first instinct is to flinch, or scream, or I don't know, just run away. I can't because I'm at work, at the gym. Despite knowing I'm safe here, I sometimes react poorly to being snuck up on or grabbed. Keeping myself composed, I reach up and finger the amethyst pendant I wear beneath my clothing for reassurance. Deep down I know it's all nonsense, but amethyst is supposed to keep away negative energy, so I've worn it since Nina gave it to me when I finished therapy so many years ago.

Roxie's face twists into a concerned frown.

"He's in a bad mood, girl. Watch yourself."

I laugh, tilting my head back to look up at the tall woman. "Jack is always in some kind of a mood, Roxie. I can handle him."

She scowls, her red lips a shocking contrast to her outrageous blue hair. "Don't let him bully you into something you aren't up for, Britt. You're too nice."

I pat her hand before moving out of reach. "And you're too sweet, looking out for me." Giving her my best smile, I weave through the equipment to the section of the gym with the cages—six cages to be exact. Fighter's League of America, full regulation-size octagons.

Roxie doesn't understand. This place, around the huge, powerful men she's always warning me away from, is the only place I actually feel safe. And it's precisely because the men *are* huge and powerful that I feel that way.

Even with being deaf in my left ear, I hear the cursing from across the room. Jackson Wolfe, aka Wolverine, resident pain in the ass and all around diva, is lying on the black rubber flooring, loudly letting everyone know how his sparring partner screwed up.

"Fucking North, kicking too late. Stupid bastard. You fucked up my back!"

Sawyer North is quite possibly the nicest fighter in the gym, yet somehow Jack always finds a way to blame the guy for all of his "injuries," and I use the word in the loosest of its definitions.

"Hey, Jack." I walk right on over and kneel next to the large, cursing man.

His angry eyes calm when he sees me. "Britt. Thank god someone who knows what the fuck they're doing is here," he grumbles.

I hide a smile. "Good to see you too. What happened?"

"Strain in the lower back," Brock, one of the trainers, answers.

"Okay, can you make it to my office?" I raise my eyebrows at the intimidating man.

Jack hisses in pain, but manages to stand and hobble all the way to my office at the back of the large, warehouse-sized training room.

"Lie facedown," I direct as I pull out the ice packs and grab some towels.

By the time I get what I need and stand next to the exam table, Jack is halfway through a story, which, of course, I didn't hear. I roll my eyes since Jack can't see me.

"Jack, I didn't catch any of that. Is it about your injury?" I suspect I know what he's getting around to, but I ask to be sure I'm not missing something important. As the sports therapist for these men, I need to pay special attention to each fighter. It's not Jack's fault I didn't hear him. I don't tell anyone about my hearing loss, not wanting to explain what happened to me ten years ago or be treated as a weak, fragile flower. I despise that.

"No, not my injury," he mumbles into the table, almost sounding embarrassed. "I was asking what you were doing later."

I sigh and grab the ice packs, laying them across the base of

Jack's spine. Sometimes I wonder how many of his injuries are merely excuses to get me alone and ask me out.

"Jack, I don't date fighters. You know this," I repeat for the millionth time since I started working here two years ago, and it's not only Jack. With the amount of testosterone flying around here, and me being one of only a handful of women who work at the gym, I end up repeating the same line to all of the guys at some point.

Honestly, I *should* date one of them. It would keep me from having panic attacks every night, alone in my little apartment. If I did, I would have someone big and strong to hold me, protecting me from the evils of the world.

Sometimes, it seems as if everyone here is hooking up except me. Lucky me, I get to listen to my coworkers gush about their weekend flings every Monday morning. I've been asked out by almost every single fighter to file through these doors. None as persistent as Jack Wolfe.

Jack attempts to roll on his side to face me. I place a hand on his shoulder, holding him still. "Don't move. You could make your back worse, especially if it's a tear."

I already know it's not a tear.

If anything, he has a minor strain. Most likely, Jack made it up or has a tiny twinge and is playing up the symptoms to corral me in my office. Despite his irritating behavior and his tendency to be a spoiled brat, I find it kind of sweet this big, intimidating guy would go so far as to fake an injury just to ask me out on a date.

"Yeah, yeah," he gripes. "I'm not moving."

I remove the ice and gently press on different muscle groups across his broad back. "Tell me if it hurts, Jack." After poking and prodding for several minutes with no reaction, I move away from the table. "You're fine. I'll put some rub on it and you can train tomorrow, but keep it light."

Jack leaves after I spread a thick layer of nasty smelling but highly effective ointment on his lower back with instructions to take it easy for the rest of the day.

By the time I clean up after my last patient, wiping down the table and countertops with disinfectant, it's late. I'm rummaging under the sink for more gauze wraps when someone taps my shoulder.

"Oh my god!" I jerk at the unexpected touch, smashing my head on the underside of the cabinet. Stars burst behind my eyes.

"Britt, I'm so sorry!"

"Max," I groan, rubbing my head where a knot is already forming.

"Shit, I didn't mean to scare you, Britt." Max moves to inspect my injury.

"I'm not bleeding, am I?" I won't tell him I'm more worried about triggering a seizure or a migraine than a small lump or cut. He'll feel bad. Then *I'll* feel bad for making *him* feel bad. Plus, I'm not discussing my condition. I refuse to be treated like a broken little bird… like my mom treats me.

Usually, I'm not easily freaked out at work. It's one of the only places I know I'm safe. Surrounded by huge, powerful men who

I know would never hurt me, who would protect me using physical force if necessary. It's the main reason I took this job. But sneaking up behind me? I'm going to be jumpy, plus, I'm the most ungraceful person I know.

Max sifts through my hair and I stiffen, afraid he'll find the ten-year knot of scar tissue behind my left ear. His fingers graze the new lump.

"Ow!"

"Sorry. God, I'm an idiot. No, you're not bleeding. It's going to be sore though."

Annoyed, I grab an ice pack from the freezer and place the cold bag on top of my head. "I look ridiculous."

Max smiles, but it's stilted. "Yeah, you do."

Laughing, I shove his shoulder to lighten the mood. "Shut up. What did you need?"

He stares at me blankly.

"Max! You came in here for something. Don't tell me you scared me to death and possibly gave me a concussion and you don't remember why?"

"Oh, right." His cheeks turn pink. "I ummmm, well, a new fighter is coming in tomorrow. Gabriel requested a full workup."

My eyebrows must fly up into my hairline. "A full workup?" No one gets a full workup unless they're going to fight in the league. "Is he an amateur?"

Max shakes his head. "Officially yes, but he's fought before. Greg says he's been training and fighting overseas somewhere.

Thailand or something. The FLA wants him, offered him a contract, so he's here."

Thailand. Muay Thai then. I've studied all the fighting styles to know what to watch for to prevent injury.

"What time will he be here?" There's a lot to do to prepare for a full workup. Professional fighters need me to analyze everything they do, looking for missteps or poor posture, which can cause injuries to muscles or bones. Plus cataloguing any previous injuries with a plan to protect those vulnerable places from repeat damage.

"Early. Seven, I think?"

I panic, staring at Max. "I can't be ready for a full workup by then. That's twelve hours from now! I've never even seen this guy fight."

"Don't worry, Britt. Gabriel knows there's not enough time for you to prep everything for tomorrow. Just meet with the guy, talk to him, and come up with a plan later." Max winks, his attempt at humor falling flat. I take my job seriously and I don't like to fail.

Scowling, I grab my laptop bag one-handed, the other hand balancing the ice pack on my head. "I'm not happy, Max."

He follows me out, laughing, as I lock the door to my office. "I know, Britt. I know."

Max kindly drops me off at my tiny Westside apartment, sparing me from walking home in the sweltering early evening humidity. Atlanta in June is unbearably hot. Yet as I stare at the door to my apartment, knowing I'm about to be alone, a cold shiver ripples through me.

"See you tomorrow, Britt."

"Bye, Max." I wave as he drives away.

Once inside, I quickly lock the three separate deadbolts on my door and start my exhausting nightly routine. Tonight, it only takes an hour to slow my racing heart, to silence the panic in my head, to stop the tingling spread of anxiety in each of my fingers and toes. Once I'm as calm as I'll get, I haul myself off the floor and force myself to eat.

After dinner, I swallow down the handful of pills necessary to keep the seizures and headaches away. It's why I only drive occasionally, why I'm concerned I hit my head at work. Anything can trigger a seizure, and doctors aren't sure if having a big one will cause enough damage to my brain to cut off my hard won independence. It's been years since I've had a seizure, but I don't want to take a chance.

One at a time, I put a bitter tablet on my tongue and swallow it with a gulp of water until they're all gone.

I take a quick shower, washing my hair, pretending not to feel the raised and twisted scar behind my left ear and being careful to avoid the new lump on top of my head. I silently curse Max and his carelessness, but can't stay angry. He means well even if he doesn't think sometimes.

Tired, I climb into bed and turn on some mind-numbing program to keep my thoughts off of the fact that I'm alone and vulnerable before flipping off the light.

With being anxious over my usual torments, plus the stress of having a new fighter I'm supposed to workup, it takes forever to fall asleep. When I do, it's the same as always. Pieces of the fateful day almost ten years ago, teeny, tiny flashes of images but never enough to trigger the memories to return, pop in and out of my mind all night long. I can only pray they never break through. I'm not sure I can stay sane if they do.

Killer

On the front step of my high-rise condo, I pull up the hood of my lightweight sweatshirt, huddling down into the fabric as I begin to jog to my new training center. Today is hot as fuck, but I'm more comfortable burning up than going without my hoodie. Being back in the U.S. still feels weird after living overseas for almost a decade. The sights, the sounds, hell, even the language seems unfamiliar.

Not even a little bit winded five miles later, I enter the enormous facility I'll be calling home for the next six months as I prepare to become the newest fighter for the FLA. One step into the building and I know this place is serious about training. It's not quite seven in the morning and the gym is buzzing with activity.

"Hello. You must be Mr. Bishop." A tall, incredibly fit woman with bright blue hair steps out from behind a counter, extending a hand.

I nod and grunt. "Yeah."

She gives me a wide smile. "I'm Roxanne Frasier but everyone calls me Roxie. Nice to meet you." She beaming and happy until her eyes meet mine beneath the hood of my sweatshirt. Roxie flinches. The movement is subtle, but it's there. I drop my gaze.

Reluctantly, I pull my hand from the pocket of my hoodie and shake hers, but don't add anything more to the conversation. My reputation for being an asshole hopefully preceded me because she doesn't question my lack of social skills or my silence.

"Gabriel is in the back. He'll show you around." Careful to avoid making eye contact again, Roxanne looks away as she turns and heads into the gym. "Come on." she says over her shoulder, again avoiding my eyes.

I follow her into the huge open space. It's clean and modern, the concrete walls painted white and the ceilings lined with steel crossbeams. This is a far cry from the small, stark facility I trained at in Brazil. And it's a whole fucking world away from the run-down place in the slums of Thailand.

We pass several men who are warming up, doing stretches or light bag work. Multiple full-sized octagons take up one entire side of the room. Rafael, my trainer in Brazil, wasn't kidding when he said this place is serious about turning out real MMA contenders.

"*Olá!*" A large, dark-haired, dark-eyed man of about fifty approaches, his hand extended in greeting. "You must be Keller! Rafael has not *stopped* talking about your talent!"

The man grips my hand enthusiastically, pumping my arm up and down, the large smile on his face never breaking.

"Killer. I go by Killer," I growl, head down.

He's not fazed in the least. "Of course! *Desculpe, desculpe,*" the man apologizes in Portuguese. "I'm Gabriel Souza."

Gabriel doesn't know I studied tapes of most of his fights from the early days of professional MMA and those of several fighters he currently trains. I know who he is and what he's capable of. He's the sole reason I accepted Rafael's suggestion to come here to prep for the FLA. Never in a million years would I set foot back in this city otherwise.

"Let me show you around," he continues in Portuguese. After living in Brazil for the last five years, I know the language well enough to keep up. The tour is brief but informative. They have everything I need to stay in peak shape for competing.

"Over here is our conditioning and sports therapist," Gabriel says, switching to English as he motions to a small, slender wisp of a blonde girl with big blue eyes as she descends a flight of stairs. "Britt, this is our newest client, Killer Bishop. Killer, this is our token college graduate, Britt Reeves."

The girl's dark eyelashes flutter and her pale skin pinks up when we shake hands, but she meets my eyes directly and never drops her gaze.

Weird.

"Nice to meet you, ummmm, Killer?" she says at a near whisper. I grunt in response, ducking my head and shoving my hands back into the kangaroo pouch of my hoodie. For some reason, I'm tense around this girl. I rub my finger and thumb together inside the pocket as I catch her studying me in my peripheral vision.

This is surprising. People are universally afraid of me. I look dangerous. My nose has been broken more times than I can remember, and my ears are halfway to becoming the thick, cauliflowered ears of a fighter, each with black gauges in the lobes. There are tattoos on my hands, arms, back, chest and neck. Most people can't look past the outside, but when they do look past it—and I mean *really* look—well, let's just say I've been told more than once I don't have a soul behind my cold, lifeless eyes.

They're right. There isn't one.

It's the reason I hide behind the hats, the hoodies, sunglasses, ink, intimidating scowl—pretty much anything I can find. Because when people look into my eyes, they see the truth.

That I'm a killer.

This girl, though? For some reason, she meets my gaze, unwavering. She isn't aware of how tainted I am, how threatening I can be. She would be wise to learn fast.

"You have time to talk to Britt?" Gabriel turns to me, an eyebrow raised. "She'll discuss any injuries you've had in the past, then watch footage of you fighting to look for problems with your form to address issues with joints or tricky spots, and help you adjust to prevent reinjury."

I lift my head and nod, my response gruff. "Sure."

Britt's eyes fly back to mine and I'm captivated by what I see. Not just the deep blue-green color, which is beautiful on its own. What draws me in is the understanding in her eyes, a common bond we share. Pain and misery skims the surface, not quite as consuming as what holds me prisoner in my own mind every day, but it's there in this girl's eyes, plain as day if you know what to look for.

What haunts Britt? What horrors does she hide behind the pretty face, quiet voice, and unshakable demeanor?

If I'm not careful, I could let down my guard around this gorgeous girl and go after everything I don't deserve. My mile-high walls are the only thing that stands between me and the crushing grief of the past. But the desire to hold her, to run my fingers through those long blonde strands, to stare into those eyes and weed out her deep dark secrets, is so tempting I have to bite the inside of my cheek to snap out of it.

I blink away thoughts of the girl and force myself to remember I don't give a shit about her or her problems. I don't care about anything, really. The only time I feel at all is when I fight. In the cage I receive the pain and suffering I deserve *if* the other man can get a hand on me. Like a ritualistic cleansing, I let out my anger and frustration and self-loathing on my opponent using my fists and feet. Yet no matter how much I fight, how much I unload on my victim, I'm never, ever clean.

"My office is back here." The girl's soft and timid voice defies her bold actions and disconcerting eye contact.

"Come find me when you're done. I'll show you your locker and you can meet the other fighters." Gabriel smiles, slapping my back before heading toward one of the cages.

My eyes follow Gabriel as he leaves. By the time I swing my attention back to the girl, she's opening a door on the far side of the room. Grumbling to myself and with no other option, I trail behind, pausing in the doorway.

The girl, Britt, is moving around the small space, clearly at ease with her surroundings. She opens a laptop and sits at a desk wedged in one corner. "You can sit." Britt points to a second chair.

Good. For a second I thought I was going to be forced to get up on the treatment table. I'm not in the mood to be a guinea pig today.

That's a lie. I don't really care what the trainers or specialists do to me as long as they make me a better fighter. It's the *girl* that bothers me, not the thought of being under a microscope. This is the only woman I've ever met who isn't instantly and irrevocably afraid of me, and the only one who has me tempted into thinking I could have *more*. More than a filthy, dirty fuck to release tension. More than someone to use for a few hours of pleasure.

Britt's obviously already damaged. As much as I'd love to peel back those layers, I don't want to give her a chance to dig out my own psychological scars, the nightmares hidden beneath a baggy hoodie and a cold stare. If I do, Britt may never recover from what she finds.

"I'm sorry," she apologizes, tapping on her computer. "I only found out you were coming last night, so I don't have much information and haven't reviewed your medical file."

She's so quiet, I strain to hear her. When I don't respond, she cocks her head and her eyes flick up to mine. *Shit.* I duck down so she can't get a good look at my face.

Fucking coward. She's going to find out at some point, idiot.

Why delay the inevitable? She'll see the same thing everyone else sees when they look in my eyes… nothing, a monster, a killer.

For the first time in ten years, the thought disturbs me.

Britt

The new fighter is… odd, to say the least. Half the time, when I ask him a question, I'm not certain if he's answered. Not trusting my poor hearing, I've taken to staring at his lips to try and decipher his words. But it's not my subpar hearing keeping me from catching his responses. It's my fascination with his lips, the flashes of pink tongue as he speaks, the gray eyes peeking under the hood of his thin sweatshirt.

Like I do to everyone else, when I directed him to sit, I made sure to put him on my good side. Despite my actions, I still can't hear him because the man is just that quiet. Even my usual trick of keeping my voice low so people will come closer, helping me to hear them better, isn't working.

And he keeps trying to hide his face. Which is strange, because he is absolutely gorgeous. So gorgeous, in fact, that I can't stop staring. Yeah, he looks like a typical fighter, slightly crooked nose, beat-up ears, scar in the eyebrow, all the usual signs. Despite his flaws, and the fact his hood keeps sliding down over his brow, it's obvious he's stunning.

"Tell me your fighting history." I roll my chair back from the desk and spin to face Killer. *I can't believe I have to call him Killer.* It's ridiculous, but whatever. "Where did you start?"

The big man ducks his head again, his voice low and steady, but still difficult for me hear. I scoot my chair closer and his head jerks up at the scraping sound. When Killer finally, for the first time since arriving, fixes his gaze directly on me, my brain stutters and stalls. My god, he's not simply stunning—he's both an angel and a devil at the same time—near hypnotizing to observe. Clear, silver eyes, unlike any I've ever seen, focus on my shocked face.

For a moment, we both simply sit there, staring at each other. It should be painfully uncomfortable, yet it's not. Killer breaks eye contact first, probably because I'm too spellbound by those quicksilver eyes to move.

"Ummmm, I'm sorry. I don't hear well. So… I thought. I mean, I needed to get closer to hear you." Beads of sweat dot my hairline, threatening to run down my temples.

Oh my god, did I just admit my hearing issues to this complete stranger? A gorgeous stranger, but still, a stranger.

Killer frowns, but answers my question after clearing his throat. "I started training ten years ago. In Thailand."

Those mesmerizing gunmetal eyes keep glancing up at me from whatever spot on the institutional tile floor he's found so fascinating.

"Very impressive." I lean back in my chair. Now that he's speaking at a normal volume, I realize how close together we're sitting. My knee is a hairsbreadth from touching his. I can feel the heat radiating from his skin. Laundry detergent mixed with his body wash, plus his undeniably male scent hits me every time I inhale, causing my head to spin.

Killer grunts at my compliment and begins picking at a tiny fray on the bottom hem of his sweatshirt.

Okay. Not much of a conversationalist, at all.

"Muay Thai then?" I ask, turning to check with my computer. "Gabriel said you did jiu-jitsu."

"Both," he mumbles, the tiny hole now a bit larger. "Moved to Brazil after living in Thailand for five years."

My head whips up. I'm astonished. "You studied in both countries? For five years each?"

Killer nods, still focusing on the fabric in his hands. By now, the bottom of his sweatshirt is unraveling from those digging fingers. Nervous tic. I'm quite familiar with those, having dealt with an involuntary one after my surgeries.

"I'm impressed," I admit. "What about injuries? Anything major?"

He shakes his head. "No."

"Minor?"

"Few sprains, aches here and there. Nothing big." Those haunting eyes lift to mine again and he lifts a dark eyebrow. "I broke my arm once. Does that count?"

"Yeah," I smile. "It counts." Reluctantly, I pull myself away and roll my chair back behind the desk so I can enter the information. "Which bone?"

"Left humerus."

"You're right-handed, though. Correct?"

"Yes."

"All right. Any problems with your arm since the injury?" I glance up when he doesn't answer. "Killer?"

"No."

"Mind if I ask how you broke it?"

The clouds must part and the angels are singing because a miracle happens. The man *smiles*, and it's so beautiful it's worth every irritating grunt and nonverbal answer he's given so far to be able to witness what I assume is a rare event. A single dimple appears on one cheek and the teeth he reveals are perfect. I hold in a gasp. With one smile he takes years off his face and appears a heck of a lot less scary.

"I refused to tap out of an arm bar."

A small smile tugs at the corner of my mouth. Ah, he's stubborn. Good thing I am too, or else the handsome but intimidating man would trample all over me and my swirling hormones.

I add his cause of injury to the file and stand up with the intention of asking a few more basic questions. Killer reacts by leaping to his feet in a motion so quick and so soundless, I stumble back over my own shoes, headed for the floor. His massive hands shoot out, wrapping around my shoulders to keep my clumsy self from going down.

Oh my god.

I find myself paralyzed in his arms, our eyes locked, my heart fluttering like a hummingbird's wings. Unable to move, I examine this strange, beautiful man, with his secrets and his quiet, gruff voice and intriguing eyes. His scent overpowers me, seeping into my skin and causing a flare of lust to spark.

Close up, I notice a smattering of freckles across his nose and cheeks. He appears almost vulnerable, not the hard-edged, take-no-prisoners fighter he claims to be. For me, there's a serenity in being in his arms. A peaceful calm I haven't felt since before "the incident."

"What's your real name?" I whisper, our faces so close his soft breaths fan across my face.

A gust of air hits me as Killer releases me, jumping back. My skin is cold without his heated touch. I didn't realize how much I would miss the unapproachable man's embrace until it's gone.

He stands a few feet away, hood pulled so far over his brow I can no longer see the silver irises that say so much about a man who says so little. His hands are fisted at his sides and his head is tilted toward the floor.

"My name is *Killer.*"

My pulse is still racing, my poor heart not yet recovered from being so close to this man, a man I shouldn't let affect me. But with that blissful calm combined with intense desire, being in his arms could easily become an addiction. To be able to let go, to shut off the anxiety, the worry, the fear… it's tempting to dive in headfirst and worry about the repercussions later.

"Well, I'm going to call you K." His head whips up in surprise and for a moment, I get a peek at that vulnerability again. I smile, but because of his tense stance, this time my smile is tense, strained. "You're too sweet for a name like Killer."

K's face goes on complete lockdown, from raw and exposed to hardened lethality in the blink of an eye. Chills break out across my skin at the transformation. Now I detect what I missed the first time around. The man *is* danger, pure and simple. His muscles are tight, bunched up, ready to attack. His body language would scream at anyone passing by to turn and run in the other direction. His mere presence should be enough to frighten even the bravest of souls, yet here I am, breathing in his scent, leaning slightly forward, wanting to reach out and climb in his arms. Be held by him. Touch him.

"No. Make no mistake. I'm not sweet. I *am* a killer." He spins on his heel and with that, I'm left alone in my tiny office. The only reminder K was ever here is the slight scent of his soap and the fact my heart is still hammering against my ribs.

I'm afraid, but not of K. The fact that I'm *not* afraid of him is what I'm worried about. Instead of heeding every warning my brain is putting out, I need to find a way to get closer to the man instead of further away.

* * *

Gabriel pulls up the correct file and hits play on his computer. The massive television set in his office lights up. The clip displayed was shot in a practice ring at a gym I'm not familiar with.

The door to an empty cage opens and two men enter. My mouth falls open in shock. The men are both fighters, both clearly in peak physical condition with cut, sinewy muscles and a lightness to their step that takes years of training to perfect.

Hundreds of fighters have passed through these doors over the last two years, so that's not why I'm gaping. It's the raw sexual appeal of the man wearing snug-fitting black Lycra shorts with red lettering, lithely bouncing on his toes, that draws me in. His entire torso is covered with ancient-looking tattoos—arms, chest, back, heck, there's even one on his neck, stretching up one side. I've never seen anything so menacing, yet so erotic.

My eyes flick up to the fighter's face. *Killer.*

"Holy crap," I murmur. He looks like a lethal jungle cat, sharp gaze fixed on his opponent. He is the very definition of sex; every movement, every sinewy ripple, every fluid step, sends a rush of blood to long-dormant places in my body.

Gabriel laughs. "I know. Wait till you see him in action, *minha filha.*"

I smile at Gabriel's endearment. He calls everyone dear to him "my daughter" or "my son." I don't speak Portuguese. I only know what it means because I asked once.

"This is only sparring with no grappling. The trainer told them to stay upright so his striking could be assessed," Gabriel adds, but my eyes are glued to the screen. I don't want to miss a single second of Killer in action.

The sound is off, but the bell must ring because the men start moving. Watching K fight is hauntingly beautiful. Like a predator stalking a kill. Every action he takes is effortless, deliberate. He moves so fast there is little time for his opponent to react. K hits and kicks the other man over and over, each strike lashing out and retreating like the flick of a whip. I'm mesmerized by his body.

A few minutes later, the two men tap gloves and the film ends.

"I need to watch it again."

Gabriel hits play and the clip starts over. It takes four more times through for me to study K's positioning, two just to stop staring at his beautiful face.

I move behind the keyboard and tap until the screen is frozen on K standing on one leg.

"See, right there." I point to the screen. "His left knee slightly hyperextends when he delivers a kick with his right leg. Eventually, if he's not careful, he can tear his posterior cruciate ligament."

Gabriel squints. "I don't see that. He seems fine to me, *minha filha.*"

Grinning, I pat the older man on the back. "I know, but trust me. Other than that, he's perfect."

Gabriel turns to me, and this time it's his turn to smirk. "Perfect, eh?"

My cheeks heat up, fire racing all the way to the tips of my ears. "I-I don't mean…"

"Relax, Britt. *Eu falo pelos cotovelos.*"

I tilt my head, confused.

Gabriel gives me a small smile. "It means I'm only joking with you."

"Right." I shift uncomfortably in my seat. If Gabriel knew what I was thinking when I watched K fight, I'd die of embarrassment.

"Okay, Britt. You can go. We can study his ground game tomorrow. Jiu-jitsu, *meu favorite*." Gabriel grins and claps his hands, rubbing them together in anticipation. "Killer, he trained with Rafael."

I nearly choke in surprise. "With Rafael? Rafael Lima?" K mentioned training in Brazil, but failed to mention Rafael Lima. Rafael is the most famous jiu-jitsu expert in the world, second only to the Gracie family.

"You will catch flies with your mouth, *meu querida*. You are shocked and you're right. He is very young to have so much training from the masters." Gabriel shrugs. "But he does, and he's here with us. Our job is to make sure he gets to use his potential in the cage."

"He doesn't need us for that," I mumble. Thankfully, Gabriel already left his office and doesn't hear my comment.

I head back to my own little room and sit at the computer. Fascinated and needing to know more, I bring up K's file and I read the scant information I find.

Who is this guy?

I don't even know his real name. Killer Bishop. That's what the file says. His date of birth shows he turns twenty-eight later this year, which makes him a little less than four years older than me. No address, no phone number, no hometown, no medical file. It's as if K didn't exist until he showed up here. The league requires him to provide all of that information to go pro.

Even though I should be afraid, I should stay detached from the man who throws up every red flag in the book, I'm not. K is a complete mystery, and I'm enthralled. He's a mystery I intend to solve.

Killer

Halfway through my second day at Souza MMA, and I'm still watching from the sidelines, itching to punch something. Gabriel handed me off to his wife, Mariana, for a tour when I arrived this morning. No one said a word about me rushing out the door after my appointment yesterday with the tiny blonde physiologist.

Britt, her name is Britt.

She isn't here yet today. Not that I'm looking. Fuck, who am I kidding, I'm totally looking for her. I shouldn't. She's all big, innocent blue eyes and rosy pink blushes. I'd take everything good about her and ruin it in a heartbeat. And god do I want to ruin her. I want to strip off those uptight clothes, force her to her knees, and grip her hair while I fuck her face.

No, that's not true. That's what I do to women, what I've done to women in the past. Use them. Get off and toss them aside. Britt… she's not like that. She's… different. And that's what makes her dangerous. This girl could easily undo everything I've created to survive over the last ten years, tear down every wall I've built, every façade I've put up.

Shit. It's like she's an obsession. I dig my fingers into my palms until they bite through the skin. Adjusting my cup under my skintight fight shorts helps to ease the pain of having a semi-hard dick trapped inside. I'm getting turned on and I haven't even laid eyes on Britt yet today.

"Killer! Ready?"

I press my lips together and nod at Gabriel. In one quick move, I reach back, yank off my hoodie, and toss the fabric to the ground.

"Good." Gabriel turns to the other fighter. "Raoul, ready?"

The man bounces on the balls of his feet and nods, his dark eyes bright with excitement.

Enjoy it while it lasts, buddy. I'm gonna knock that smug expression right off your face.

I follow Raoul up the steps into the cage. The door closes with a satisfying *clink* behind me. Gabriel moves to the center, urging us to come forward.

"Okay, *meus amigos,* this is only sparring. No hard hitting. We're concentrating on form, speed, and footwork." He shoots us both a stern glare. "Not is not the time to show-off your hotshot moves."

Raoul acknowledges Gabriel with a quick salute and a grin, his teeth hidden behind his bright yellow mouth guard.

"Killer?"

My eyes flick back to Gabriel, and to the trainer's credit, he doesn't flinch under my scrutiny. Most men do. Waiting another second, I dare him to break eye contact with the monster. When Gabriel stays fast, I finally grunt, nodding my chin toward this man who never wavers.

"Good. Five minutes." Gabriel pulls out a stopwatch and holds it out. "Go!"

I brace my feet on the mat, letting my opponent strike first. Raoul does exactly what I predicted. He raises his hands, protecting his face, and goes at me with a left hook. As his fist comes toward my face, I tilt back on my left leg and rotate my hips, bringing my right foot across to collide just beneath his exposed ribcage, hitting him slightly above the liver.

Raoul's punch whiffs past my chin and he collapses to the mat in a loud, whining heap.

"Fuck, man! I thought we were sparring," he groans from the floor. Raoul staggers to his feet with Gabriel's help. "I think you cracked a rib."

Pussy. I went easy on him. If I hit him where I wanted to, he would have been unconscious from that liver strike. Idiot showed too much in his warm-up. Karate. Those guys always try for hits to the face and they're shit at watching for Muay Thai kicks.

Emotionless, I stand with my back against the chain-link cage. Gabriel walks Raoul out, the man clutching his midsection and glaring at me.

"Crazy fucker," he hisses as he passes by.

The shit talking doesn't faze me in the least. I know what I am and I've been called worse.

After they depart, I figure this session is over so I leave the cage. Maybe I should have let him get a few hits in first so I could at least get a workout of some sort. Ignoring the whispers and stares of the other fighters and employees, I snatch up my hoodie. As I go to shrug it on, I catch sight of her out of the corner of my eye.

Britt is watching me. Our gazes meet and I expect her to flinch or turn away. She doesn't. Those clear blue eyes stay fixed on mine. When I realize I'm standing with my hoodie halfway on, I yank it over my head, pissed I let this woman get under my skin. A tiny little girl. With cock-sucking lips and a tight round ass and the ability to completely distract me.

I flip up the hood, letting it fall over my brow. The feeling of being watched doesn't diminish. Another quick peek has me locking eyes again with the petite blonde.

What the fuck? Why isn't she afraid?

I don't like this at all. People are supposed to turn away, not study me. If they look too hard, they might see everything I don't want exposed. And Britt? She's already closer to exposing me than anyone I've ever known, and it's only been twenty-four hours.

I have a feeling when it comes to Britt, fate has already determined I'm screwed.

* * *

"Come in and sit, Killer. *Por favor.*" Gabriel directs me to his office by extending his hand.

I follow, knowing what's coming. It's nothing I haven't heard before. My temper, my strength, my inability to control myself in the cage—more bullshit lecturing, I'm sure. Gabriel grabs the chair behind his desk, bringing it around the front to face the only other chair in his office.

"Sit." His tone is firm but kind. Not one you argue with, so I comply, staring at the hem of the sweatshirt with my hood pulled up over my eyes.

Gabriel takes his own seat and I wait for the verbal thrashing. Nothing happens. He makes soft noises—breathing, the slight rustle of clothing, but no words.

The silence overtakes the room, crawling up my legs and making my skin feel too tight. My heart is pounding in my chest. What the hell? I love silence. I live for silence. How is he using it to make me so uncomfortable?

Against everything I am, I tilt my head to go eye to eye with Gabriel, bracing myself for the anger. The fear. When our gazes meet, Gabriel gives me a huge grin.

Is this guy crazy?

"There you are," he chuckles. "I was wondering if you were ever going to look at me when we talk."

My mouth falls open, but nothing comes out.

He laughs again. "I can do all the talking, Killer. Don't worry."

His humor is disconcerting, but encouraging. "You're not mad?"

Gabriel is nonplussed. "Why am I supposed to be mad? Because Raoul can't take a hit? Or because he didn't think to block it?" He waves an uninterested hand my way. "*Não*. Of course not. You spar, you get hit. That's the game."

"But..." I blink rapidly. "But you said no hard hits."

The kind man puts his elbows on his knees, leaning forward and steepling his fingers in front of his mouth. "I know what a liver kick will do. Did you hit him hard?"

I shake my head and huff. "No."

Gabriel smiles, leaning back. He spreads his hands wide. "*Bom*. So no problem."

My mind flicks through all the reasons Gabriel should be furious right now. Just as quick, I calculate all the reasons he wouldn't be.

"You know I didn't hit him hard or where I wanted to. You know I held back."

He laughs, a rich, throaty laugh. "Of course I know. I watched your film. I talked to Rafael. Hell, *meu filho*, just looking at you I know your striking potential is much, much higher than what you showed me with Raoul. I'm certain he would been knocked out by that kick if you used your potential." Clapping his hands together, Gabriel traps me with his dark gaze. "Now, you're the one who has to deal with Raoul complaining. I think that is punishment enough." Gabriel winks.

I'm floored. This man, he gets me. Like really gets me. And oddly enough, he's not intimidated by me in the least. He sees something in me most people don't. Potential.

Britt

Today is K day. That's what I've called it in my head all week. It's a full day of watching K train, offering advice, and helping out when needed. He's only been here a week and a half but it seems like much longer. Probably because I spend every free second thinking about him or stealing glances in the gym.

When did I turn into such a basket case?

I laugh. Who am I kidding? I'm always a basket case, just not usually at work, and definitely not over a fighter.

I grab a drink to soothe my dry mouth and smother the flames of desire building at the thought of watching K fight. Clutching the bottle, my hand trembles so much a tiny bit of water splashes out, splattering on my desk and keyboard.

Of course.

"Crap." I grab a roll of paper towels and mop up the mess. Thankfully, only a few drops hit the actual keyboard and the rest landed on my desk.

I've been a wreck, obsessing over K, wanting what I shouldn't want. Craving more of that feeling I had when wrapped in his powerful arms when I should be avoiding him. But if K can bring me the kind of peace I've struggled to find…

With an irritated huff, I let it go and finish wiping down the desk.

By the time I'm done cleaning up, I'm a sweating, nervous wreck. I toss the wet towels in the garbage and wipe my forehead with the back of my hand. Still unsettled, I straighten out my clothes, checking that my amethyst is in place. I wore my usual khakis and short-sleeved sweater set, needing to appear as a professional amongst the fighters. The clothes are a little frumpy, but they make the fighters respect me in a way they wouldn't if I hung around in sloppy sweats all day.

"Britt?"

I let out a startled yelp, spinning around to face the door.

"Sorry," an embarrassed Max says. "I really need to learn not to sneak up on you."

I feel bad about deceiving Max, but damn, the guy always catches me unaware. He doesn't know I can't hear well, so it's technically not his fault he always manages to sneak up. Plus, because of K, I'm on edge today, which adds to my usual clumsiness. Still, I would think Max would figure out another way to approach after surprising me the same way so often.

"I'm okay, Max," I lie. My blood is pulsing hard through my veins. First from my anxiety over working with K all day, then from Max startling me—I wouldn't be surprised if I keeled over from a heart attack right about now.

"I just wanted to let you know they're about to start." He jerks his thumb over his shoulder.

"Oh. Okay, thanks." I run a hand over my straight blonde hair, making sure it's smooth. Max scowls before turning and storming out of my office.

Huh? What is that about?

Whatever. I have no idea what Max's problem is and honestly, I'm not in the mood to find out. Right now, my job is to watch—no, *study*—Mr. Sexy and Mysterious for the next six to eight hours. I grin. My job is awesome sometimes.

When I step into the main gym, I catch sight of K on one of the large mats, stretching his lithe body in ways that should be illegal. Desire flares, racing up my spine, igniting every nerve ending until my entire body is on fire. My breath catches when K's hooded head slowly turns my way as if he can somehow sense me behind him.

Surrounded by shadows from the fabric pulled around his face, silver irises peek out, meeting my own, ensnaring me. Even from halfway across the room I see his pupils dilate a fraction. I lick my lips as a peaceful sensation calms my anxious mind, soothing my ragged nerves. I begin to wonder if K is the man who can give me what I need. That unknown entity my college boyfriend couldn't manage to find. That even I can't seem to figure out. After an eternity, K's body unfolds, rising from the mat, his eyes never leaving mine.

Oh god. Can you die of lust?

"Britt! We're at cage three today."

Gabriel's shout breaks me from the hypnotic spell. My ears and face burn as I hurry over to the cages, somehow managing to not trip over anything. What the heck was I thinking, staring at K and openly lusting after him like some kind of creeper? Ugh, he'd have to be an idiot not to see that I want him.

For the first time since I met the withdrawn man, I'm thankful he doesn't speak much. Otherwise, I'd worry he would embarrass me for drooling over his sinfully flexible body. Jack, on the other hand, would think nothing of loudly calling me out in front of the entire gym if I looked at him in such a hungry, desperate way.

"*Olá*, Britt." Gabriel nods in my direction. Turning, he greets K, who somehow slid in next to me without my knowledge. His arm is right next to mine, causing the skin below my short sleeves to tingle, the tiny hairs on my arm standing on end as if he's sending out electrical pulses. "Killer." Gabriel gives us his warm, fatherly smile. "Are we ready for a long day of hard work?"

I manage to turn the corners of my lips in a half-grin, half-nervous frown in an attempt to hide my reaction to K. I'm sure it makes me appear demented. Holding up my laptop, I announce, "I'm all set."

Max sets up the camera, aiming the lens at the cage to record K's work. Later tonight or tomorrow, Gabriel and I will both study the video, meeting afterwards to share our thoughts.

K replies with his usual grunt.

"Great. Killer, Max will help wrap your hands, then I'll meet you in the cage." Gabriel slaps K's back with a huge hand and walks away to talk to one of the other trainers at a neighboring cage.

While K has his hands wrapped, I take a seat on a bench and open my laptop, getting ready to take notes, focusing on breathing to calm down my out of control libido. It's important I pay attention and not spend all my time staring at K's ass. I'll need to reference the notes later while watching the tape to remember what my thoughts were as K made each move.

Max finishes wrapping K's hands and fastens his thin gloves. The fighter's fingers are now interwoven with wide bands of black leading up his wrists. His glorious, half-naked body bounces up the steps to the cage. Before he starts fighting, I greedily take in every single mark on K's tan skin, examine every tattoo, trying to put a story behind each dark stroke of ink as I imagine tracing the lines with my tongue.

"Do you need a towel for all of your drool?" Max snaps as he drops to the bench next to me.

Shocked at his vitriol, and a little embarrassed to be caught gawking, I turn and gape at Max. "What is your problem today?"

"Nothing." Max shifts away and focuses straight ahead. His jaw clenches as he pretends to watch Gabriel speak to K in the cage.

For god's sake.

I am so not in the mood to deal with Max's little hissy fit right now. Besides, I need to pay attention to every little movement K makes without distractions—lust, longing, Max—I can't let any of them keep me from watching K fight. My job is to make sure his form is absolutely perfect so he doesn't injure himself when he stands in the AFC octagon for a regulation fight.

K gets into his stance, Gabriel in front of him with pads on his hands and head. K's muscles tighten and coil, his beautiful inked skin rippling over the sheer power it contains. Gabriel nods and they begin.

Oh god.

I pray I'll be able to do my job when all I can think of is how well that body could move against mine.

* * *

Pausing the video in my office, I check the caller ID before answering my cell phone.

Mom.

I glance back at the laptop, K's exquisite form frozen mid-downward roundhouse kick. My preference is to continue watching the delicious eye candy rather than talk to my mother. Heck, I'd rather undergo Chinese water torture than speak to her.

We don't talk much anymore because I continually refuse my mother's demands to speak at events or help her with SASS, the anti-school violence organization she now works for. She doesn't, or won't, understand my desire to *live*, not rehash the past over and over again. A past I can't even remember.

In a moment of weakness, my finger slides over the screen to answer the call.

"Hello?"

"Britton?"

Holding back a sigh, I already regret picking up. "Yes, Mom. It's me."

She huffs. "Don't be smart with me, Britton."

"Sorry." *I'm totally not sorry.*

"Anyway," my mom begins, the tone of her voice indicating I'm not going to like whatever she called to discuss. "Your father and I were hoping you'd come to dinner tomorrow night. It's been forever."

I wonder why that is, Mom?

"Dinner?"

My mom must notice my lack of enthusiasm because she jumps right on the guilt train, steering it full speed ahead to mow me down.

"Britton Shelton Reeves—" Wonderful, she's gone and pulled out the full name. "We are your parents and want to see you. Don't you miss us?"

I miss my parents, but not the arguing about my "poor life choices" and "unwillingness to help others" through difficult times.

"Tomorrow?" I groan.

"Yes."

"Friday would be better." I hedge my bets, hoping I can come up with a suitable excuse to bail out by then. "There's a new client and it requires me staying late at work. I'm still at work now."

My mom tsks, clucking her tongue in disapproval. "Alright, Friday. Seven o'clock. Do you need me to send Raymond to pick you up?"

Driving is something I avoid whenever possible, but I don't want to be indebted to my parents. Maybe I'll cab it. "No. I'm good."

I sense my mom's disdain through the phone, but for once,

she lets it go. "Fine. See you then." Before I can reply, she hangs up.

Tossing the phone down on the desk, I focus back on the screen and K. Even the thought of studying his gorgeous body can't get rid of my dark mood. Irritated, I shut down the laptop and head out, my mind going over a hundred different excuses I can use to avoid what is sure to be a disastrous dinner on Friday.

I need to remember—*I'm* in charge of my life, not my mom, my dad, or anyone else. Me.

Killer

"Killer! You're here early," Roxie chirps from behind the front desk. She's too happy all the time. It's annoying. Especially since I know for a fact I make her uncomfortable even without the fake cheer in her voice when she speaks to me. She's gotten a glimpse of the monster. Yet those huge eyes of hers combined with her joyful tone always succeed where others fail.

She gets me to speak.

"I have a meeting with Britt."

"Well, she's already here, so go on back."

I keep my head ducked as I slink by so Roxie can't see my eyes. No sense letting her meet the monster again when she's the only one who manages to get an actual verbal response out of my sorry ass.

After a couple of weeks here, most of the fighters and staff don't bother talking to me anymore. I keep my hood up and eyes on the floor whenever I'm not sparring or training, and I never do pleasantries. Being ignored helps people understand they shouldn't speak to the new guy. I heard some whispering and know I already have a rep for being a complete fucking douche, and that's the way I want it.

Britt's office is in the back of the gym. As I approach, I spot one of the employees standing in her doorway. Being as quiet as I can, which is pretty damn quiet, I walk up behind the man. He's not talking and neither is Britt. When I peer over the guy's shoulder, which is easy because I'm a good four or five inches taller, I realize she's absorbed in reading a file on her desk and doesn't even know he's there.

Is he fucking spying on her?

The hairs on the back of my neck stand up and a tight coil of anger sizzles in my chest. My vision shimmers with a red-tinged haze as this douchebag molests innocent and sweet Britt, *my Britt*, with his pervy eyes. I'm surprised by the possessiveness of my thoughts, but I'll worry about that later.

"Excuse me," I bark, shoving past him and shouldering my way into the room. He stumbles forward, ready to snap out with a biting comment, but when he recognizes me, his face blanches and his mouth snaps shut.

Britt turns around at my loud entrance, her wide gaze flicking back and forth between me and the motherfucking pervert gaping next to me.

"Max? K? Is…is everything all right?" Her brow wrinkles in

confusion. She's astute, catching on to the fact something strange just transpired.

I stare at Max, fixing my hard gaze on his shocked face. His skin is flushed a bright crimson, and I watch in satisfaction as the red drains out when Max makes eye contact. He understands what he's looking at. He sees the truth. The monster. The killer behind my cold eyes.

"I-I..." Max staggers back toward the door, stammering like the pussy he is. "I'm s-sorry, Britt. I'll catch you later." Wide eyed, he darts out the door.

Fucking coward. Not so ballsy when faced with someone he can't fool with his bullshit nice-guy act.

Britt tilts her head questioningly towards the empty space previously occupied by Max. I give her a noncommittal shrug. She smiles, facing me. Once again, those blue eyes don't waver as they meet mine. Chills trickle down my spine at Britt's ability to hold her own when coming face-to-face with the monster. I wait for her to scream, to run away, to see me for what I am and turn away.

Instead, her pupils dilate, and the icy cold is replaced by a smoldering heat that ignites deep inside me. Quickly—too quickly— flames begin to flicker across every inch of my skin, fire spreading like molten lava. She's everything a man could want, beautiful, kind, with a sort of innocence about her. She the type of woman men would fight for. *I* would fight for her.

Ultimate control over my body is one of the only things I pride myself in, so when my cock begins to stir in my shorts, I flinch in disgust at my lack of restraint.

"Hi," Britt says in her soft, pleasant voice. She glances back down at her desk, shuffling the stack of papers she had been flipping through when I caught that bastard Max spying on her. "You can sit if you like." Britt glances up as I drop into the same chair as my first day here.

She picks up the chair behind her desk, once again bringing it out to sit next to me. Reaching over, Britt flips her laptop around, the screen now facing us.

"Will this be okay? Or is the screen too small?" Once more, Britt makes bold, direct eye contact, but as usual her voice is low and timid, almost hesitant. My heart stutters at her close proximity, at the warmth of her body and the alluring scent of her skin.

"It's fine," I grunt rudely. I need to remember I'm not here to be nice or make friends or even get laid, though I can't count the number of times I've imagined undressing Britt and worshipping her body. I'm here to fight, to train, to motherfucking make use of my pathetic life.

We spend two plus hours going over different highlights from the last few days. One thing I notice being this close, is that Britt is young, really young. She's glaringly out of place in this gym, a tiny blonde innocent amid the blood and violence and testosterone. Yet at the same time, despite the diminutive appearance and tiny voice, Britt is *far* from out of place. She's brave, unintimidated by the massive fighters, and as the day goes on, I realize she's a fucking genius at what she does. One more reason to credit Gabriel for his ability in spotting talent and using it to strengthen his team.

After a quick bite to eat, we're ready to go into the ring to try out some of Britt's modifications. Gabriel stands to one side while I torque my body into each requested position.

"Okay, see here?" Britt taps the inside of my left knee. "You need to be like this." Her small hand wraps around my thigh to manipulate my leg where she wants it. Electricity from her touch burns from my leg up and over my entire body, scorching me from the inside out. I say a prayer of thanks for my athletic cup. Without it, my cock would be jutting right into Britt's face since she's on her knees in front of me.

It's near impossible to concentrate without my brain going to thoughts of those thick lips wrapping around my dick, but years of exerting near obsessive control over my body helps to mask the urge. Helps, but doesn't stop it completely. Britt is my weakness, my kryptonite. If I'm not careful, she'll burrow under my skin, break down my meticulously crafted defenses, and reduce me to a weak, emotional mess.

Britt releases my leg and stands up, her face flushed. Is it possible she feels it too? This thread between us? One that keeps tugging me in as I fight to get free. Even if she feels it, I doubt Britt is feeling the same level of desire as me. It's as if before we met I was suffocating, and now, when I'm near her, my lungs are filled with precious oxygen, allowing me to breathe easy for the first time in a decade.

"Try a few kicks," Gabriel says, stepping aside so the camera can catch my new form. I execute a few downward roundhouse kicks, slamming my foot into Gabriel's padded hands. "Well?" They both wait for me to say something.

What the hell do they want me to say?

I shrug. "It's good."

Britt smiles, her full lips pulling back to reveal brilliant white teeth. Her bright blue eyes and sweet face send another bolt of lightning to my blackened heart, this sweet, innocent angel trying to resuscitate a soul that died a long time ago. I don't do angelic. I don't do sweet. And I sure as fuck don't do innocent. I can't ruin her. And if I touched her, that's what would happen. She'd be ruined. Dragged down into the blackness of my life, to never be the same.

I turn away from Britt's smile, unable to continue looking at something I can't ever have.

As we're packing up at the end of the day, I catch that asswipe Max out of the corner of my eye. He's lingering by the front desk all creepy as fuck. Britt locks up her office and heads toward the door where the two of them exchange a few words. I grind my teeth in aggravation as I watch. The urge to hit something is nearly overwhelming when Britt follows Max out to the parking lot where she climbs into his car.

Son of a bitch!

I'm not a good guy, not by any stretch of the imagination, and I don't deserve a woman like Britt, but I'm positive Max might be the worst thing for the naive sports therapist, even when compared to me.

CHAPTER 4

Britt

After dodging Max's offers to drive me home the last few days, he traps me by the front desk. "Britt, you headed out?" His smile is forced, likely a result of my recent avoidance tactics. He's been acting strange lately, especially around K, and it has me on edge. More so than usual. Work is my sanctuary and Max is ruining it with his bizarre behavior.

"Yes," I respond as cheerily as I can manage seeing as I'm going to my parents' house for dinner tonight. It's hung over me all day. I'm dreading dinner more than a trip to the dentist's chair.

"I'm about to leave myself. It's pretty hot out so I figured you wouldn't want to walk."

It's hot every damn day from May through October, I think. Instead of voicing my sarcastic response, I accept his offer, unable to come up with a reason to decline except the fact that Max makes me nervous lately.

"Sure. Thanks, Max."

He grins, the smile more natural now that I agreed to the ride, which allows me to relax a little.

Max cranks up the A/C, letting the blazing hot car cool off a little before pulling out of the parking lot. "So," he begins, his eyes never leaving the congested streets. "What's up with the new guy?"

"Who?" I play dumb, knowing exactly who Max is asking about.

I catch Max rolling his eyes. "Killer. What a stupid name."

Although I agree on the name thing, I'm not going to give Max the satisfaction of knowing he's right. Plus, the way he's always putting down K makes me defensive for some reason.

"He's doing well. Once he hits the circuit, he'll be unstoppable."

Why I want to rub K's success in Max's face is a mystery. I guess it's the fact that no one else here bothers to look past the tough exterior K projects. No one else sees or understands the similarities we share and hide from the world. Despite his attempt to cover it up, I see him. Inside, he's damaged. Like me. And that makes him even more attractive in my eyes.

Max scowls. "We'll see about that."

"We will," I agree.

Max pulls into my apartment complex and stops in front of my building. I grab my purse and when my hand reaches for the door, Max speaks. "Did you maybe want to get something to eat tonight?"

My head whips around in shock, wondering if I heard correctly since he's on my left. "Are you asking me out?" I blurt without thinking. Max turns bright red and drops his gaze to the steering wheel. His thumbs rub back and forth over the worn leather on the wheel.

"Yeah, I think I am." Nervous eyes flick over to my face.

Crap. I don't think of Max that way. How are we supposed to work together if I turn him down?

"Ummmm, I'm having dinner with my parents tonight," I stammer.

"Oh." He looks crestfallen, biting on his lower lip. "Okay. I'll see you Monday, Britt."

Nodding, I hurry out of the car, eager to be away from such an uncomfortable situation. Once inside, I lock the door behind me and sag. Jesus, I need Max asking me out like I need a hole in my head.

I hunch over and start giggling uncontrollably. I *did* have a hole in my head. It shouldn't be funny, but for some reason I can't stop. After fifteen minutes of ridiculous, near-hysteric laughter, I wipe my eyes and check the clock.

Crap.

Now there really will be something for my mother to be mad at. I'm going to be late.

* * *

I park my cherry red BMW coupe and hurry up the fancy paved stone stairs leading up to my parents' front door. I don't drive much, but I didn't want to be at my parents' mercy when it's time to leave. The house hasn't changed much over the years. It's still massive, pretentious, and way too big for three people, let alone two.

I raise a hand, feeling for the amethyst pendant under my

shirt. My finger hovers over the doorbell, and I realize I'm being ridiculous. This is, or was, my house until two years ago when I moved out. I open the door, stepping inside the two-story foyer.

"Britton?" My mom's voice echoes in the large space. Her heels clack on the hardwood floor as she makes her way toward me.

"Hey, Mom."

"You're late, dear," she chastises before I can even take a single step off of the expensive imported rug in front of the door.

"Sorry, Mom. I came as soon as I got out of work."

"Well, dinner is ready. Come. Your father is waiting."

I follow her into the ridiculously huge dining room, lit by two crystal chandeliers hanging over the twelve-person table.

"Britton, you're looking lovely tonight." My dad stands up and gives me a hug. I sink into the embrace. He's not around much, having worked a lot over the years. Heck, he still works a lot. But I know my dad always loves me no matter what I do or say.

"Hi Daddy." I lay my head on his chest and accept the comfort. It reminds me of a time before "the incident," when I was a normal kid and not someone damaged who needed to be taken care of and told how to run my life.

"If you're ready, Lina is bringing out dinner." My mom's voice snaps me back to the present.

Daddy pats my arm and releases me. He holds out my chair, pushing it in for me as I sit.

"Thank you, Daddy."

My dad smiles, his blue eyes sparkling. "You're welcome,

sweetheart."

My parents' housekeeper brings in dinner, setting plates in front of each of us before scurrying away. I pick at the dish, eating a few bites. For some reason, my appetite always vanishes when I eat here. My mother opens her mouth and I remember exactly why that is.

"So, Britton. The tenth anniversary of 'the incident' is coming up in September," she mentions calmly, as if bringing it up it isn't the equivalent of dropping a nuclear bomb on the table.

I continue focusing on my plate, not giving her the satisfaction of a response.

"Anyway," she continues. "The school is doing a memorial service with the help of SASS, and I think you need to be there to speak."

And there it is.

That's why she wanted me here tonight. To guilt and bully me into speaking at her event. The exact type of event I've insisted over and over I want nothing to do with.

"No." I clench my hands under the table, away from my mother's prying eyes.

The single harsh word hits its mark. Mom's eyes go wide a split second before she can control her face. Then her mask of cold disapproval slides into place, turning her into the mother I've known for most of the last ten years.

"Britton, don't be so selfish. The families of the victims need you there," she insists, her mouth turned down in the corners.

Heat floods my face and I swear, if I were a cartoon character, smoke would be billowing out of my ears. "Selfish?" I reply, my voice rising. "*I'm* selfish?" I push back my chair, shaking with anger, my half-eaten dinner going cold between us.

"Britt," my dad interjects, attempting to coax me into calming down. He's got to be as tired of the fighting as I am.

"No!" I swing my gaze from my dad over to my mom. "I will not be made to feel guilty for not wanting to revisit the worst day of my life! I repeatedly tell you I need to move on with my life, and yet you ignore my wishes again and again!"

"Now wait a minute, young lady," Mom lectures. "I gave up my career to help you recover, to keep you up to date with your peers by homeschooling you so you wouldn't fall behind or have to feel unsafe at school. I thought you'd come around—"

"And I appreciate what you did for me, Mom. I do. But I didn't ask you to give anything up. Just like I didn't ask for a bullet to be put through my skull." My breath hitches as I try to hold in a sob. "It's infuriating that you refuse to acknowledge my need to put all of this crap behind me. I don't remember any of it and I won't let it define my life."

"I'm only trying to—"

I cut her off again. "I don't want excuses, Mom. You don't get to decide for me. Whether you mean well or not, I'm not doing those speeches or attending any events. Ever."

Spinning on my heel, I march toward the front door. As I leave the room, I hear my dad trying to calm my mother down. "Let her be, Rose."

Thankful for his intervention, I slam the front door and hurry outside, the oppressive humidity of Atlanta in June smacking into me like a wet blanket to the face. Tears burn at the backs of my eyes and I have to calm down before driving home. Before I can sort myself out, the door opens behind me. I tense up, waiting for the angry scolding to continue.

"Britt, do you need me to take you home, sweetheart?"

"Daddy?" I peek over my shoulder, finding my father holding his keys. He stares at me with an odd expression on his handsome but tired face. Not pity, it's more than that. Respect?

"No, I'm okay. Thank you, Daddy."

My dad steps forward and engulfs me in a hug, wrapping his strong arms around my small frame. It's been so long since I experienced loving human contact of any kind. My parents aren't the touchy-feely types and my last, my *only* boyfriend, was back when I was an undergrad, and because he knew about "the incident" he treated me like an untouchable porcelain doll.

My dad kisses the top of my head. "Anytime, sweetheart. Anytime."

Killer

Jackson Wolfe might just be the biggest prick I ever met. And I've met a lot of fucking pricks.

"Come on, *Killer*," he taunts from across the cage. "Who

cares what Gabriel says? Let loose so we can find out what you're made of."

A small crowd of trainers and fighters has gathered outside the octagon. We're supposed to be practicing speed and agility, light hits only. This idiot apparently feels the need to prove his alpha status amongst the other men by egging me on in front of everyone.

It infuriates him when I don't answer. In fact, I refuse to speak a single word to the jackass. I reviewed his FLA fights. He's sloppy and too cocky for his own good. He wins because his reach is long and luck is on his side… so far.

I continue training as instructed, swinging at half-strength, dodging his blows when they manage to get anywhere close to me, which isn't often.

"What's wrong with you, man? You're creepy as fuck." Wolfe grins, his face looking more like a caricature of the Joker than anything remotely attractive. His mouth is too big, his eyes too small, and his attitude might even be worse than mine. Silent and brooding beats cocky motherfucker any day.

I survived six months in prison by ignoring the barbs and taunts thrown my way. In my first week I learned what happens if you let emotions take over when another inmate gets under your skin. Nine days in the infirmary taught me a lesson and shut me up damn quick.

Maybe Wolfe needs that experience.

He comes at me again with every intention of landing a hard jab to my ribs. Using only a fraction of the power I normally put behind my punches, I easily deflect his fist, pivot on my back foot, fake a right jab, and hit him with a perfect left cross to the jaw, following up with flying knee strike to the chest. The moron goes down like a house of cards.

"Fuck! You motherfucker!" Wolfe lets loose a string of curse words as he rolls around on the ground, gasping and whining like a baby. "Fucking asshole! We're only sparring."

I duck my head to hide my smirk, struggling to keep my face neutral and uninterested as he loudly blames me for giving him exactly what he asked for. The cage door opens and a trainer rushes in to help the poor diva patch up his boo-boos. I use the distraction to slip out unseen. With a backdrop of Wolfe's cursing and complaining, I pull off my gloves and slip on my hoodie.

No way did I hit the asshole hard enough for him to put on such a display. Once my hood is up over my head, I allow myself a smile at my victory, which slides right off my face when I realize Wolfe's endgame. Britt hurries across the gym in a tiny blonde streak and hops into the cage, kneeling at Wolfe's side.

That sly motherfucker.

He might not have been expecting my hits to be that hard, but he sure is milking it for everything he can—such as garnering plenty of personal attention from the pretty blonde therapist. Anger and possessiveness surge, boiling my blood until it's pumping hot lava through my veins.

One of the trainers helps Wolfe to his feet. It was a simple punch kick combo, for fuck's sake! He's acting like I collapsed one of his lungs! Wolfe and Britt cross to her office and the door shuts behind them. Watching him touching her nearly drives me to grab his hair and punch him in his stupid face. That's when I discover my fingernails are digging into my palms hard enough to draw blood and my jaw is so tight the muscles are beginning to ache.

Fuck! I don't give a shit what Wolfe does with Britt. It's none of my business. Pissed off for letting it get to me, I throw all of my stuff into my bag and head for the door. I'm angry at Wolfe and his scheming bullshit. I'm angry at Britt for falling for his act. But most of all, I'm furious with myself because I handed Britt to Wolfe on a silver fucking platter.

I shouldn't care, but goddamn it, I do.

* * *

Gabriel stares at me from behind his desk, his dark eyes steady. It makes me nervous, how he can look right at me and not turn away or freak out like everyone else. The man has to see the monster inside. He's not stupid or naive.

"You're almost ready for your first fight, Killer. Are you going to be able to handle this?" I scowl, and my face must answer his question. Gabriel laughs. "I know you can handle the fighting, *meu filho*. It's everything else that goes with it I worry about with you."

I sit back in my chair. "Like what?"

"You can't go into the ring, fight, and be done. There are interviews, parties, fan meet and greets, all kinds of social activities you will be expected to take part in." I cross my arms over my chest and let my hood fall over my eyes. "You can keep up the silent, brooding act if you like." I glance up, about to interrupt when Gabriel holds up a hand. "But, you will take part in league events. It's in the contract."

"Shit."

"Yeah, shit," he replies, laughing. "You can do it, Killer. I see past this cold façade you display for everyone." He waves his hand in my direction. "There's a good guy in there somewhere. You just need to give him a chance."

I narrow my eyes at Gabriel. "I'm a lot of things, Gabriel, but one thing I'm not, is a good guy."

He folds his hands on top of his desk and shrugs. "You say that, but I don't believe it."

Familiar defensiveness and hostility flare up in my chest, sizzling, burning until they work their way into every cell in my body. Rage and self-loathing swirl inside, churning and clawing their way out, begging to be released in a flurry of violence. Seething, I hold back the urges, speaking through clenched teeth.

"It doesn't matter what you believe. I know what I am."

"Oh, but it does. It very much matters. I wouldn't train you if I didn't believe in you. This would be a waste of my time, no?" Before I can respond to his bullshit psychobabble, he continues. "Britt is waiting for you in her office. She wants to talk to you about one of your takedowns." The dismissal isn't harsh, but it's clear.

Tense and ready to snap, I jump to my feet, eager to get out of the cramped space. "Fine."

Without sparing him a final look, I storm out of Gabriel's office and make my way to Britt's treatment room. Her back is to me when I enter the room and drop into my usual seat.

As quiet as I am most of the time, today I'm thoroughly irritated and therefore pretty loud when I stomp in and take a seat. Oddly, Britt doesn't seem to hear me at all. I clear my throat so I won't startle her like that asshole Max loves to do.

Britt glances my way and smiles, her eyes lighting up at the sight of me. *What the fuck?* Why is it the only two people in the world who treat me like I'm human both work here, in the very city where my humanity was stripped away? It pisses me off that they don't get it. Mostly because being treated kindly makes the guilt even worse, gnawing at what little is left of my hollow insides. I can't allow her to see me as human when I'm not.

"K, you're early," she chirps, just as happy and normal as could be.

I grunt out a response. "Yeah."

As usual, she pretends I'm polite instead of a massive dick.

"Okay, give me a minute to boot up my laptop. I want to show you something quick, then we can move out to the cage."

Also as usual, Britt yanks her chair from behind her desk to cozy up next to me so we can both see the computer screen at once. Her loose blonde hair brushes my shoulder and I catch the faint scent of citrus. When her hand accidentally touches mine, I nearly fly out of my seat. It's as if a million tiny sparks ignite my skin, blazing hot, the heat singeing me from the base of my spine to the top of my skull.

I'm so fucking confused and stressed out, I don't hear a word Britt says. My body wanted Britt the first time I laid eyes on her. I held back because she's too good, too innocent, and certainly not deserving of the shitty treatment I'd give her. Yet Britt sparks an emotion in me I thought died with my little sister. Something besides the need to satisfy raw animal lust.

Desire? Affection? Adoration?

Shit, I sound like a pussy. By the time I pull my head out of my ass, Britt is staring at me, waiting for me to speak. When I don't, her pink lips turn down in the corners.

"K?"

"What?" I snap, annoyed at Gabriel, annoyed at the way Britt dredges up feelings I gave up on years ago, annoyed at myself for having any feelings at all. Hurt shines behind those wide blue eyes, but Britt collects herself quickly and it's gone in a single blink.

"Are you ready to try out the new positions?"

My mind instantly goes to all of the positions I want to try with Britt and my dick gets embarrassingly hard—pounding her from behind, thrusting into that inviting mouth… Shit. Once again, I silently thank my athletic cup for saving me from humiliation. At this rate, I'll need to wear it all the damn time.

"Uh," I swallow, nervous for the first time in god knows how long. "S-sure?"

Britt is momentarily stunned, certainly a result of the rare crack in my armor. She shakes her head and stands. "Let's go."

Britt

K is acting weird today. Okay, he's always weird, but this is different. He's almost… shy? Embarrassed? Either way, the silent confidence he projects is gone, or flickering in and out, allowing me a few wonderful moments with the real K. The one I'm certain he hides behind that big old tattooed alpha exterior.

Without saying a word—big shock—K follows me to cage six. The grappling dummy, a black and red leather figure, is splayed out obscenely on the mat, waiting for us. Heat floods my face. Max positioned the damn thing on its back, legs spread and pointing upward, as if held in place by invisible gynecological stirrups.

"What's up first?"

"Eeep!" K's sudden presence at my side draws a humiliating noise out of me and I wobble. Catching myself, I turn to face him, unprepared to control my reaction. My mouth drops open at the sight. K is already shirtless, exposing a tantalizing expanse of tan skin, defined muscles, and dark black slashes of ink. All within inches of my now itchy fingers.

"Sorry," he grunts, his huge hand wrapping around my wrist to keep me steady. The touch sends a spark straight between my legs.

Oh. My. God.

"Ummmm, I… I'm okay. Thanks." Our eyes lock and my heart leaps into my throat. Mesmerized, I stare at his molten silver irises as the black of his pupils enlarges, eclipsing nearly all of the extraordinary color.

Those eyes.

I can't put my finger on it but they remind me of… of something. Something just out of reach, but I'm not sure what it is. It's like déjà vu but not quite. Without thinking, I raise my hand to touch his face, desperate to understand, desperate for physical contact, desperate to see if K can give me the serenity I crave.

"Are you guys ready?"

Max's loud question breaks us apart. I yank my hand back to my side. K actually cringes and if I didn't spot the crimson streaks on his cheeks, I would never have believed the man could actually blush.

"We're ready," I reply with more confidence than I should be able to manage.

"Good." Max snaps, entering the cage, K hot on his heels.

Oh great. First K, now Max is in rare form today.

I stand by the cage, confused by the images running through my mind. K's eyes, they seemed… I can't explain it. Familiar? And not because I've been obsessed with their unique color since the first day he arrived at the gym. He so rarely allows eye contact, it's not as if I've gotten anywhere near as acquainted with them as I'd like. I could stare into them for hours at a time.

The unsettling sensation has my heart beating wildly, which is irritating considering I have no idea *why* I'm so unnerved.

"Earth to Britt!"

Once again, I'm caught spacing out. In the ring in front of

me, Max and K are staring, waiting for me to join them. Max has his hands cupped around his mouth to amplify his voice.

"No need to shout, Max," I retort, stomping up the steps and letting myself into the cage. "We won't be filming today, so you can go."

Max frowns, his entire body going rigid at my dismissal. "I'm supposed to help," he insists.

The hostile expression Max shoots my way sends chills down my spine and an uneasy ache into my stomach. Max is pissed off to say the least, only I don't know why and frankly, I don't care, but my voice catches in my throat, along with any argument I had at the ready to tell Max off.

K must sense my discomfort, because he does something I've never, ever seen him do. Something I never imagined he *could* do. He gets visibly pissed and shouts. *Loud.*

"Did you hear what she said?" K takes a deliberate step into Max's space. Max blanches, his hands trembling just enough to notice. "Don't fucking look at her or talk to her like that again," K growls, fists clenched and brows pulled tight over hardened eyes. Eyes that aren't hidden by a baggy hood.

Max stumbles back. "I-I wasn't—"

"Leave!" K's voice is so thunderous the entire gym goes silent. It's probably the first time most of these people have heard his voice. I stand, shocked, as Max scrambles for the stairs, hurries out of the cage, and up the stairs to the employee lounge.

I glance around, unsure of what to do next. Everyone is

staring. K doesn't seem to care or notice. He steps out of the octagon and walks over, his loud, booming voice now a soft, near-whisper.

"Are you okay?"

I flush and a nervous giggle escapes. "Are you really asking me that?"

The corner of his mouth quirks up. "Yeah, I guess I am."

"I'm fine. I'll *be* fine," I correct when one of K's eyebrows lifts accusingly. "Max just… I mean, he's never acted like this before, but lately he's just off. I'm not sure what to make of it."

Now, confused instead of furious, K's brow furrows over those stunning eyes again. "I don't understand you," he admits.

K is willingly meeting my gaze. Only this time it's K trying to figure *me* out instead of vice versa.

"Not much to understand," I lie. "I'm not very complicated."

K leans in closer, only a scant few inches between us. "I disagree. You're very complicated and I want to figure out every single thing about you." Hypnotized, I stare into those deep, silver pools. My stomach flutters, the same sense of déjà vu returning, only to slip away before I can make sense of it.

"I-I'm really not."

K frowns, as if it pains him to continue. But he does, and it's the most I've heard him speak at one time.

"Britt, you're the only girl… no, the only *woman* who isn't afraid of me. Who…" He pauses, his Adam's apple bobbing as he swallows.

Is K nervous?

"You're the only one who doesn't see it," K whispers.

God, I want so badly for him to throw his arms around me, wrap me up in his strength, comfort me and shield me from danger while I spill my secrets to this broken, shuttered-up man. Right now though, it seems he's the one who needs to be held, to be reassured.

"I don't know what you're talking about. I like what I see."

This time, K cringes at my words, inhaling a shaky breath as he responds. "That's the problem."

CHAPTER 5

Killer

"You're ready." Gabriel clamps a heavy hand down on my shoulder, his face lit up with a grin. "AFL has you down for your first fight next month."

"Where?" I allow Gabriel to steer me toward his office, but at the last minute, he surprises me by pushing me into Britt's.

Britt is sitting behind her desk when we enter, me stumbling forward and Gabriel hanging back a few steps. She stops typing and stands.

"You told him?" she asks, her eyes darting back and forth between Gabriel and me.

"Not yet. I was waiting to tell him with you," Gabriel says proudly.

I wait, silent, as the two of them do some sort of wordless dance involving a lot of wide eyes and lifted brows.

"Fine, *mina filha*. I will tell him." Gabriel faces us both but makes eye contact with me. "You will be on the same card as the welterweight title fight. This is a big deal for a newcomer."

I must be gaping like a fish, because Gabriel and Britt laugh, indulgent smiles on their proud faces.

"The Battaglia vs. Gomes card?" I trained with Hugo Gomes at Rafael's gym in Brazil. He's amazing.

"That's the one." Gabriel gestures toward Britt. "Britt here will be traveling with us to Las Vegas for the fight. We need her to make sure you stay in top form."

I'm at a loss for words. Not only will I be fighting on a major card in Vegas, but these two people, people I only just met, honest to god believe in me. As a person, not just a fighter.

"I'm speechless," I admit.

Britt snorts. "Like that's new."

Gabriel laughs loudly and I can't help myself, I join in, my face splitting in a huge grin. Maybe my laugh isn't as big or attractive as theirs, but it's real. This is the first true moment of joy I've experienced in ten years.

"Well, *meu filho*," Gabriel rubs his hands together in excitement. "I'm going to plan our trip. I need both of you in my office at three to go over the details."

Gabriel smiles before leaving Britt and me alone in awkward silence. At least, I find it awkward. Britt has no problem being alone with me or filling the silence.

"How exciting!" Britt squeals, her blue eyes bright and shining with pride.

I can't think of a response to her delighted outburst, instead standing stupidly and picking at the hem of my hoodie. Silent? No. Awkward? Yeah, still awkward.

Her enthusiasm must overwhelm her because next thing I know, Britt's arms are around me, pulling me into a hug. My shocked brain takes a minute to catch up. When it does, I hesitantly lift my hands to place them on her back.

I must give off some sort of signal when my arms close around her, because Britt instantly melts into my chest and lets out a tiny sigh. Her body relaxes and when it does, I realize how tense she her muscles were. Did *I* relax her? My touch wouldn't unwind her. I *cause* fear and pain, not take it away. People do *not* come to me for comfort.

Completely out of character, I go with my desires and duck my head, burying my nose in her hair and inhaling deep. Citrus combined with the soft scent of femininity hit me hard. How long has it been since I've held someone I care about?

I nearly laugh with the ridiculousness of it all. I've *never* held a girl I cared about. I've had sex. That's it. Dirty, raw, sex. No emotions, no connections, nothing but selfish pleasure. But this? It's different.

And now, I want more.

* * *

"Hey man, congrats on the big card."

I spin around to come face-to-face with Jackson Wolfe. *Wolverine.* The nickname makes me want to roll my eyes, but I refrain. Like I can say anything. I'm called Killer, but at least I have a reason. I'm pretty sure he's not an actual wolf. I stare at the other fighter curiously. This is the first time he's spoken to me since I knocked him on his ass a few weeks ago. The way he manipulates Britt irritates me to no end, and the phony smile on his face practically invites another punch.

Instead, I keep my expression neutral, as usual, giving him only a slight nod of acknowledgement.

Jackson frowns, not getting the response he desired. "I'm on the same card, so I guess we'll be traveling together." He smirks. "And Britt, of course."

Fuck. Dealing with this idiot while prepping for the biggest fight of my fledgling career is not what I need right now. Plus, he's right, Britt will be with us as well, so I'm certain my emotions—what very few I have—are going to be in knots. If he starts using Britt to piss me off, it won't take much to push me into losing my temper.

Instead of answering, I turn and walk away, leaving *Wolverine* to stew over my obvious brush-off. Fuck him. It's not required for me to like him. I only have to tolerate him. And be sure not to beat him to death.

Britt and Gabriel are waiting for me in his office so we can start our meeting. After my interaction with Wolfe, I'm seething and frustrated. All I want to do is jump into the cage and beat the fuck out of something, release this shit building up inside. Confusing new emotions like jealousy are dueling with my usual focused, raw fury.

The dark, hollow place in my chest isn't equipped for this. I fight, I fuck, I exist. Nothing more, nothing less.

Furious, I walk over to Gabriel's office and shove open the door. It bangs against the wall with a loud *crack*, causing Gabriel to frown and Britt to cry out. Just like that, she drops to the floor, curling into a ball and covering her head with her hands.

Gabriel leaps to his feet, hurrying around his desk to crouch next to a huddling, quivering Britt. Stunned, I stand at the door frozen, unsure what is going on or what I should do.

"*Meu filha*! Britt! What is happening?" Gabriel's voice hitches as he tries to pull Britt out from under his desk. His head whips around to face me. "Killer! ¡*Venha aqui e ayudar!*" *Get over here and help.*

I cross the space in two quick steps, approaching Gabriel's desk from the opposite side. Britt's tiny frame is tucked into a tight ball, her knees pulled to her chest, head ducked, and arms curled protectively over her head.

Protecting her from what?

"Britt," I say in as composed of a voice as I can manage, which at this moment, isn't saying much. Not a lot freaks me out, but right now, watching Britt fall to pieces, has me struggling to keep calm. "Please, come out."

Britt is quietly sobbing, her body shuddering in fear. Watching her in such obvious distress sends a stabbing pain through my chest. Not sure this is the best thing for her, but not knowing what else to do, I crawl under the desk. Being as large as I am, I can only get my head and shoulders in next to her.

Gabriel slides into nervous, staccato Portuguese. "I will leave you to take care of her. Let me know when she's feeling better and I will return." He stands and leaves the room, gently closing the door behind him.

He left me with her?

What the fuck am I supposed to do? At a loss, I do the only thing that comes to mind. It worked to relax her before, so why not? I gather her tiny, trembling body up in my arms, and hold her. Britt immediately unwinds her arms, clutching me tight, burying her face into my shirt, her tears dampening the fabric.

On the floor in my trainer's office, lying half under a desk, a tiny shard of my black soul becomes human again.

Britt

My frantic pulse slows down the moment K pulls me into the protective circle of his arms. There's just something about him that brings me peace. He's able to take away my anxiety with a single touch.

The gunshot-like sound of the door hitting the wall triggered some sort of flashback or deeply buried memory of "the incident." I've remembered bits and pieces of that day here and there, just flashes, never enough to put together anything concrete. The loud bang, however, somehow managed to dig into the deep recesses of my damaged brain to unearth something horrific. A memory.

Me, hiding under something as gunshots ring out.

I shudder, ice trickling over my skin, goose bumps pricking as I replay the memory. Suddenly, K's hands are there, rubbing up and down my back, warm and comforting. The ice thaws quickly, turning my fear into a flush of heat.

"You okay?" he whispers, his breath ruffling my hair.

I tilt my head back, gazing into those cool, silver eyes. "Y-yes. T-thank you. For…" I swallow, my throat tight as desire burns hot between my thighs. My eyes drop to K's mouth. Even scowling and bewildered, he's beautiful.

Is it the memory that makes me so reckless? Is it the fact that we're tangled together on the floor, our bodies pressed together? Is it the change in K's carefully detached expression to one of concern?

I have no answer. All I know is when I lean forward and press my mouth to his, everything in my world becomes right. For the first time in ten years, I'm exactly where I belong.

K is hesitant at first, his bulk tensing up under my hands. I part my mouth, gently swiping my tongue across his full lower lip, and he gives in. With a groan, K opens his mouth to tangle his tongue with mine, the slick, velvet surface sliding into my mouth. I sink into the kiss, letting K take what he wants, giving me what I need.

A small moan erupts unbidden from low in my throat and it demolishes the rest of K's control. His huge hands leave my back to wrap around my waist, nearly spanning the entire circumference. In one swift move, he spins me around until we're out from under the desk and I'm straddling his lap, chest to chest, face to face. From this position, I can feel beneath me that K is excited. Very excited.

He uses his big hands to press my hips down on his hard length, dragging a gasp out of me. Electricity crackles in the air around us, charging the tiny room. The rub of his groin against mine sends hot sparks of lust up and down my spine to swirl and grow until I'm writhing on his lap and we're both panting and groaning. I nearly tip over the edge right then and there on the floor of Gabriel's office.

K must be close too, because he slows his kisses, allowing both of us to catch our breath. His eyelids are half shut, his mouth swollen and red and slick, his skin flushed with desire. He's so beautiful I can't believe he's real.

Without warning, K jolts upright, as if he just awoke and realized what was happening. Hazy silver eyes pop open in disbelief and refocus on the present. "Oh my god. I'm sorry," he mumbles, attempting to push me off his lap so he can stand. I resist, clinging to his body like a barnacle, refusing to part with his strength, his calm, the comforting way he silences my inner demons.

"Don't," I whisper. "Please don't let go."

K gives me a grim look, but stays. His muscles are still bunched up under my hands, as if he's ready to bolt at any second. I press my good ear to his broad chest, listening until the pounding of his heart to slows to a steady rhythm.

"What happened, Britt?" K's voice is strained.

I tuck in closer, not wanting him to see the lie. "I-I don't know."

"Britt." K shifts, pushing my shoulders back until we're face-to-face. "I don't believe you." Before I can protest, his eyes go soft. "I'm not going to make you tell me, Britt. As you've probably guessed, I'm not exactly a… discuss your feelings kind of guy."

And just like that, K once again took my fears and

demolished them. I giggle at his description of himself. "No, you're not."

He grins. That single dimple appears and I melt. "As much as I love the feel of you against me, can we get up off the floor?" he asks. "I think my ass fell asleep."

In a very unladylike manner, I snort. K's eyes go wide and we both crack up, laughing until we're finally able to stagger to our feet. It's strange to see this stoic, angry, defensive man let down his walls. I thought he was attractive before, but now? Now I fear I may be hopelessly addicted to someone who may never be what I want. Never be what I need. Someone who will always keep himself at arm's length.

The jovial mood from moments ago vanishes when K reaches for the doorknob. "Wait." I grab on to his wrist to keep him from leaving. Shining silver eyes lock on to mine and that sensation of déjà vu sends chills up my arm, raising the tiny hairs on my neck. "Thanks, for helping me."

K nods, brushing his thumb across my lips. Then he's gone.

I slump into a chair, taking a moment to recover from the whiplash of shifting emotions so quickly. From paralyzed with fear to nearly orgasming on K's lap to laughing and joking around with the usually reticent man—my head is spinning.

Now that I'm no longer in the safety of K's arms, anxiety floods my system and I begin to shake. My teeth actually chatter from the adrenaline letdown. I reach into the neck of my shirt and pull out my pendant, squeezing it in my hand. Memories… *my* memories are coming back. Visions of huddling under the desk in the school's office flicker through my mind. And K's eyes. What is it about them?

Thankfully, no one enters Gabriel's office while I fall to pieces. The only thing worse than remembering would be everyone knowing why I freaked out.

CHAPTER 6

Killer

I've never been so relieved to get on a plane in my life. The last two weeks have been brutal. Between cutting weight, training, dealing with that idiot Jackson and that sick fuck Max, plus having no clue how to process my feelings for Britt after what happened in Gabriel's office, I'm a fucking wreck.

I close my eyes and think about that day. Seeing the normally fearless girl—the *only* one who can look me in the eye—so vulnerable, huddled on the floor cowering in fear, was shocking. And it takes a hell of a lot to shock me, especially since I don't usually *feel* anything. But having her pressed against me, it was so right, so perfect. The desire to have that again is so strong, it's all I think about when she's around.

I tried to avoid Britt after mauling her like an animal, but every time I turned around she was there, too close, too warm, smelling too fucking good. If I didn't know how sweet she was, how innocent and good, I would have thought she was getting some perverse pleasure in torturing me with her presence.

The empty seat next to me sinks down and I inhale a soft breeze of citrus. It wraps around my dick, jerking it from soft to hard in a heartbeat.

Fuck.

"K." Britt's voice caresses my stiffening cock, making it throb painfully in my jeans. "Are you nervous for the fight?"

My fingers tighten around the armrests. How the hell am I supposed to talk to her here? We're in an extremely small, enclosed space, she smells so good, and now my dick is so goddamn hard. All I want to do is push her to the bathroom, push up her obscenely short skirt and bury myself in heaven. Three weeks since I kissed her and I'm more obsessed than ever. I don't even need her sitting next to me to get me hard. Hell, Roxie made me a citrus protein shake the other day and I started to sprout wood at the front desk of the gym just from the scent.

"No, Britt. I'm not nervous," I grit out through clenched teeth.

"Oh."

She sounds odd, unlike the perky girl I'm used to. Against my better instincts I give in and turn toward her sitting in the aisle seat on my right. Sunlight is filtering through the small window to my left, highlighting every inch of her gorgeous face. High cheekbones, a delicate nose with a slight upturn, a smattering of light-colored freckles across the bridge and continuing beneath those piercing blue eyes—she's stunning.

And I'm staring.

"Sorry." I slouch down in my seat until my hoodie covers my eyes. If I let her in any more than I already have, Britt could easily peel back my defenses until I'm exposed and squirming under her gaze. Better to hide, to keep her at arm's length so she won't figure out I'm not the man she thinks I am. I'm not a man at all. I'm a monster. A killer. She deserves better than half a human with a black heart and no soul.

"I didn't mean to bother you, K." I flinch when her warm hand curls around my wrist. Against every rational thought I have, I push back my hood and meet her intense gaze. She's leaning out of her seat, her entire body turned toward me. "Jack kept bugging me." Britt uses her thumb to point over her shoulder and rolls her eyes, smiling.

Of course he is. That fucking douche is begging for a flying knee strike to the face.

My revulsion must be evident. "Don't worry," Britt laughs. "I can handle Jack."

"I'll handle him if he doesn't fuck the hell off," I growl.

Britt's eyes widen and she shoots me a huge grin. Her hand tightens around my wrist. My calmed-down cock fills up again in less than three seconds.

"That's sweet of you."

What? She thinks it's sweet that I want to rip Jack's arms off his body and beat him to death with them?

Britt gives my arm one last pat before sitting back and placing her hands in her own lap. She pulls a book out of her bag, cracks it open, and begins to read. Naturally, I'm gaping at her like a teenager who saw his first pair of tits. Great, now I'm thinking about her tits.

Britt stops reading and tilts her head in my direction. "Is it okay if I sit here? I can't deal with his chatter."

Unable to think past the image of running my mouth all over her breasts, biting and leaving dark red marks in that creamy white skin to claim her as mine, I nod. Cheeks burning, I sink down in my seat, adjusting my hard-on as discreetly as possible stuck between the window on my left and her sitting six inches to my right, and close my eyes. I think every hideous, non-sexy thing possible to cleanse my mind of Britt and how badly I want her. I can't have her. Not when I know I can never be worthy.

Britt

The schedule the week of the fight is so crazy, I've hardly had two seconds to speak to K even though we spend nearly all of our time together. There's always something to be done or someone else with us—Gabriel, Max, Jack, journalists, AFL officials, fans—it's insane. Even though he's a rookie in his first fight, K has garnered massive amounts of interest. I'm not sure if it's his unheard of training experience in Thailand and Brazil, the scouting reports, or if it's just K, all tatted up and scary-looking, but excitement surrounds us wherever we go.

As do the women. Lots of them. Half-naked, desperate, clingy women all over K every minute of every day. Three days in Vegas and I want to scream, put my hand up, and shove them away by the face. Only the fact that K ignores every last one of them, his signature hood pulled down low over his eyes whenever we're in public, keeps me sane and gives me smug satisfaction. It's not like I haven't noticed I'm the only woman he makes eye contact with.

I'm watching K spar in the cage at our Vegas training facility, a gym owned by a good friend of Gabriel's. The week before a fight is crazy busy, but the workouts are cut back to about seventy-five percent to prevent burnout by fight night.

Truthfully, he doesn't really need me here. K's form is perfect. Every kick, punch, jab, and takedown is fluid and beautiful to watch.

Max drops onto the bench next to me, huffing. He motions towards K. "Jesus, you'd think he's the second coming of Anderson Silva with all the freaking fuss being made."

My mouth twists up, but I don't acknowledge Max's dig at K. He's been unreasonably hostile this week when it comes to K, especially over the attention K is getting from the media and fans.

Naturally, Max continues ranting, clueless to the fact that we're supposed to be here to help K succeed, not to cut him down over petty bullshit. "I mean, he's not that special."

I twist my head to face Max. He's been my friend at work for the last two years, but I can't let him continue to badmouth any member of our team. And we are supposed to be a *team*.

"Can you just shut up?"

Max's mouth drops open in shock. Never in a million years did he think I would go off on him, but he doesn't know I've been playing the passive-aggressive game with my mother for the last decade. I'm an expert at recognizing it.

"I... but... seriously?" he stammers. "You're defending that stuck-up asshole?"

Now I'm flat-out fuming. "Stuck up? What on earth are you talking about?"

Max quickly works himself into a frenzy, his arms flailing all over the place. "He thinks he's so much better than everyone else! Never speaking to anyone, turning his nose up at all of us! Fuck him for being such a dick."

Don't punch him.

I inhale deep, attempting to calm down enough to respond rationally instead of yelling. "Max, did it ever occur to you that maybe he's like that for a reason?" I think of how tortured K looks sometimes and it makes me sad. I've spent hours wondering what happened to break such a strong man.

"Uh-uh. No way!" Max jumps to his feet, towering over me, still gesturing wildly. "He's a fucking—"

I don't hear the rest of Max's tirade, because one of his flailing arms swings wide and he accidentally backhands me across the right side of my face. Stars explode behind my eyes and the hearing in my right ear fades in and out. His hand hit so hard I topple backward off the bench, landing on my shoulder.

Blistering white-hot pain shoots down my arm and I let out a cry.

"Oh my god, Britt! I'm sorry!" Max is kneeling beside me, hands hovering, unsure what to do.

I'm about to tell him to back off when a gust of air ripples over me and Max vanishes.

"What the fuck is wrong with you?" At first, my hearing is still wavering, so I don't know who's shouting. Dazed, I begin to sit up, using my good arm to push off the ground. Gabriel appears at my side, helping me back onto the bench.

"Sit here, *meu filha*. I need to stop K before he disqualifies himself."

Max's panicked voice rings clear. "I didn't mean to—"

Bewildered, I glance around and my stomach clenches at the sight in front of me. *Oh no.* K is holding Max up off the ground by his shirt, thumping him against the concrete wall like a rag doll.

"I don't give a shit what you meant, you sick fuck!" K roars.

Now I know why I didn't recognize the voice. K is raising his voice. It's so rare, most of these people have never even heard him speak, let alone shout loud enough to be heard by every hotel on the strip.

"I know what you are," K hisses, his face less than six inches from Max's pale visage. "Don't go near her again." He slams Max against the wall again. I flinch when his head bounces painfully off the painted cinder blocks. "Don't ever touch her, don't look at her, don't fucking go near her." His voice is chilling.

"*Meu filho. Por favor*, let go. You will be *disqualificado*." Gabriel puts his hands over K's, gently, but firmly, prying his fingers out of Max's shirt.

I don't notice who hands me an ice pack for my face. Numb, I simply take it and press it to the throbbing ache.

"I'll have someone take you back to the hotel. You need to

calm down." Gabriel waits until K steps back from a wide-eyed Max. "Take Britt with you. She needs to rest for later. We have a press conference and dinner tonight."

Gabriel turns to me, waving me over. I gather my notebook and purse one-handed, balancing the ice pack with the other. "Go to the hotel with Killer," Gabriel instructs.

"But—" K frowns and takes a step toward Max, causing Max to scurry back in fear.

"No." Gabriel's voice is firm and final. "I will take care of this one." He flicks his hand at Max. "Both of you leave, now."

There is no arguing with Gabriel when he's like this. The only option is to do as he says. I step forward and take K's wrapped hand. "Come on, K. Let's go." I can see the raw fury in his eyes, the reluctance to leave without his pound of flesh. He *is* a fighter after all, but a good fighter must also be able to control his urges no matter the circumstances. I tug on his hand and he finally relents.

Ten minutes later, we're dropped off in front of our hotel. The silence on the short ride was excruciating. I wanted to crawl into K's lap and kiss him senseless for defending me, and then chastise him for endangering his career. The AFL and the Nevada Athletic Commission can and will suspend his license for bad behavior outside the cage.

We enter the crowded hotel elevator without saying a word. K dips his head, letting his hoodie cover half his face to hide from any AFL fans. When the elevator stops to let more people on, K grabs my waist, tugging me to his side possessively. My heart leaps into my throat and I have to hide a smile. He's so close I can smell the seductive combination of sweat and man and K.

I squirm uncomfortably and catch him glancing at me from under his hood. His eyes land on my cheek and go cold, the silver turning the color of hard stone.

"It's okay," I whisper.

He shakes his head but says nothing.

After an eternity and about five different stops to let other guests on and off, the elevator finally reaches our floor. K slides his arm from my waist, effortlessly finding my hand and entwining our fingers. The sweet gesture is so contradictory to the man I know, I nearly melt into a puddle on the floor.

"Come to my room." His voice is rough, strained. Like he even has to ask. I'd do anything he wanted. Anything.

"Okay."

With a sharp nod, he leads me down the hall. K deftly removes a card from his pocket and opens the door.

"Go sit." He points at the bed. "I have some first-aid supplies."

I drop onto the pristine white duvet. "What?"

"A medical kit. I have to fix you up."

A medical kit?

He brought me to his room to give me first aid? The thought is more depressing than I imagined. Maybe that kiss in Gabriel's office was a one-time thing, a mistake in K's mind. Either way, I don't need or want his pity, or anyone else's for that matter.

"I'm fine, K. I'm not bleeding. Ice is really all I can do for it." I move to get up and K pins me in place with his eyes. The argument drains out of me and I sit back down.

K scowls. "No. You need anti-inflammatories. It's going to swell and it's going to hurt. Fuck." K squeezes his eyes shut, his beautiful face twisted as if he's in agony, the tendons in his neck bulging. Those haunting silver eyes pop back open, locking on to mine. "I wanted to kill him for touching you."

Stunned at his admission, I pat the bed. "Come sit with me."

His lethal expression vanishes, replaced by uncertainty. The bravest man I know takes a step back. "I shouldn't," he whispers.

I stare at this big, strong fighter as he attempts to turn away. *No.* I refuse to let him do his usual dodge and flee routine. This time, he's going to answer my questions. "Why not?"

"I'm… I'm not a good person, Britt. Things I've done." K licks his lips and swallows, his throat rippling. I want to lick and bite my way across the rough skin, lave my tongue over it, taste his sweat, rub my body all over his until I'm coated in his scent. K's eyes roam over my body. He shudders and I feel it in my groin. "Things I want to do to you. I can't… I refuse to ruin you."

I stand up, determined to see what he'll allow. K watches as I walk over, only stopping when my body is a fraction of an inch from touching his. My hands find the hem of his hoodie and I slip them inside, gliding my fingers up over each ridge of his abs, stopping when I palm his wide chest.

"You won't ruin me, K. I'm stronger than I look. I just

need… I don't know what I need. I've been looking and can't find it. Whatever it is, I think you can give it to me."

K twists his mouth as he thinks about what I said. Before I can react, he grabs my hips, tugging me forward. I feel the hard length of his erection digging into my abdomen. His head drops to my left ear and I quickly duck around him so his mouth is on my right. "What kind of things do you think you need, Britt?" His breath tickles my ear and neck, causing goose bumps to spread over my sensitized skin. "Because I'm not a nice guy. The things I want to do to you, they're harsh and depraved and filthy."

His words have me panting, grinding my pussy against the thick muscle of his thigh. I skim one hand further up to his chest, finding a nipple. Not really knowing what I'm doing, I twist it between my fingers. The action turns K feral; growling, he grips my backside in his huge hands as he spins us around. My back slams against the wall and I groan with pleasure. K yanks my arms out from under his shirt to pin them above my head. With a sinuous ripple of his lower body in a move that would make Magic Mike jealous, K rubs his crotch against me, pushing that huge thigh up into my aching pussy.

If the wall weren't behind me, I'd drop my head back in ecstasy. "God," I moan. "I need… I need your strength… and power. I need to feel safe…" I gulp down air between breathy words.

"Safe? What does that mean?" K skims his mouth down my neck to where it meets my shoulder. Before I can explain he bites the soft flesh and tight tendons… hard.

"Oh Jesus." My knees weaken and I would collapse if K weren't holding me up. "Yesssssss."

He releases my stinging skin, laving his hot tongue over the area. "You like it rough?" K breathes into my ear.

I convulse with pleasure. "I-I don't know."

"You like to be restrained?"

"I-I…" My legs are now quivering.

"Pain?"

I throw my head back, my chest heaving, my underwear wet from my body's reaction to K's husky words. I'm not thinking, merely reacting when I answer. "God, yes."

"Fuuuuuck," he groans. K lets me go, taking a step back. I'm about to beg him to come back when he reaches behind his shoulders and yanks off his sweatshirt, tossing it to the floor. Mesmerized, I stare as he shoves his shorts down and kicks them aside, standing gloriously naked in front of me.

"I don't know why, Britt, but I can't stop thinking about you. You make me want things… things I don't deserve. But I can't fight it anymore. The need for you is stronger than me."

His words make me melt and I lick my lips as my eyes drift down. *Oh god.* I have no idea what to do first. I'm eager to taste the wide expanse of skin on his pecs, those pebbled copper discs, to trace my tongue over every line of ink on his body. Then my eyes find his thick cock, erect and waiting for me to take it in my mouth. He's stunning.

"Strip," he commands. I whimper when K wraps a big hand

around his length and begins to stroke. The sheer power contained within his body, all hard muscle and cut ridges, has me writhing. He's like a gorgeous, coiled panther, ready to strike, and he's staring at me like I'm his prey.

"Oh my god." Suddenly, I can't get naked fast enough. Because he was training in the cage today, I'm wearing casual Capri leggings and a lightweight T-shirt. The clothes come off quickly, dropped somewhere on the hideous hotel carpet.

"Fuck, you're beautiful." K's eyes shine with lust and a hint of danger. I should be afraid, but I'm not. I'm more turned on than I've ever been in my life. One step of his long, sinewy legs puts K directly in front of me. His arm darts out, a strong hand threading into my hair, the other wrapping around my waist.

I let out a throaty cry. K yanks me forward, tightening his grip in my hair just to the edge of painful. The burn on my scalp wakes up every nerve ending in my body. A scorching ripple of heat rushes across my skin.

"This what you want?" K's mouth is an inch from mine. I attempt to lean in for a taste, desperate to have those thick lips on mine. K is having none of that. He grinds harder against me and I light up like Times Square.

"Oh god." His grip on my waist is the only thing keeping me on my feet. My pussy clenches with pleasure.

"You don't decide what you get. I decide. You think I can give you what you need, then you let me give it." His eyes are locked on mine. They're feral, the silver nearly eclipsed by huge black pupils.

I nod, panting with desire. Without speaking another word, K's grip on my hair tightens and he shoves me to my knees in front of him. K repositions his hands in my hair, one tangled on either side of my head, holding firm.

I nearly pull away when his fingers come dangerously close to the scar behind my ear, but I come face-to-face with his gorgeous cock, the wide head glistening with evidence of his desire, and any worry is gone. I close my eyes and inhale. His scent is sweaty and masculine. I groan with desire. I couldn't stop now, not for anything, not even if the building started crumbling down around us.

"You want it?" he asks, staring down at me with a look so hungry, I moan at the sight.

"Yes."

K growls. "Then show me."

I reach up to grip the heavy shaft but am stopped when K holds me back by my hair. The pain is sharp enough for me to let out a half-cry, half-moan, and the temptation to touch my quivering pussy is nearly overwhelming.

"No hands. I want to fuck that gorgeous, innocent mouth of yours before I fuck that hot wet pussy."

I swallow hard and open my eyes, suppressing a shudder. Looking up, I meet K's hungry gaze. Everything wrong in my life suddenly becomes right. *This*, this is what I need. "Yes."

K tilts his hips forward, the blunt head of his cock sliding across my lips. "Open that sweet mouth, baby." Without breaking eye contact, I do as he says and take what he gives me as K slowly slides his length into my eager mouth.

I tighten my lips around the smooth, hot skin and suck… hollowing my cheeks. K hisses and those silver eyes flutter closed, his head dropping back in ecstasy. Using my hair to hold me in place, he begins to thrust in and out, using me, using my mouth purely for his pleasure.

K is in perfect control of his movements, never giving me more than I can handle. His hips jerk forward and he nudges the back of my throat with the flared head of his cock, holding it there until I'm desperate for a breath of air. I don't panic, trusting him completely. At the last possible second, K pulls back, allowing me to inhale through my nose before he goes deep again. Over and over, he plunges slowly in and out until his chest is heaving and he's moaning and letting out a string of filthy words.

"Fucking hell, your mouth is so tight." *Thrust*. "You're so gorgeous like that, on your knees for me." *Thrust*. "You were made to suck cock, weren't you?" *Thrust*. Eventually, I can't contain all of my saliva. It leaks out, slicking my chin and dripping onto my bare breasts.

I can tell K's control is unraveling. His muscular thighs are trembling and the salty taste of his release is near constant in my mouth. The next time he pulls back, I swirl my tongue around his shaft and flick it across the sensitive skin beneath the head.

"Fuck!" With a sharp tug on my hair, K pulls me off and pulls me to my feet.

Before I can catch my breath, his lips are on mine. K devours me, his tongue plunging deep. The soft, velvety texture of his lips and tongue contrast with the rough way he claims my mouth. When he breaks the kiss, K snags my lower lip with his teeth, sinking them in hard enough to break the skin.

"Ahhhhh!" I cry in surprise, my eyes flying open. The tang of copper hits my tongue and I moan in ecstasy, trembling, desperate for the pleasure I know he can give me.

"You're incredible." My eyes widen at K's praise. The lust and raw need is still visible in his silver irises, but now I also see pride and admiration. The grip on my hair loosens and he gently caresses my face, his expression almost reverent. K's jaw twitches. When he speaks, his voice is husky with desire. "Get on the bed."

After a moment's hesitation to process his words, I scramble up on the thick mattress, my heart pounding a mile a minute. It's been so long since I've had sex, and K will only be the second man I've ever been with. Eric, my one and only boyfriend, treated me like glass. Because he knew about my history, my injury, "the incident," sex with Eric was gentle and predictable. And completely unsatisfying.

K rummages in a bag, pulls out a condom, and drops it on the bed.

"Please," I beg, squirming, not sure what I'm asking for or even what I need. I just need... *something*, anything. I need K.

"Shhhhh." K climbs on the bed, crawling toward me. He forces my legs apart with his knees. Heat ripples up my body as his eyes skim over my exposed flesh to stop on my face. "I want you so badly, Britt." His large hands rest on my thighs, rubbing up and down. "How much can you take?"

"I-I don't know."

His brow furrows. "You don't know?"

My face flames up. "I've never—" I swallow and fist the duvet. "I'm not a virgin," I blurt out. K scowls at my admission. "I just haven't done anything like this before," I say quickly. My eyes dart to the side and my face heats up. I'm too embarrassed to look at K.

"Hey!" Thick fingers grip my chin and force me to face my lover. "Don't turn away from me. I want your honest reactions. All of them." In a blink, his angry expression calms. "We'll play this by ear then. I want to take you to the edge and make you fly. Just tell me if it's too much."

Somehow, I know he's not expecting a verbal response. K releases my jaw and skims his fingers lightly down my arms, sending a chill down my spine and a flood of liquid heat between my legs. When K reaches my hands, he holds them tight and brings them over my head, placing them on the headboard behind me.

"Do I need to tie you down or can you keep them here?"

I nod. "I can do it. I trust you, K. Make me feel alive." My heart feels like it might burst out of my chest it's beating so hard. I shift on the bed and lift my hips, seeking contact. I'm so turned on. A single touch to my clit might make me explode.

"Fuck, Britt." K's neck and chest are flushed red. His lips part and he growls, his face crumpling into a harsh, heated glare.

"You asked for it. We'll see if you still trust me when we're done."

K lets go of one of my wrists. I hear the whistle of air past my ear and the loud *crack* before the pain registers from the open-handed blow K landed on my thigh.

Breath rushes out of my lungs. "Oh my god." I've never been this sexually stimulated in my life. My pussy is literally throbbing. I want to press my legs together to relieve the ache, but K is firmly planted on the bed, his thick, muscular thighs keeping my legs apart.

"That was for moving. Stay still."

My chest is rising and falling with each rapid breath. K leans forward, his hot mouth skimming along the side of my neck, finding the spot he bit earlier. K swipes his tongue over it and I moan, throwing my head back. Sharp teeth sink into the already tender flesh.

"Ahhhhhh." My back arches, forcing my head into the pillow. The pain sparks a fire deep inside me that quickly flares up into a roaring inferno. Heat zaps through millions of nerve endings, electrifying every pleasure center in my body. The harsh contact of a second blow to my thigh drags another moan from me.

K releases of the throbbing skin on my neck and slides further down, circling one breast with his tongue.

"Oh god." Again, my hips buck up off the bed. Once again, a sharp slap resonates in the hotel room. "Jesus, ohmygod."

"Stay still or I'll stop." His voice is as ragged as mine.

"S-sorry," I whimper. My body is aching—pain, pleasure—all of these new sensations swirling together, combining to create the perfect storm of ecstasy.

K's mouth clamps around one nipple, his hand finding the other. He sucks hard while his fingers twist and pull.

Staying still takes more concentration than I thought possible. My body's instinctual demand to seek out relief is overwhelming. Sweat trickles down my brow and I clench my jaw at the effort. My fingers clamp down, digging into the wood headboard.

Then K uses his teeth on my sensitive nipple and I lose it.

"Oh fuck!" I arch back, crying out as my muscles tighten and spasm. Pleasure tears through me, the orgasm surprisingly strong despite the fact that K hasn't gone anywhere near my pussy.

Tremors are still wracking my body when K grips my legs and flips me to my stomach. As I continue to shudder, I hear him tear open the foil packet. He yanks my hips up so my backside is high in the air. A strong hand holds down my head, pressing one of my cheeks into the mattress.

Another loud crack and my ass is on fire. Then another. As the third blow smacks across the sore flesh, K plunges into my aching depths, driving that thick cock deep, not stopping until he bottoms out.

"Ahhh! Oh my god, K..." I gasp at the fullness of having K inside me.

"Fuck, you're so tight. Your pussy is incredible... Jesus, Britt." K holds still, one hand still shoving me down brutally while the other clutches my hip, his fingers digging in painfully. Slowly, so slowly, he drags his cock back until it's almost out, and thrusts in again. Hard.

I let out a strangled cry and he cracks my sore ass again. "You like this, baby?" My muffled groan is the only answer I can manage. K pistons in and out as I wail into the pillow. "You didn't even know you needed this, did you? Need to be fucked, to be dirty and used, to feel pain."

"Yes!" I shout as he snaps his hips. Each time, his cock rubs across a spot deep inside that lights me up all over. Flashes burst behind my closed eyes and I begin to tremble uncontrollably. K stops to growl in a low voice.

"I'm going to fuck you now, Britt."

Oh god. He hasn't been fucking me? I'm going to die. He's going to fuck me to death.

All of the breath is punched out of my lungs when K begins to pound in earnest. He is relentless, thrusting hard over and over until reality becomes hazy and sensation takes over. Held down and helpless, all I can do is feel, absorb what K gives me.

"Jesus, Britt," he huffs. K leans forward, his sweat-slick body covering mine. The hand on my hip reaches for a breast and he twists my nipple. The pain sends me over the edge. I scream while K continues fucking me through my second climax.

Right when I think I might pass out from the intensity, K roars, slamming in deep one last time as his release tears from him.

I'm floating—a pleasant, drifting semi-awareness. I feel K's heat, the weight of him splayed on top of me, but it's as if I'm watching from above. I must lose time, because the next thing I know, K is pulling down the covers and climbing into the bed. His heavy arm comes around my waist and the hard ridges of his body press against my back. K brushes his thumb over my abdomen, the affectionate gesture an absolute contradiction to the harsh, physical sex we just had.

I want to think about it more, the kind, sweet man who peeks through the rough, frightening exterior, but I'm too tired.

My eyes are heavy, my mind still flying high as I sink into sleep. The final thought that flicks through consciousness before I let the darkness take me is *finally*... I finally found exactly what I need.

No. Exactly *who* I need.

And I won't stop until he gives me everything.

CHAPTER 7

Killer

My eyes fly open at the piercing ring of my phone. I sit up, disoriented. Where the hell am I?

Drinking to oblivion and passing out isn't something I've done since I learned the control and discipline necessary to excel at Muay Thai. Only, I didn't drink last night. I rub my eyes, the stupid phone still blaring.

Irritated, I swing my feet over the bed and follow the sound. The room is dark, but a few slivers of light filter through the edges of heavy curtains. I paw through a pile of clothes on the floor. Shorts, pocket, phone.

Finally. I answer with a rude, incoherent grunt.

"Killer? Where are you? Did you take Britt to her room? I can't find her." Gabriel's voice is not angry, but laced with concern. *Britt?*

Oh fuck.

I drag a hand down my face, trying in vain to rub away the idiocy of my actions. Cringing, I glance over my shoulder and confirm what I already know. Blonde hair is spread across one of the pillows of the king-sized bed in my hotel room.

The one time I lose control of myself and it's with Britt. What was I thinking? For fuck's sake, I work with her! My plan to treat her like I treat all the other women I've been with, dirty and degrading, backfired in my face. Sweet, innocent Britt loved every minute of it—the pain, biting, spanking, being restrained. Fuck, just thinking of it has my dick waking up for more. I thought she'd be a missionary, making-love kind of girl and I'd scare her away. Instead, all I did was make it impossible for myself to not want more.

"Killer!" Gabriel begins yelling in rapid-fire Portuguese. "Are you listening to me? You and Britt are supposed to be at this press conference in fifteen minutes. Where the fuck are you?"

Shit. Shit. Shit.

"I'm coming. Sorry. I'll bring Britt with me." I hang up before Gabriel can ask why Britt is with me and what I'm doing with her. Damn, he's going to be so pissed.

I'm pissed at myself.

No time for regrets. Right now, I have to get her up and both of us need to go downstairs ASAP. The AFL press conference is a big deal. It's mandatory for all of the fighters to take part.

"Britt." I hover over the bed, unsure of the best way to wake her up. When she doesn't move, I speak louder. "Britt."

"Mmmmmhhmhphh." She tugs the sheet up higher and rolls away. She's gorgeous. Rumpled and relaxed, like a beautiful angel.

Jesus Christ, I am so stupid. I'll never get enough of her.

"Britt!" I shake her arm at the same time I shout her name.

"What?" She bolts upright, recoiling. Her eyes are wide with fear.

I hold up my hands to show I'm not going to hurt her. "The

press conference. It's starting in fifteen minutes." Without waiting for a reply, I scoop up her clothes and toss them on the bed. "Hurry!"

Realization sinks in and Britt springs to action, babbling for me to give Gabriel her apologies as she tugs on her pants. I rush into the bathroom and turn on the shower. While I'm busy taking the fastest shower known to man, I hear the door to my room close.

She left.

I don't know if that makes me relieved or angry. Fuck it. No time to worry. Who am I kidding? I never worry. In order to worry, you have to care, and I definitely don't care.

I quickly throw on a T-shirt with Souza MMA emblazoned on the chest and pull on a clean pair of jeans. Out of the bathroom, the evidence of what we did is everywhere. Rumpled bed, clothes on the floor, used condom in the wastebasket, the scent of sex permeating the room—just thinking about Britt on her knees, swallowing my cock while looking up at me with those big blue eyes is getting me hard again.

"Goddammit!" The urge to punch something is near overwhelming. I inhale and struggle to calm down. Control over my mind and body is second nature, but today it's not so easy. It takes me a few minutes before I'm able to relax.

I snort and hurry down the hall to the elevator. Control over my mind and body? I'm good at it. No, I'm fucking perfect. I have absolute control over my mind and body.

Except, it seems, when it comes to Britt.

The tiny blonde physiotherapist with the exterior of an

innocent angel that conceals a seductive temptress who didn't know she craves pain and rough sex. If I let her, she'll unravel everything I've worked for, everything I've built to block out the unnecessary things—things like feelings and emotions—things that make living impossible for me to endure. Yet, as I argue with myself as to why it's a bad idea to be with Britt, I already know I'm going to go down the rabbit hole again if offered the opportunity. Being inside her once isn't enough for me.

I can easily see Britt becoming an obsession. One with the potential to either save me or destroy me.

The question is, do I want either?

* * *

"Mr. Bishop, do you feel you're adequately prepared for Saturday's fight?"
"Mr. Bishop, is it true you trained at Dragon Muay Thai in Bangkok with former world champion, Sirichai Wattana?"
"Killer. Where did you get that name?"

The questions go on and on to the point I want to shove the microphone off the table and knock some of these journalists into next week. Most of them are pushy to the point of rude and cross the line of decency more than once.

"We are done." Gabriel stands from his seat next to me and I do the same. "We must get ready for the dinner tonight. Thank you for your time."

Gabriel moves back, letting me go first off the makeshift stage. I hear his heavy footsteps behind me and I brace for the inquisition.

"Killer, in here." Gabriel stops at an open door in the long hall of empty conference rooms and offices and larger ballrooms.

Without a word, I follow. Gabriel is right to be furious. Whatever he *thinks* I did with Britt, the reality is sure to be much, much worse.

Gabriel spins around to face me, but his expression is concerned, not angry. "Killer. Are you sure you can handle what you are doing?"

I tense. Not only is his worry surprising, but I'm not certain what it is exactly Gabriel is implying I can't handle.

Defensive, I cross my arms over my chest. "I don't know what you mean."

"*Meu filho*, come on. Don't play stupid. I see the heat between you and Britt." Thank god I have ten years of practice controlling my reactions, because Gabriel just blew me away. "You didn't think anyone noticed? Think again." He laughs. "The two of you practically go up in flames whenever you're near each other."

"What? I'm not—"

He waves me off with the flick of a wrist. "Save it. I don't need excuses. I'm Brazilian. We are passionate people." Gabriel turns serious, holding my gaze. "Britt is a sweet girl, but troubled, lonely. A lost soul, like you, no?"

Britt is lost and troubled? Okay, yeah, I can admit I noticed something like that. She admitted as much earlier.

"And you," he continues without waiting for my confirmation. "You act so strong and proud and as if you have no *sentimentos* inside." His arm extends and he thumps on my chest with a closed fist. "You think you are empty?" I open my mouth to reply. "Pffft," he brushes me off again. "I know people. I trained many men over many years. You're a fighter. You know I am trained as you are, to study the opponent, to learn to pick out the weaknesses and strengths in a man. I know you."

Fuck.

Heat floods my neck and face. I'm not sure if it's anger or embarrassment, but either way I don't like it. I don't react to other people. They don't affect me.

But now they do. First Britt, now Gabriel.

"Be careful," Gabriel says. "I give you both my blessing. I think you could be good for each other. But if you are incapable of being what Britt needs, stop now. I will not see her hurt."

And there it is. The warning I was waiting for.

I swallow and drop my gaze, my bravado quickly disappearing with Gabriel's ability to see right through me.

"Dinner. I will meet you in the lobby bar at seven. Don't be late this time."

Gabriel pats my shoulder and leaves. My mind is a jumbled mess of thoughts, which is exactly why I don't allow myself to have emotions. They're too messy, too complicated, bring too many painful memories. Only, with Britt, it doesn't feel messy or complicated, or painful. It feels…right.

The fact I feel *anything* should let me know I'm headed in the wrong direction, headed down a path of darkness, destruction, and failure. A path that will dig out memories so painful I've created an entire persona to avoid dealing with them. Yet I know—I'm going down that path headfirst, no questions asked, no matter the outcome.

I might be a monster, but I'm a selfish one.

Britt

It's Thursday night. My hands tremble as I lay down the hair straightener and smooth the last few flyaways. I step back from the sink in the cramped hotel bathroom. The bright red Herve Leger bandage dress is short, tight, and leaves a sinful amount of skin bare.

I exhale, placing my hands on my churning stomach. *You can do this, Britt.* My little pep talk does nothing for my nerves. Neither does the risqué dress I spontaneously purchased in the hotel's upscale boutique to show K I'm far from the innocent girl he sees when he looks at me. I'll be paying it off for the next year, but it will be worth it if it keep K coming back for more.

After fleeing K's room earlier, I sat on my bed and reflected on his words.

"I'm not a good person, Britt. Things I've done."

I don't get it. I fail to see anything bad about him. Yeah, he's intimidating as hell and very unapproachable. But bad?

"I can't…I won't ruin you."

How could he ruin me?

I just can't reconcile the horrible person K believes himself to be with the man who held me on the floor of Gabriel's office until I stopped shaking. My only regret is K seeing me vulnerable that day. If he thinks I'm broken or weak, he won't touch me or offer a repeat of the fantastic, life-changing sex we had. Sex that lights up my body and silences my mind.

No. I don't believe he's bad.

He's a good person. Despite what he says, I feel it. I *know* it. And tonight I'm going to make him see I can take whatever he wants to give. I've thought about the sex I had with K a lot. More than I should. I've been flailing for so long, and after being with K just the one time, it's all become so clear so fast. I need a strong man to give me pain and depravity to feel alive and displays of strength to feel safe. Weak, innocent Britt is saying goodbye and sick, twisted Britt is going after what she wants.

I slip on my four-inch designer heels and pose in front of the floor-length mirror on the back of the closet doors. Vampy red lipstick slicks my lips and a layer of concealer hides the bruise on my jaw. When I pull one corner of my mouth into a slutty smirk, I feel ridiculous. Whatever.. I huff and snatch up my clutch, stuff my keycard inside and decide to let the proverbial chips fall where they may.

This dress is either going to blow K's mind, or send him running. Somehow, I don't foresee this night ending any way except with me wrapped around his sinful body, my skin humming with the satisfied sting from his hands.

Time to find out.

* * *

I show my badge to the slack-jawed man in a tuxedo at the door to the ballroom. Grinning, I give him a wink. "Thanks."

His reaction tells me the dress isn't a complete waste of money and will hopefully serve its purpose. Right inside the door, a lovely woman in a forest green gown greets me. "Name?"

"Britt Reeves."

She scans her clipboard, her eyes lighting up when she finds my name on the list. "Here you go, dear." The woman hands me a tiny card. "Table five. They're numbered but it's in the center." She points me in the correct direction.

"Thank you."

The ballroom is three-quarters full already. I wasted a good twenty minutes freaking out before leaving my room, so I know I'm a tiny bit late. At least my phone isn't blowing up. I'm surprised Gabriel didn't send a text wondering where I am.

"Britt?"

I startle and spin around to come face to face with Jackson Wolfe. "Jack?" He's can't keep the shock out of my voice. I'm used to seeing him in fight gear, shorts, sweats, stuff like that. Tonight, he's wearing a dark, custom-fitted suit with a bright blue and black tie to match his fight colors.

"Holy fuck, Britt!" My cheeks flame up as Jack gapes, blatantly scanning up and down my body. "Christ, I knew you were hot, but hell." He continues his visual assault, not once looking up at my face.

"Jesus, Jack. Do you think you could at least pretend I have a head attached and look up here while you speak to me?" Irritated and embarrassed, I cross my arms over my chest and scowl.

Now it's Jack's turn to blush, something I never thought possible. "Sorry, Britt." He actually looks honest to god ashamed at his behavior.

"It's okay, Jack. I understand this dress will attract a certain amount of…" I pause to snag a glass of champagne off of a passing tray and take a big sip. "Attention."

He grins, laughing. "Yeah. You could say that. Hell, Britt. You know you're at an FLA dinner, right? Filled with hormonal men. Every fighter in the room is going to follow you around drooling."

No, I didn't think of that. I was too fixated on K seeing me as someone other than good-girl Britt, I forgot about the forty or so other testosterone-fueled fighters here tonight.

Jack chuckles again. "From your expression, I'm guessing you didn't think of that."

I shake my head and down the rest of my drink, the bubbles tickling my nose. "No."

"Don't worry. I can always pretend to be your date and keep the men off of you." Jack smiles earnestly. Without question he would do it. But having Jack hanging off of me all night isn't the best way to garner K's attention. Well, it is, but not the attention I want, or the attention K needs. A fight with Jack at an AFL dinner would have him disqualified in a heartbeat.

"Are you ready for the fight Saturday?" I change the subject, scanning the room for another waiter with champagne, and a certain silver-eyed man.

"As ready as I can be." My eyes flick back to Jackson to catch him shrugging. "I have no doubt I'll win."

Cocky as ever.

From the corner of my eye, I spot K and Gabriel near the bar set up in a corner of the huge room. Before I can decide if I should go straight over to them or get another drink first, everyone is asked to take their seats.

Here goes nothing.

An arm slips through mine. *Jack.* "Let me take you to our table."

I can't say no without coming off like a bitch, so I smile and nod. God, I need another drink. Jack deftly weaves us through the crowd, puffed up and smug as other men stop to blatantly stare at me and my teensy red dress. I swallow down my embarrassment, instead focusing on the sight of K, dressed in a beautiful silver suit with a red tie, converging on the same table as Jack and me.

Maybe this dress was a bad idea.

K's shock when he notices us couldn't be more obvious if he tried. His usual expression of stony indifference is gone, replaced by bulging eyes, clenched hands, and a jaw hanging open so wide it may as well be dragging on the ground. Then those shrewd silver eyes, accentuated by the fine gray fabric of his suit, zero in on Jack and his face goes from gaping to enraged in the span of a heartbeat.

K begins to walk around the table toward me and my palms become slick with sweat. Lust and anger war in his expression, and as screwed up as I am, I love it. Before K reaches us, Gabriel steps in front of him and whispers something in his ear. K nods and Gabriel steps aside to let him continue on his way. K reaches my side and I tense, waiting for the explosive confrontation with Jack.

Instead of shouting or striking, K gives me a wide smile, that dimple making a rare appearance, and holds out a crooked arm. "May I escort you to your seat?"

"What the fuck, Killer?" Jack tries to maneuver between K and me, which makes me stumble in the impossibly high heels I'm unaccustomed to wearing.

"Don't touch what's mine, Wolfe," K hisses, darting around him to steady me with a strong hand on my waist. K's words, combined with the heat of his touch, singe my skin through the fabric of my dress. Desire builds low inside and I burst into flames, the heat unfurling quickly, flaring up, licking over every nerve ending. I gasp at the intensity and our eyes meet.

I'm trapped. Ensnared by his mesmerizing silver gaze. The familiarity of it warms me further, but that funny sensation of déjà vu is still there to send an icy ripple down my spine and back up to the base of my skull. The scar beneath my hair throbs and I have to tear my eyes away. My heart is pounding in my chest, a cold sweat beading up between my shoulder blades.

What is it about his eyes that is so familiar?

"Britt?" K's breath tickles my ear and I shiver. "I want to throw a sheet over you and hide that unbelievable body from all the men in the room. You're going to pay for letting them see what's mine." I gasp at his words. Then, as if he didn't just get me hot and bothered, he changes the subject. "Let's get you in a chair."

Breathless, I allow him to maneuver me into a seat. He takes the one to my right, threads his fingers through mine, and pulls my hand into his lap. K's thumb gently strokes across the back of my hand, soothing little caresses no one would believe could come from a man so intimidating and fierce.

Yet without me saying a word he somehow knows what I need.

The gesture is tender and sweet and so unlike the brooding, angry man he projects, yet it's so *him*. It's another glimpse into the real K, whoever he is.

"You all right?" His question is without ulterior motive or jealousy. He honestly wants to know if I'm okay.

I shake my head, tilting it to meet his inquiring stare. "I-I don't know. Maybe too much champagne." *Maybe being near you blows my mind.* I give a forced smile and K squeezes my hand under the table.

From the way he presses his mouth into a tight line, I'm pretty sure he doesn't believe me. Or maybe he's pissed over the dress. Thankfully, K doesn't press for more. I couldn't explain how I feel even if I wanted to, which I don't. How do I tell him his eyes make me uneasy, but at the same time his presence sends a warm, protective feeling straight to my heart?

K glances over, dropping his gaze to the low-cut red dress and my voluptuous breasts. He gives me a dark, hungry look that leaves no doubt what he's thinking.

Oh hell. I'll never make it through dinner.

Killer

"*Meu filho*, where is your head?"

I flinch at Gabriel's question. "I'm here, just… getting in my zone."

He laughs loudly as he weaves the red wraps around my fingers and palm. "You? You're always in the zone. You *are* the zone!"

I ignore the teasing. He's right. I'm off today. My wandering mind won't make a bit of difference on the outcome. Once I'm in the cage, I'm one hundred percent focused on my opponent, on the only thing I'm good for… fighting. Even if I'm not all there, I'll still slaughter the other guy. I'm that confident in my skill.

Britt made herself scarce after fleeing dinner Thursday night. It didn't make any sense. To let me fuck her into the mattress, show up in that dress, flaunt her delectable body, making me burn with jealousy, give boners to every single fighter and AFL executive in the room, and then take off without so much as a goodbye tossed my way.

We crossed paths briefly at weigh-in yesterday. Gabriel asked if I needed to consult Britt for any last-minute problems or issues. I could have used the opportunity to confront Britt, to ask what the fuck happened, but I decided it's better to let her go. I'm not the guy who sits down and hashes out *feelings*. I don't have feelings.

And she doesn't owe me a goddamn thing.

Jackson Wolfe, however, needs to be at the receiving end of my fist sooner rather than later. When I saw him touching Britt Thursday night, I nearly jumped over the table and strangled him in a rear naked choke. The bastard is lucky Gabriel reminded me I would be disqualified if I made a scene. If he hadn't, a hospital room was in Wolfe's immediate future.

Fortunately, my memory is long, and waiting is something I can manage. I'll be back in Atlanta and in the cage with Jack soon enough.

"Come, come!"

Gabriel claps his hands, waving the team in. The team consists of Gabriel, my cutman Pete Emery, that creepy little prick Max, and myself. I hate ritualistic bullshit team building crap, but I respect Gabriel, so I put my hand in the center of the huddle with everyone else and shout the proper cheer when prompted.

The door to our prep room opens, and a man in an AFL polo and a headset signals for us to follow.

Gabriel grins. "Let's go!"

The man brings us to a halt at the doors to the event center, waiting for our cue. The beginning notes of Skillet's "Monster" flood the arena and it's time. AFL employees fling open the double doors, exposing thousands of fans screaming in the darkness, bright spotlights highlighting the octagon, and the undeniable thirst for blood hanging low in the rafters.

I start down the path, following a man who walks backwards with a massive camera aimed at me. The lyrics of the song convey what everyone who looks in my eyes knows to be true—I hide a monster, caged and locked up until the moment I step into the octagon, where the layers peel back and the monster is exposed.

Gabriel and Pete stop at the stairs leading into the cage. Journalists and who-the-fuck-knows who else form a tight, raucous ring around us. Gabriel grabs the back of my neck, pulling me close until our foreheads touch.

Gabriel's dark gaze meets mine without fear or hesitation. It's unnerving, and Gabriel notices the tension in my eyes.

"Stay focused, *meu filho*. You got this one, easy." He removes his hand, smacking my shoulder.

Pete puts in my mouth guard after offering me water. "No problem, Killer. You're gonna slay him." He slathers Vaseline all over my face and brows and steps aside for the official.

I nod and turn to the AFL official. He pats me down, skimming his hands over my skin and doing all the required ringside checks—ears, hands, groin, feet—and has me open my mouth to check for my mouth guard. Satisfied, the ref does the same for my opponent, Darius "Demon" Fernandez. Like me, the guy is new, but this is his second fight.

The minute I'm in the cage, everything around me falls away—the crowd, the flashing lights, the cameras. Only I can't shake the image of Britt, who I spotted in the front row when Max took his seat next to her.

I crack my neck and force my attention away from the girl with the miraculous ability to break through my impenetrable walls. Right now there's can only be me and the unlucky bastard I'm about to destroy.

When the pre-fight bullshit is done, the announcer steps up to get this thing going.

"Ladies and gentlemen, the next fight on tonight's card is an AFL middleweight regulation bout." I zone out while he explains the rules, laser-focused on studying every move Fernandez makes. Jiu-jitsu is his specialty, but he's nowhere near as good as me. Plus, his striking sucks.

"In the red corner, from Atlanta, Georgia, representing Souza MMA, weighing in at one hundred eighty-one pounds, Keller *Killer* Bishop!"

If the crowd responds, I don't notice. The announcer turns to the opposite side of the octagon and I do something I never, ever fucking do during a fight. I glance outside the cage and lock eyes with Britt.

"In the blue corner, from Fort Worth, Texas, representing Youngblood MMA, weighing in at one hundred eighty-three pounds,

Darius *Demon* Fernandez!"

The announcer's voice fades from my existence as Britt and I remain locked together, blue and silver. The corner of her mouth turns up and she mouths *"you got this…"*

"Fighters to the center of the ring!"

That snaps me out of whatever the hell just happened.

The three of us come together in the center of the cage, two fighters and the ref. I pinpoint the exact second Fernandez makes eye contact with me. The cocky attitude, the arrogant spark in his eyes, vanishes like a puff of smoke.. He probably doesn't recognize his own reactions. But I do.

He's seen the monster, and he's afraid.

The ref steps back and the bell rings. He should be afraid. It's time to unleash the beast.

Britt

Keller. His name is Keller.

Hearing the announcer broadcast K's real name reminds me of the paperwork I read yesterday. The legal paperwork required by the AFL for every fighter before they step into the ring.

Keller Bishop. It explains the Killer nickname, but not the odd, churning sensation in my gut when I hear it over the loudspeaker.. It doesn't explain the strange sense of déjà vu I get when I run the name Keller over and over in my head. It's the same creepy, "ice water in my veins" feeling I get when I look into his haunting silver eyes.

Max drops into the seat next to me. We're in the front row at K's corner, Gabriel and Pete about a yard away.

"You think he'll do okay?"

I turn to gape at Max. He hasn't spoken a word to me since K—no *Keller*, nearly took his head off at the training center the other day.

"I-I…" Max stares at me as I start to speak, his mouth twisted, his eyes sending out a silent challenge. One that says I'm either with Max or with Keller, depending on my answer.

Challenge accepted.

I straighten up in my seat and shoot him my own confident stare right back.

"I think he'll demolish Fernandez in the first round," I say with confidence.

The hurt in Max's eyes is obvious, to the point I almost feel bad for taking Keller's side. Then I remember—there *are* no sides. Max is the one pitting himself against the new fighter, with my friendship as the prize.

I turn back to the cage and feel the weight of Keller's, heavy gaze on me. He gives Max a quick glance, his lip curling into an almost imperceptible sneer. Those quicksilver eyes return to mine, sparkling under the bright lights of the ring. A ripple of heat spreads from between my thighs, sending a shudder of pleasure through my body. Reflexively, I lick my bottom lip. Keller's eyes widen and the fire inside me explodes into animal lust.

I'm practically panting, reeling from the ability of something as simple as a look from Keller turning me into a puddle of hormones.

The bell rings and my moment of dazed bliss ends.

Fernandez immediately tries to crowd close to Keller. He knows that Keller is a better striker and being a jiu-jitsu style fighter himself, Fernandez needs to prevent Keller from landing any kicks or hits, and get him on the ground as soon as possible.

Fernandez executes a swift jab to Keller's chin. Keller does nothing to block the shot, the other man's fist landing flush against Keller's jaw. His head barely moves from the blow. I blink several times in shock. This is the first time I've seen anyone land a hit on Keller. The corner of Keller's mouth pulls up in an almost imperceptible smirk.

He let Fernandez hit him on purpose!

Feeling brave, Fernandez leaps again, this time his fist swooshing past Keller's face as Keller leans back just out of reach. Keller's response is to grin, taunting Fernandez. The other man scowls, determined to land another blow, and starts aggressively pursuing Keller. Every step Fernandez takes forward is met by a step backwards by Keller. Over and over, they dance around the cage. Finally, a growling Fernandez runs out of patience and goes for it, leaping into Keller's space, determined to grab his waist and bring him down.

Anticipating his move, Keller lands a quick jab to Fernandez's face, shoves him back by the shoulders, and executes a perfect diagonal kick to the side of his head.

Fernandez crashes to the mat in a sweaty mound. Keller jumps on top of him, immediately maneuvering him into an arm bar, threatening to break his joint at the elbow if he doesn't tap out. Fernandez makes a weak attempt to get out of the hold, but he's still too dazed from the blow to his head to do anything effective.

The ref is about to call the fight when Fernandez taps his hand on Keller's leg, which is wrapped tightly around his neck.

Keller lets go and gracefully leaps to his feet, leaving a gasping Fernandez on the ground. Gabriel and Pete cheer from the corner where Keller accepts a bottle of water.

The crowd in the arena is going crazy, cheering and shouting in disbelief. Twenty-four seconds. That's how long it took for Keller to get his first AFL submission. Did he even break a sweat? I watch Keller drink, the long, sexy curve of his throat working to swallow the water. He hands the bottle back to Pete and his eyes search out the front row until he finds me. Chills rush over my skin and can't hide the pleasure wracking my body from his pointed stare. His eyes say what he can't—*I want you, I did this for you, this isn't over between us.*

"Fuck, that was fast," Max mumbles.

The officials enter the cage, pulling Keller away to announce his victory. The moment between us over, I turn to Max. The desire to rub Keller's win in his face ricochets loudly in my head. With a sigh, I tamp it down, not wanting or needing any more animosity between the two men.

"Yeah, it was," I agree, and stand up. "I'm going back to

make sure everything is okay."

"You're not going to watch Jack fight?" Max looks both surprised and irritated at my decision.

I frown at Max. "I'm the therapist. I have to check on the fighters," I snap. I'll be back in time." I walk off without further explanation.

So much for no animosity.

It takes forever to push through the throngs of spectators, employees, and reporters to get to the training room backstage. With all the jostling, the nearness of so many strangers, an uncomfortable tightness begins squeezing my lungs. With each accidental shove or bump, the feeling increases, sending my pulse skyrocketing. I clutch my chest, spots beginning to appear in my peripheral vision. *No, no, no.* I've been doing so good. I can't have a panic attack on the floor of the Nevada Desert Arena. Trembling, I focus on putting one foot in front of the other, blindly making my way to the hallway lined with training rooms.

After an eternity, I grab the knob with a sweaty hand and duck inside, slamming and locking the door, leaving the loud group of nosy journalists on the other side.

"You okay, Britt?" Gabriel is staring at me, concern marring his kind features.

Keller is sitting on the edge of the table, his hands out for Gabriel to unwrap. His dark head of hair lifts and shining gunmetal eyes lock onto mine. Keller's mouth drops open for a brief moment before his expression changes from shock to rage.

"What happened?" Keller demands, jumping off the table to stalk over to me. Sharp eyes rove over my body, checking for injuries. "Are you hurt? Who did this to you?"

"W-what?" I'm still recovering from the adrenaline that flooded my bloodstream, so my mind is slow to respond. "I-I don't..." I close my eyes and shake my head. "What did you ask?"

"Gabriel!" Keller's loud voice startles me, sending my poor heart stumbling back into overdrive.

"Yes?" Gabriel is behind Keller's shoulder.

"I need a moment alone with Britt."

Gabriel's brow furrows as he thinks over the request. His dark eyes find mine and somehow, I manage to nod that it's okay.

"All right, Killer. Congratulations. I will go talk to those sharks." He jabs a thumb at the door.

Numb, I allow Keller to maneuver me out of the way so Gabriel can exit the room. The door clicks softly behind him and Keller locks it before scooping me up in his arms to set me on the padded exam table. He nudges my knees apart until he's standing between my legs.

"Britt, tell me what happened?" His tone is soft, calm, but I can tell he's far from calm. Keller runs his hands over my skin, searching for injuries.

I squeeze my eyes shut, lowering my head. "Nothing. Just..."

"Hey. Look at me, baby."

I swallow, forcing my eyes open. Keller is inches away, his bare chest nearly touching me. I drink in his skin, the dark ink slashing across taut, sweaty muscles. He brings his huge, taped hands to gently frame my face. "Tell me what happened so I can kill whoever made you feel like this."

Those words, coming from someone as dangerous and as lethal as Keller, should frighten me. It's a clear warning to run far away without looking back, because I have no doubt he would do exactly what he says. But to me? The words are a blanket of comfort, a warm fire to curl up in front of on a cold day. They're the words I need to hear to feel safe, to silence the forgotten trauma that unnerves me each and every day. The time apart has only made me crave him more.

Without thinking, I lean into one of Keller's hands. His thumb caresses my cheek, soothing, calming. My heart slows and I'm able to sort out my thoughts as the panic recedes.

"It's just the crowd.. I get a little… freaked out sometimes."

His eyes narrow as he thinks over this new information. "*You* get freaked out?"

I nod and lick my dry lips.

Shockingly, Keller chuckles, a sound I never thought to associate with him. "I don't get it. You're one of the bravest people I know and you're afraid of a crowd?"

Shame rushes down my spine, releasing a flood of heat across my skin. "I'm not brave," I whisper.

Keller lifts my chin and stares right into my eyes, our noses almost touching. "You are more than brave, Britt. You're fearless. I'm in awe of you."

The rough pad of his thumb leaves my cheek to brush over my lips. "I'm not." My mouth scrapes against his thumb. The desire to pull it into my mouth and lave it with my tongue, to taste his salty sweat, is near overpowering.

Keller tilts my head back, our mouths a fraction of an inch apart. "You're not afraid of me."

I don't hesitate to respond. "No. I'm not."

"You should be."

His mouth crashes down over mine, the kiss punishing yet somehow tender. My body melts and fire rips through me, sparking nerve endings that explode in a burst of white-hot desire. I grip his waist, pulling his hips flush against the edge of the table so I can wrap my legs around him. Keller groans into my mouth, his hands dropping to grab my backside so he can grind his hard length into the soft space between my thighs. He curses and reaches into his shorts, tossing his required cup to the floor.

"God, Britt. You make me so fucking crazy. You make me want things I haven't thought of in years." Keller lets go of my face to tug my shirt off. He bends me back, easing me down until I'm lying on the exam table, Keller still standing between my legs. "These need to go," he snarls, yanking down my leggings and panties, leaving them around my ankles to bind them together.

I whimper as he draws a lone finger across my skin to the pulse point at my throat. He continues down, over my collarbone, between my breasts, stopping at my navel. My back arches into his touch, craving more, needing more.

"Harder," I gasp. "Make me feel."

"Shhhhh." That wicked finger dips lower, tracing a path to my slick pussy. "You'll get what I give you, baby. I know what you need." Bending over, Keller bites one of my breasts through the thin lace of my bra. As the glorious pain shoots through my body, Keller thrusts several fingers inside my tight channel.

"Oh god!" My hips buck off the table and I scrabble for something to hold on to, my hands gripping his thick hair.

Keller withdraws his mouth and hand, stepping back.

"No!" The loss of his touch has me aching. Keller smiles, his eyes alight with desire.

"I would finger your pussy all day if I could." Without a word, he grabs my hips and flips me over, landing a stinging blow across my ass. His large hand presses down on my lower back. "If I move my hand will you stay still?"

Panting, I control the urge to squirm and beg. "Yes."

His hand vanishes and I can hear him rummaging around the room. When he comes back, he's in front of me. I'm draped over the exam table, my feet on the ground, tangled in my pants, my naked ass in the air, and my torso laid out over the table.

Keller takes my hands and begins winding a red hand wrap around my wrists, over and under, again and again until he's satisfied. "There. Don't move," he growls.

I test the bindings as he circles the table and a sharp, blistering slap lands across my backside.

"I said, don't move." Keller leans over me, the silky softness of his shorts sliding against my upturned ass. His tongue finds my left ear, plunging in, sending shivers rippling down my spine.

If he says something, I can't hear it on that side, nor do I care. Keller puts one hand on each of my shoulders and drags them down my back, his blunt nails gouging into my skin.

"Ahhhhhhh!" My neck arches back at the sting of the scrapes.

Smack! Another blow hits my ass, then another. Slaps rain down on me until my skin is on fire and my entire body is trembling for release, making me forget everything—the crowd, the anxiety, the past. Keller moans his approval, his voice husky. "God you're so fucking hot, Britt. So responsive. You want to feel alive? What you don't know is that you have it all wrong. *You* make *me* feel alive."

Keller reaches down between my legs and pinches my clit, twisting it, and I fall apart. Wailing, I shatter into a spectacular climax. The blunt head of Keller's cock presses at my entrance and without warning, he slams in deep. What was merely an orgasm has now become a transcendental experience. Fast and hard, he fucks me through my climax and I swiftly peak again.

When Keller grabs my shoulders, holding tight as he fucks me, I swear I nearly black out from the pleasure. My body is floating, soaring, *living*. From somewhere, I hear Keller shout out his own string of obscenities as he falls over the edge, but I'm still flying too high to take much notice.

I've finally found someone to make me feel alive and there's no way I'm letting him go.

CHAPTER 8

Keller

Sweat drips off of me as I lean over Britt. For a moment, I think I've fucked her unconscious, but even though her eyes are closed, her pink lips curve up into a smile.

Happiness like I haven't felt in almost a decade has me grinning like an idiot. How is it possible that this tiny, timid-looking girl, can make me feel about ten feet tall? She makes me feel... human. Fuck, just the fact that she makes me feel *anything* is a goddamn miracle.

I pull out and tuck my dick back into my shorts. Working fast, I unwrap her wrists, gently massaging the circulation back into them. Britt is so blissed out, she lets me manipulate her like a rag doll, her head lolling from one side to the other as I turn her over and pull her pants back up from her ankles, sliding them over her gorgeous red ass.

Britt finally comes back from wherever she's been, blinking those big blue eyes up at me. I help her sit up, and she reaches one hand out to touch the side of my face. "Keller."

Like the flip of a switch, the sound of my name on her lips turns my good mood dark, sending frigid blood pumping to my black, shriveled heart. I can't stop the sneer that spreads across my face. "My name is Killer."

Britt's eyes narrow and her pert nose wrinkles up. Before she can argue, someone bangs loudly on the door. Neither of us can look away, sapphire versus gray, trapped in a bizarre silent standoff. I watch as a deep blush stains her cheeks and she finally drops her gaze, those long lashes brushing her skin.

"Oh god. Someone probably heard us," she whispers. Britt pushes off the table, searching for her shirt. Finding it hanging off of a nearby bench press, she shrugs it on. The loud banging begins again. Shoulders back and head high, Britt marches over to open the door.

"Wait!" I grab her arm, not sure what just happened to change the energy between us from blazing hot to ice cold. I only know that something feels wrong. If I let the moment end like this, everything will change, and not in a way I find acceptable.

Britt stares at the spot where my hand grips her arm and flicks her gaze up to my face. An odd look flashes in her eyes, gone before I can analyze what it means.

"What do you want, *Killer*?" Her pretty mouth twists into a sneer as she spits out my name.

What do *I want?*

It's obvious Britt wants me to let her in, to drop the mask and let her see the real me. What Britt doesn't know is that Keller is dead and gone. Killer *is* the real me, he's all that's left in this shell of a body. I lower my hand, unable or unwilling to explain my past. It's better Britt thinks I'm an asshole than for her to know what I truly am, what I did.

The pounding gets louder, more determined. Frustrated with myself—for hiding, for letting Britt down, for being a coward—I march over to the door and fling it open. "What the fuck do you want?"

An irate Jackson Wolfe shoves his way in, kicking the door shut behind him. His eyes are wild and his chest is heaving.

"Jack?" Britt moves closer. "Aren't you supposed to be fighting soon?"

Wolfe's crazy eyes flick from me to Britt and back. "What the hell were you doing to her in here, you sick fuck?" he snarls, shoving his way into my personal space.

Already agitated from the thought of losing Britt, and thrown off by her calling me by my real name, I step forward, bumping chests with Wolfe. "None of your fucking business, douchebag."

Wolfe's eyes widen, shocked to actually hear my voice since I almost never speak to him. He sneers, putting up his fists as if to fight me.

"Jack," Britt jumps between us. "Are you crazy? You'll be kicked out of the league."

"Britt, this guy is a sick piece of shit. Can't you see it? The thought of him touching you—"

"Is none of your business," Britt interrupts, her voice firm.

My blood pressure is sky high, my pulse throbbing in my temples, and my carefully composed façade cracks. "Who the fuck do you think you are, Wolfe?" I step forward, forcing him to step back. "Get the fuck out of here before I hurt you." My still-wrapped hands curl into fists. Adrenaline courses through my body, starting in my core and quickly radiating outward until my limbs buzz with energy.

Only two things make me feel alive, Britt and fighting. If Wolfe doesn't get out of my face, he's going to meet the *real me* he claims to see. The unleashed version, not the tame, restrained one he's encountered at the gym.

"You motherfucker," Wolfe growls.

He leaps, arms swinging. I see it happening a split second before it becomes reality. There's not enough time for me to pull Britt out of the way, and goddamn it, she's always in the way! The pussy that he is, Jack shoves me instead of throwing a punch. As I stagger to maintain my footing, my elbow makes contact with the side of Britt's head and she falls to the floor. The sound of her skull smacking on the solid concrete will haunt my memory forever.

"Oh fuck!" Wolfe shouts, panicking. He attempts to kneel down next to her, but I push him back, so furious I'm bordering on homicidal.

"Go get Gabriel, you fucking idiot!"

I cradle Britt's head in my lap, pushing her long blonde hair off her face. Feeling around her skull with my fingers, my hands come up clean. No blood. Right as Gabriel bursts through the door, Britt's eyes roll back in her head and she begins convulsing.

My heart leaps into my throat as her small body begins to thrash on the floor. "Protect her head, Killer!" Gabriel turns to shout at Wolfe. "Get the paramedics in here! They should be in the medical room."

Wolfe takes off to get the medics as Britt continues convulsing. I hold her head as still as possible without accidentally injuring her neck. The tremors continue, and with each passing second a long buried part of me struggles to surface. The human part, the part with emotions and messy, complicated feelings. I failed Kinsey. I wasn't there to protect her. I'll be damned if I'm not going to be here for Britt.

Uniformed medics rush into the room, working together, lifting Britt onto a stretcher. I watch, helpless, tugging at my hair as they strap her down.

"I'm riding with her," I insist, finding my hoodie and pulling it over my head.

Gabriel gives me a withering look, which I challenge with one of my own. "Fine, *meu filho*. Stay with her. I'll meet you at the hospital after the press conference. I'll make your excuses."

The paramedics wheel her out as I stuff my feet into my unlaced shoes. I hurry to keep up, shoving gawkers out of the way in the crowded hall. They load her up and I swing up into the back of the ambulance, sitting next to the stretcher. Outside, I catch a glimpse of Wolfe, his face drawn and pale, and decide then and there that he will suffer for what he did to Britt.

And I'll be the one to make it happen, enjoying every minute of it.

Britt

Familiar, pale silver eyes fill with tears that overflow down ruddy, freckled cheeks. I'm cramped, my body curled up tight, shaking like a leaf while pressed against the person with the haunted eyes. My nostrils sting from the smell of industrial cleaner and the acrid burn of sulfur. Heavy boots thud into view.

Pop! Pop! Pop!

I jolt awake, the sudden movement sending a streak of pain through my skull.

"Ow." I try to reach up to touch my scar, but someone is holding my hand.

"Thank god, you're awake! Jesus, Britt. I was so fucking scared."

"Keller?" My voice is hoarse and my throat is dry. His warm hand squeezes mine.

"Let me get the nurse." He tries to untangle his fingers from mine and I panic, clinging to his arm.

"No! Don't leave me!" Memories of being in the hospital after waking up from brain surgery and a weeklong coma have me freaking out. The beeping of the heart monitor gets faster and faster, a loud alarm drawing unwanted attention to my distress.

"Okay. It's okay, baby. I'm here." Keller squeezes my hand before reaching over and pressing a button to summon the nurse.

"What happened?" I croak, licking my cracked lips. Keller lifts a cup and puts a straw between them. The cool water soothes my raw throat.

Keller's hand tightens on mine. "Don't worry about that right now."

I want to push for more information, but a harried nurse enters the room. She gives Keller a scathing look that lets me know he's most likely been a nuisance.

"Hello, Miss Reeves. Welcome back. I'm Mona. I need to check your vitals and then Dr. Wetzel will be in to see you." Mona fusses with various buttons and my IV line, throwing a scowl or two Keller's way. At some point, Keller threw his hood up over his brow, hiding most of his face, which probably aggravates Mona even more.

Her work done, Mona stalks out of the room in a huff with a promise to find the doctor.

"Why am I here?" I ask Keller again. He winces and his face turns red. Even under that hood I can see he doesn't want to tell me. "Tell me, Keller!"

Sighing, he pushes back the hood, letting it fall against his back. Troubled gray eyes meet mine and I gasp. Flashes of tears, of screams, of the metallic scent of gunpowder assail my fragile mind. Frightened, I twist, yanking free from Keller's grip and press the heels of my hands to either side of my head.

"Britt? Britt? What the fuck? Hey! Help! What's happening?"

I curl up, screaming while pushing on my temples to try and purge the horrific visions. The machines attached to my body go crazy, beeping in a loud cacophony that only adds to my agitation.

"Move back, please." A commanding voice enters the room.

"Fuck you, I'm not leaving her!" Even while I'm falling to pieces, the panic edging into Keller's voice is obvious. Keller is on the verge of losing it.

"Sir, if you don't step aside, I'll have security remove you from the premises. You are not family and we can keep you out."

"Fuck!"

Keller must do what they ask because several sets of hands touch me at once, causing me to flinch and let out a strangled cry. A stranger speaks. "Britton? Can you calm down?"

Blood, gunpowder, silver eyes, burnt rubber, more blood, so much blood… memory after memory pummels my mind as it splinters into fragments—ignorant bliss on one side, reality demanding to be set free on the other.

"Mona, push one milligram of Versed, IV."

A soothing chill enters my vein and before I can piece together the images, my world goes dark.

* * *

When I wake up, it's nighttime. The bright lights of the Vegas strip shine through the huge windows on one side of the room. Disoriented, I push myself to a sitting position.

The furniture is familiar. This is definitely my hotel, but not my room. A quiet snuffle next to me answers the question as to whose room it is. Keller is lying on his stomach, arms under his pillow, his face slack with sleep. My eyes trace over the intricate, traditional Thai sak yant tattoos on his back.

How did I get here?

My bladder cries for relief, so I slide out of bed and quietly take care of business. When I return, I sit on the edge of the mattress to watch Keller for a few minutes. He's handsome all of the time, but without all of his hard edges and angry scowls, he is positively stunning. Sleep wipes away the constant fury, the hostility, the walls he puts up. I see Keller as he's meant to be, young, relaxed, gorgeous—it breaks my heart that he's filled with such anger and self-hatred.

We all have our demons.

Keller rolls to his side, slinging an arm out across the bed. His hand finds my waist and as strong as he is, I don't stand a chance. Keller pulls me to his body, tucking me into his side and dropping a soft kiss on the back of my neck.

I melt into his touch, letting the safety of being in his arms quiet the noise in my head. There are so many questions, but do I really want to know the answers if it could jeopardize what I have with Keller? For the first time in a decade, I feel calm. The constant anxiety I carry around has been shed like dropping a heavy, dead outer husk, leaving me light and free to live without fear.

"Hey." Keller's muffled voice breaks me from my thoughts.

"Hey."

I twist to see over my shoulder and Keller presses a chaste kiss to my forehead. Such a tender gesture from such a violent man. "You feeling better?"

I shift to sit up and Keller joins me, rubbing the sleep from his eyes. His dark hair is matted in the back, sticking up in every direction. Beneath his gray eyes are heavy, dark circles. Keller looks tired. And adorable.

"I'm fine. I just... what happened? Please, tell me."

Keller throws off the sheet and stands up, his perfect body on full display. Wearing only a pair of tight black briefs, he stalks over to the window, bracing one arm on the glass over his head, pressing his forehead to the smooth surface as he stares out at the lights of the strip.

"You... a... then... scary..."

I move closer—with his back to me, my bad ear prevents me from catching what Keller says. I run my hand down the silky skin over his spine and his chest rumbles with pleasure. "I'm sorry, K. I didn't hear you."

Keller breathes in and out slowly. I can see the muscles in his jaw pulsing. He still won't look at me, blindly staring outside. "You had a seizure, Britt."

My blood runs cold and my hand drops to my side. I take a step back, not wanting to hear the rest.

Keller spins around, his face a combination of fury and anguish. "That fucker Wolfe shoved me and..." He squeezes his eyes shut, causing the tendons in his neck to pull taut. "I hit you with my elbow." Speaking through clenched teeth, he continues. "That asshole made me hit you and you hit your head and started convulsing. Fuck, Britt..." Keller swallows, his Adam's apple bobbing, his eyes still closed.

"I'm sorry," I whisper, taking another step back.

Keller's eyes pop open. "What are you sorry for? It's that motherfucker Wolfe who's going to be sorry. Seeing you in that hospital… Jesus." Large hands run through his mangled hair and he stares up at the ceiling. I've seen Keller upset, but this is beyond angry. Keller's eyes glint with lethality.

But my mind isn't focused on Keller or his desire for revenge. All I can think of is if I was in the hospital for a seizure, the doctors would have seen my scar. My heart races, throbbing painfully inside my chest. Did they tell Keller about my injury? I can't have him treating me differently. He'll be afraid to touch me. He won't give me what I need. He won't help me feel safe.

I retreat another step, surprised when the back of my legs hit the mattress.

Keller's hands fall from his head and he focuses on me. Tilting his head, he gives me a strange look. "Where are you going?"

"I'm…" I glance around the room, searching for my clothes so I can get the hell out of here before I have to see the pity in his eyes.

In a flash, Keller is in front of me before I can come up with an excuse to flee. His thick thighs pin mine to the bed, while his wide hands and long fingers span my waist, holding me firmly in place. "What's wrong? Why are you afraid of me?"

"I-I'm not. I just… I need to get back to my r-room. To clean up."

"I had all of your things moved here. You're not staying by yourself. I'm not chancing you having another seizure with no one there for you." Keller barks out an unamused laugh. "Fuck that. No way. You're not leaving my side ever again."

I wonder if I get a say in the matter, but decide not to argue... yet.

"How did I get here?" I change the subject, trying to remember the events between waking in the hospital and waking up here, and fail. There's only darkness, and the horrific, haunting images of "the incident."

Keller raises an eyebrow and brings up a hand to brush my hair back behind one ear. "You don't remember? You were awake, but kind of out of it. They said you would be like that from some of the medications they gave you. You signed the discharge papers and everything."

"Oh."

I wait for the questions. My heart is pounding so hard I'm shocked it doesn't crack any ribs. Any minute now, Keller will mention the scar, the brain injury. He'll want to know. He'll see me differently. Back to being treated like delicate glass. My lungs constrict, and I'm suddenly desperate for air.

"Britt?"

Pins and needles prick at my fingers and toes, ice racing up and down my extremities as my chest squeezes tighter.

"Britt? What the hell?"

Suddenly, I'm being swept off my feet and laid gently on the center of the huge bed. Keller wraps his body around mine, throwing a leg over my hips and an arm over my shoulders. He pulls me close, whispering into my hair.

"You're okay. Jesus, I'm going to kill that fucker Wolfe for doing this."

Gritting my teeth, I take deep, measured breaths through my nose, in and out, in and out, until the shimmering edges of unconsciousness recede from my vision and my heartbeat slows.

"Don't hurt him."

"What?" Keller pushes up on one elbow, leaning over so he can see my face. "You've got to be kidding."

"Don't hurt Wolfe. It's not his fault."

"Britt—"

"Please, Keller."

Keller

My stomach twists as Britt's big, blue eyes bore into me, unwavering in their quest to see right into my soul. For the first time in a decade, the sound of my given name doesn't dredge up feelings of loathing and resentment.

I try to put the wall back up, the protective armor that has surrounded me for so long, but Britt reaches over and with gentle fingers, caresses my rough cheek. Just like that, the wall she's been chipping at since we met, crumbles to dust.

"Don't shut me out," she whispers. "I can't…" a sob rips from her chest. "I need you."

Fuck.

I have to look away. Images of my sister hit me hard. Kinsey needed me and I fucked up. Who's to say I won't do the same with Britt?

"Please?" She scoots closer, brushing her lips over mine. "Keller." My name is a soft whisper against my skin.

I breathe in her scent, citrusy and soft. Desire coils in my spine, along with an odd, knotted sensation in my chest. Britt parts her lips and kisses me passionately. My dick very much wants in on the action, but the new, unfamiliar feeling has me pulling back.

"No. I can't. You're injured." I untangle myself from Britt's embrace and climb off the bed, confused by my warring reactions. I want her like I've never wanted anything, anyone, but what kind of an asshole would I be if I fucked her one day after she cracked her head and had a seizure?

Britt leaps to her feet on the other side of the bed, her face and neck flushed crimson. Her beautiful mouth is pulled into an angry scowl. "I'm not broken and I'm not made of glass, Keller!"

What the—?

I grab my shorts, yanking them on. "I didn't say that."

"Fuck you," she snarls, snatching her own clothes off the floor and dressing quickly.

"Britt, what are—?" I begin to circle the bed to get to her, my head spinning from the sudden fury emanating from this tiny girl. I need to touch her, breathe her in and let her scent fill my soul.

"No!" Britt holds up a shaky hand to keep me from approaching. Her eyes are panicked and wild. "I need to get out of here."

I move toward her again, and this time, her reaction is shocking. She holds up both hands to stop me and shrieks.

"Stay away! There's nothing wrong with me! I don't need your pity!" Britt snatches her purse off the couch and storms out of the room, leaving me stunned.

My instinct is to go after her, throw her over my shoulder, toss her down on the bed, spank her ass red, and fuck her into submission. I groan, clenching my hands and reining in my lust. Britt just had a fucking seizure and spent time in the hospital. I can't toss her around like my plaything, even if she begs me for it.

Confused by her reaction, I collapse on the bed, tugging at my hair in frustration. It's so much easier to be a cold bastard— unfeeling, uncaring. Then I remember the icy fear I felt when Britt collapsed on the ground, convulsing, and I wonder if I'll ever be able to be that emotionless guy again, to be Killer.

If Britt is going to shut me out, I won't have a choice in the matter. If she doesn't need Keller, I don't need to be him. Killer doesn't have feelings, Killer doesn't miss anyone's touch, Killer doesn't need anything but the cage.

I clench my jaw and rebuild my shattered walls.

* * *

Thwack! Thwack! Thwack!

The heavy bag shudders under my relentless attack. I flick the sweat out of my eyes and switch to knee strikes, kicking the bag over and over until every muscle burns and my lungs scream for relief.

"Killer, come with me."

I grab a towel and rub it over my head and face. "Not now, Gabriel." I toss the towel and get into my stance to continue my workout.

"Now! Get in my office!" His Portuguese is sharp and his tone indicates he's not to be argued with.

Frustration boils over, scorching my veins. Britt hasn't been to work in four days. It's been six since she stormed out of my room in Vegas, leaving me bewildered, with no explanation whatsoever. She went from passionate kissing to furious screaming in the span of a heartbeat, and I have no fucking clue as to why.

The powerlessness I feel has me on edge, snapping out at anyone who dares to cross my path. The entire gym has noticed. Hell, just the fact that I'm not ignoring everyone is enough to earn me strange looks and hushed whispers whenever I'm around.

Fuck them. I didn't care before, and I sure as fuck don't care now.

I yank off my gloves and enter Gabriel's office.

"Close the door," he says, still speaking Portuguese. "Sit." Gabriel glares, pointing at a chair.

I scowl, ready to argue, but he won't have it.

"Now. Don't talk, sit."

With a huff, I drop into the chair and cross my arms over my sweaty chest, focusing on a seam in the tiled floor. Damn, I wish I remembered my hoodie. I feel exposed. I'm losing my edge. My armor isn't what it used to be and Gabriel is an astute man.

"I want to talk about Vegas." Gabriel puts his elbows on his desk, tenting his fingers in front of his mouth.

I continue to stare at the ground, wholly unconfident of my ability to be Killer, and desperate to keep Gabriel from seeing Keller.

"Look at me." Gabriel snaps his fingers in my face.

Pissed, I whip my head up. I'm not a damn dog. Gabriel's demand causes a snarl to rip from my throat.

Gabriel smiles. "Ah, there he is. I've been wondering where my fighter went."

Yeah, me too.

"Listen to me, son. I don't know what is going on with you and Britt." I open my mouth to deny it, but he holds up a hand. "I don't care. I only care that you both are happy." Gabriel's eyes soften. "Britt, she is like a daughter to me, but you must know, she is proud. Independent. But inside," he thumps his chest with a fist. "She is broken, scared."

"Scared of what?" Gabriel grins and I realize he sucked me right into a conversation I didn't want to have.

"That is for her to tell. Anyway, I don't know what it is that troubles her. You must not regard her as weak. That I *do* know. I've seen her tear down men twice her size when they treat her as delicate."

I consider this information, connecting Britt's fury to me rejecting her advances because she had a seizure.

"She has demons, that one." Gabriel stares right at me, unwavering as usual, unafraid of the monster staring back. "Just like you. Maybe you are good for each other, maybe not." He stands up, circling the desk to lean on it in front of me. "But if you hurt her," Gabriel bends down until we're eye-to-eye, nose-to-nose. "You will regret it."

Who is he to assume what or who is good for me?

"Gabriel, I don't want or need a shoulder to cry on, a buddy, a friend, a girlfriend, or any of that goddamn bullshit. I've been alone for ten years and it works for me."

"Does it?" Gabriel stands up straight, clapping me on the shoulder. "Now, you focus on fighting. Let Britt figure it out on her own. Go." Gabriel waves me out. "You have another fight in two months, mid-September. I will meet with you and Britt in two days to discuss technique."

I hurry out of his office, my mind reeling at the thought of seeing Britt in forty-eight hours. When I start to get excited, I shove that shit right back down.

Fuck it. If she needs time, that's what she'll get. Killer doesn't give a fuck how long she takes to figure shit out or if she ever comes back. Killer doesn't feel hope or get fucking butterflies in his stomach. I feel the walls snap fully back into place, strong and tall and impenetrable. As they should be.

I should have known Keller couldn't still exist inside my hollow, blackened heart. Not after ten years of hard, cold living as Killer. Britt wants to be treated like everyone else?

You got it, sweetheart. I hope you're prepared.

CHAPTER 9

Britt

The phone rings from the other room. *Ugh!* I don't have the energy to deal with whoever it is, so instead of answering, I bury my head under my covers where I've spent the last five days, too afraid to leave my apartment.

The memories dredged up in the hospital plague my dreams at night, my thoughts during the day, my every single moment. I can't escape them. They're so real—the smell of the gunpowder, the trickle of sweat down my back, the arms of another girl around me as we shiver with fear.

I exhale, my entire body shaking. A panic attack is on the horizon—the signs are all there. If I can just get to the gym, surrounded by my tough, strong fighters, the anxiety will recede. Unfortunately, I can't seem to get out of bed to get there.

I need Keller.

The phone rings again, its shrill sound piercing the quiet in my gloomy apartment. When it stops, there's a minute of silence before it starts up again.

My heart thrums, the familiar tightening in my chest making it difficult to pull air into my lungs. *Stop it, Britt.* The door is locked, no one else is here. On some level, I know I'm safe, but my brain refuses to accept the truth. Trembling, I force my legs over the side of the bed.

My mind is torn in half. I feel too much. I don't feel enough.

Deep breaths, in… out, in… out.

I remember my physiotherapist, Nina, and her kind encouragement in rehab. Heel, toe. Heel, toe. Slowly, so slowly, I whisper the words, putting one foot in front of the other until I reach my phone on the dresser.

My hand shaking, I collapse onto the couch, curling up into a ball, cradling the phone. "H-hello?"

"Britt?"

"Max?" I'm not sure who I expected, maybe my mom, but the last person I thought would be on the other end of the line is Max.

"Are you okay? You haven't been to work and I heard what happened with the hospital, and—"

His familiar rambling helps ground me in reality. The panic recedes somewhat, if only temporarily. "Max, I'm fine."

"You don't sound fine. Can I come in?"

"What?" Suddenly tense, my eyes dart over to my door. The three separate deadbolts are all in place.

"I'm outside. I brought you some food. I was… I was worried about you."

Max brought food? Even after we argued at Keller's fight? Strange, but he's a familiar face. He doesn't give me the comforting aura of safety the fighters do, but he's here. I won't be alone.

"Okay. I'm coming."

I hang up and on wobbly legs, walk to the door, sliding each lock open.

"Britt!" Max comes inside, holding a takeout bag in one hand and pulling me into a hug with the other.

I stiffen in his embrace. It feels... wrong, weird. I wriggle out of his hold and lock the three deadbolts behind him. Max wrinkles his brow at the sight of so many locks, but says nothing.

"I uh, brought tacos from your favorite place." He stares at his feet uncomfortably and holds out the bag.

"Thanks, Max." *Stop stressing, Britt. This is Max.*

I relax, finally able to think somewhat rationally. Max isn't a fighter, he can't protect me, but having someone else here with me is better than being alone. I head into the kitchen and pull out a couple of plates, quickly dishing out the food.

Once seated at my tiny table, Max begins his interrogation. "So, are you okay?" His eyes take in my disheveled, unwashed appearance.

I should be embarrassed, but I could care less right now. Looks are the last thing on my list of things to worry about. "I'm fine. I'll be back at work Thursday."

"Not tomorrow?"

I shake my head. "No. I'm having lunch with my mother. I haven't seen her in a while and she's... talkative."

Max lets out a strained laugh, but if he only knew. I'm sure my mother is making a last-ditch attempt to bully me into attending the upcoming ten-year anniversary of "the incident." Why I agreed to meet her, I don't know. I was at the airport in Vegas, fleeing Keller's rejection—that look of pity he gave me. I was so distraught at the time, I said yes to my mom without thinking.

We finish eating in silence. Max helps bring the dishes into the kitchen. He doesn't seem to be in any hurry to leave, and it's awkward. I walk to the door, hoping he'll take the hint.

He does, following me, stopping much too close. I back up, pressed against the door, the locks digging into my spine.

"Britt…" Max raises a hand to touch my face.

I flinch, turning my head to the side to avoid his fingers. The panic I finally had under control surges in my chest, squeezing, tightening, closing in on all sides.

"Don't," I whisper.

His hand drops, curling up at his side. "Why him? Huh, Britt? He's a fucking psycho. You deserve better."

I'm both shocked at Max's hostility, yet I expected it at the same time. "I'm not explaining myself to you." I shimmy to the side and unlock the bolts, holding the door open. "Thank you for dinner."

Max scowls. I see him struggling to hold his tongue. With a narrowing of his eyes and a quick nod of his head, Max slips out the door. I slam it shut, flipping the bolts.

My lungs constrict, the panic I held back bursting though the dam, flooding my body. I sink to the floor, lightheaded, numb, alone, and curled up in a ball.

Keller. I need Keller.

Keller

Done with practice, I sit on a bench to pull my gloves off with my teeth and begin unwrapping my hands.

"Good session, man." Sawyer North, one of the other fighters, nods in my direction.

I throw on my hoodie and cover my head, letting it fall over my eyes. "Yeah."

We grappled for about an hour and while he's good, he's no match for me. I held back several times just to make it challenging.

North leaves without another word. He knows. He saw it in the cage, the monster. Freaked him the fuck out, too, I could tell. At least I know Britt didn't turn me completely soft. I pack up my stuff, slinging my bag on my shoulder.

Tomorrow, I'll see Britt again. I have to stay detached. So we fucked, big deal. I've fucked lots of women. I don't need her and I don't feel anything. I *can't* feel.

"Hey, *Killer.*"

As much as I want to avoid everyone here, the snide tone has me turning to see who the asshole is. *Max.* Creepy little fuck. He's got balls of steel to speak to me, I'll give him that.

I wait, staring, letting the icy silence speak for me.

He sees me, but I see him. We're two different types of monsters, but both monsters all the same.

"So… I saw Britt yesterday," he says with a smirk.

My entire body goes rigid. That sick piece of shit was with her?

In three long steps, I'm standing in his space, towering over him. Max's confidence wavers and I watch him swallow nervously.

"What did you say?" I growl, inching closer.

To his credit, or maybe his sheer stupidity, the idiot stands his ground. "Yeah, I had dinner with her at her place. She looks good."

Motherfucker. He knows I can't hit him or I'll be thrown out of the league. My hand itches to wrap around his skinny throat and squeeze.

"What's your point, Max?"

I tilt my chin down, giving him a clear view into my eyes, my empty, heartless soul. Only, he doesn't react and I sure as fuck don't feel empty. I feel angry and defensive. The need to claim Britt as mine courses through my veins hot and electric, waking those buried emotions again.

I feel... alive.

"Fuck off!" I hiss, stepping around Max, "accidentally" bumping him with my shoulder on my way to see Roxie at the front desk.

She's chatting with someone, but I could give a fuck. "Roxie!"

The tall woman startles, spinning to face me. She doesn't flinch either, her gaze steady and somewhat annoyed.

Am I losing my touch?

"Yes?" Roxie puts her hands on her hips. Her bright blue hair is slicked back today, making her look like a comic book heroine.

"I need Britt's address."

She puckers her lips, having an internal debate over whether or not to give it to me.

"Please? I'm worried about her." I push the hood off my head.

Roxie's eyes bulge. Certainly no one here has ever heard me ask for anything, let alone say please. Dumbstruck, she reaches under the counter, producing a small address book.

"You better not make me regret this," she says as she scrawls the address on a scrap of paper, pushing it across the counter.

"Thanks, Roxie." I snatch it up and hurry outside.

The oppressive summer heat has me instantly dripping with sweat. I punch the address on the paper into my phone and realize Britt only lives a few blocks away. As I start to jog in the direction of her apartment, I try to figure out what exactly I'm going to say when I get there.

Britt

Why did I agree to this? I stir my sweet tea with my straw, watching the ice cubes dance around the glass.

"Britton Shelton Reeves, I'd appreciate it if you'd at least pretend to pay attention when I'm speaking to you."

"Yes, Mother." I sit up straighter and grab my fork, poking at the food on my plate.

"So have you given it any more thought? The city is closing government businesses for the day so everyone can come to the school, and Mayor Cheetham will be speaking. Plus, Robin Bateman, the daughter of the principal is going to speak in his honor."

I stare at my food, unblinking, until my vision goes fuzzy.

"Britton? Did you hear me?"

"Yes, Mother," I reply automatically. It doesn't matter what I do or say—she doesn't listen. She'll never understand. My only saving grace in all of this is that immediately after "the incident." my parents had the foresight to keep my name out of the press to protect my privacy. Yet now she wants me to stand up on stage and tell everyone who I am.

"Are you hearing a word I say?"

What a joke. If anyone isn't hearing what someone is saying, it's my mother. My eyes roll of their own accord, earning me another verbal slap down.

"Don't roll your eyes at me, Britton. It's disrespectful."

That's it. My blood pressure soars. I feel my skin prickle with heat. The dreams, the memories, the seizure, Keller, the anniversary, her nagging… it's too much.

"If anyone is disrespectful, it's you, Mother!" My mom's mouth falls open in shock. "For ten years I have told you I'm not going to play the victim. I refuse to be the face of this… this tragedy, to live it over and over in front of crowds of strangers when I can't even remember what fucking happened that day!"

"Don't use such foul language," she hisses, glancing around the fancy restaurant to see if anyone is listening.

"Then don't ask me again! No. The answer is no! I'm not

going. Until you can respect my wishes, I think it's better if we don't speak for a while."

I stand up and grab my purse.

"Britton, stop making a scene."

"Ha!" I laugh humorlessly. "You worry more about appearances than you do about me. When you get a clue, call me. Until then, don't bother."

I spin on my heel and storm out of the upscale restaurant, not caring who stares or who whispers about me "making a scene." I broke down and drove today. Turning the engine and driving off, I make it all the way down the block before the tears start to flow. I'm not one to pity myself. Hell, I'm not Britton Shelton Reeves, victim, survivor, or whatever label people want to slap on me. I'm Britt Reeves, a young woman trying to live her life without being crushed by constant fear and anxiety.

My mother will never understand the fact that even though I don't remember that day, I carry the burden of it on my shoulders just as undeniably as the concealed scar on my head. Pity makes it worse. Standing in front of crowds, all of them feeling sorry for me… No. I can't. I won't.

Thankfully, my apartment isn't too far. The ten minutes it takes to drive home leave me emotionally exhausted. The crying leaves me hollow and drained. I stagger up the flight of stairs to my unit, too tired to even feel my usual anxiety.

I stop in the hall to dig out my keys when I hear my name.

"Britt? You drive? I didn't think you had a car."

My head jerks up in time to see Keller climbing to his feet, glancing between me and my shiny red BMW, a gift from my parents when I finished school.

Keller was sitting outside my door?

Speechless and overemotional, I feel the keys slip from my hand and clatter to the floor. Keller begins to approach, but hesitates, his eyes showing rare uncertainty. "Keller," I choke, running into his arms.

When his strength envelops me, every wrong becomes right, every anxiety melts away, every doubt disappears. I feel calm, safe, whole. The spark of life that's been missing inside burns bright, lighting me up like a solar flare, sizzling white-hot through my veins. Keller brings me out of the darkness and into the light.

Keller spins, slamming my back against the wall, caging my head between his thick biceps. He thrusts his hips forward, pressing his hard length into me.

"Keller." I slide a hand under his shirt, letting it rest over his heart. Its rhythm is strong and vital, offering its strength to me.

"God, Britt. Why can't I stop this?" He brings his mouth down on mine, lightly at first, skimming his tongue over the seam of my lips. I open up, giving him full access. Keller groans, his hips bucking forward again as he thrusts his tongue into my mouth, sensual and deep.

His hungry mouth devours the small whimpers I make. Keller grabs the sides of my face, angling my head so he can plunge even further inside. I slide my other hand into his shirt and drag both down his muscled back, digging my nails in, marking him as mine.

Keller rips his mouth away, panting, his eyes glazed over. "Inside."

I scoop up my discarded keys, taking a painfully long time to undo the deadbolts with Keller behind me, pressing his hardness into the cleft of my ass.

The door opens and we stumble through. Keller kicks it shut and grabs me for another kiss. I'm about to protest, needing to lock the door. But this is *Keller*. He'll keep me safe. He leans in and bites my lip, drawing blood, and I gasp. All thoughts of deadbolts fly out of my head.

"Bedroom," he rasps, trailing his teeth down my neck. Electricity crackles from the base of my spine, making me aching and near desperate to have Keller fill me up.

He pulls back, landing a hard slap on my ass. "Bedroom," he repeats, sharper this time.

Lust coursing through me, I lead Keller down the tiny hallway to my room, wondering what I'm doing. Why is he here? What could we possibly have together beyond sex?

Then I think about what Keller is offering, here and now— the chance to relax, to sink into pleasure without worry or fear, to live, to claim that spark even if it's only for a few hours—I can't say no. But can I stay detached?

As we undress I decide that I'll take whatever Keller gives me, even if I eventually break. I'd rather feel alive for a little while than never feel anything again.

And right now, I want to *feel*.

Keller

I follow Britt down the tiny hall to her even tinier bedroom. I should win a fucking award for the restraint I show in not just shoving her, face-first, against the wall and plowing into her tight pussy.

The minute we step inside the room, I wrap one arm around Britt from behind, curling it around her waist. My other hand slides around her throat, fingers spanning ear to ear, holding her against my chest.

"You're mine." I punctuate my words with a hard thrust of my hips, digging my cock against her lower back.

Britt hisses before sucking in a sharp breath. She tries to roll her head back to rest it on my shoulder, but I tighten the grip on her throat, keeping her in place.

"Answer me," I growl, nipping at her ear. "Tell me you're mine."

She whimpers, but refuses to answer. I keep her still, using the hand on her neck, while the other shoves her leggings down to her knees and my own shorts as well, releasing my aching cock. By walking forward, I maneuver Britt to the edge of the bed and push her down, holding her in place with a rough hand to the back of her neck. With one foot, I kick her feet apart as far as they will go with her leggings still around her ankles. The moan coming from her sparks fire in my aching balls.

"Tell me you're mine, Britt." I fish a condom out of my shorts and quickly roll it on. When the only noise out of her is a quiet keening, I bend my knees and thrust up into her, driving deep until my thighs rest against hers. "Fuck, you're so goddamn tight. Tell me I'm the only one who can have you like this." I lean over her body, pushing her T-shirt up so my sweaty chest can slide against her soft skin.

"Yesssss," Brit lets out a long, wailing moan. I fist her hair, wrenching her head down into the bed so I can bite the soft flesh at the juncture of her neck. Beneath me, she writhes and screams out, "God yes, Keller. I'm yours!"

"Fuck yeah." I straighten out so I can grab her hands. Britt's groan is muffled by the pillow when I yank them behind her back. Both of her wrists pinned in one of my hands, I jerk them up to the point of strain on her shoulders. It's easy to hold them in place at the uncomfortable angle while continuing to slam into her pussy over and over.

Fuck, the things she lets me do to her. My mind is spinning with all the ways to degrade, to ruin, to worship her body with mine.

Britt turns her head to the side so she can breathe. Her eyes are glazed over, her mouth parted. I want to bite and suck on those plump, wet lips, but refuse to release her arms to do so. She must want the same thing, because she begins to struggle to get out of my iron-clad grip. The resistance sends a jolt of ecstasy through my cock, pulling my balls tight.

"Oh fuck." My head rolls back and my eyes close for a brief second, fighting the intense pleasure that threatens to spill over from having Britt at my complete and utter mercy. "Fight me, baby. Go ahead. You'll make my fucking day." She gasps and her body ripples around my dick, tightening, milking me right to the edge of release.

"Keller…" Her breathing is ragged. Britt's pussy begins to clamp down and spasm.

"You're just dying for it, aren't you? You want me to hurt you, to take you, to do whatever the fuck I want to you," I growl. Her mouth opens and closes wordlessly. I thrust harder, each snap of my hips stealing her breath so she can't respond. I lean over her bound hands until my mouth is as close to her ear as I can get. "I'll give you what you need, Britt."

With my free hand, I slide it beneath her body to wrap around her neck again. Carefully, I squeeze her throat just enough for breathing to require effort. Britt cries out and her pussy clenches so hard it disrupts my rhythm.

"Jesus! God, Britt. Fuck, I'm gonna come."

"Keller… I need…"

"I know." My hand leaves her throat and glides down her abdomen to her slick, hot pussy. I find her swollen clit and pinch it between my fingers. Britt shatters beneath me, screaming my name as she comes.

I let go of her arms and pull out. In one quick movement, I flip Britt onto her back to ram back inside that wet channel while she's still climaxing, and drive home hard and fast. I slap her clit with an open palm and her eyes roll back in her head, her entire body shuddering. My balls tingle, squeezing tight, and my own release roars through me, jetting out of my cock so hard I nearly black out from the intensity of it.

On my final thrust, I collapse on top of Britt, both of us sweaty and panting. When I pull out, I feel her shiver from the loss. After tossing the condom, I lift her legs and place them on the bed, then curl up next to her, holding her tight against my side. Britt's hand lies over my chest, her fingers drawing gentle circles on my skin.

It's so faint, so quiet, I almost miss when Britt whispers, "Thank you," right before she falls asleep.

The words pierce right through my walls, the tough outer shell I've kept in place for the last ten years. They act like a defibrillator, zapping my black, soulless heart into beating again, and I know right then and there, I can never, ever go back.

Britt

"There's been no further damage, Miss Reeves. Your EEG is normal, your vision unaffected, and your nerves are all responding properly." Dr. Marshall slips his penlight in his pocket and steps back from the exam table. "I'd say you are a very fortunate young lady."

"So, I'm okay?"

Dr. Marshall's mouth curves down. "You did not suffer lasting or permanent effects from your recent head injury or the seizures."

HEATHER C. LEIGH

"You didn't answer my question." I fiddle with the hem of the threadbare cloth gown they made me wear for my post-hospitalization follow-up visit with my neurologist.

The kind doctor leans against the cabinet that holds a sink and other medical supplies and crosses his arms over his chest. "Because *okay* is not a word that will ever describe you, Miss Reeves. You suffered a severe brain injury. Yes, time has passed and you haven't had any further complications, but you won't ever be back to the way you were before the incident."

"The incident"—even my doctors use that term to describe the day that took so much from so many people.

"I know that, Dr. Marshall. I'm asking if I'm the same as I was before the recent seizures."

"Then yes. I see no evidence of any progression or changes in the electrical output of your brain." I exhale in relief, but it's short-lived. "However, it is even more imperative that you take extra precautions to avoid any further head injuries. Especially after having proof that a blow to the head can and will bring on very serious seizures. Take your medications exactly as prescribed and be very, very careful."

I nod, swallowing down the knot of anxiety that blossoms in my throat. "Okay. I will."

He smiles. "Great. I'll see you in three months for a repeat EEG and MRI."

"Thanks." Dr. Marshall leaves the room. As I get dressed, the worry comes back. I can't tell anyone at work about this, about how I

180

have to be cautious not to bump my head again. I'll just have to be extra vigilant on my own. Just the thought of everyone at the gym tiptoeing around me like I'm made of glass makes me nauseous.

And Keller. I can't lose what I have with him. I need him, his strength, the safety of his arms, the way he makes me feel. Without it, the memories straining to burst free from my mind will take me down in no time, reducing me to an anxious, cowering mess.

No. Just like everything else in my life, I'll handle this on my own.

* * *

"You're going to need to go easy for a day or two. Ice and rest, no sparring, light stretching and workouts only."

I pat the fighter's ankle and tell him he can go. He grimaces, but manages to give me a weak smile before sliding off the exam table. Sawyer North is one of my favorite fighters. Always calm, always polite, he's unflappable under stress.

"Thanks, Britt."

"Anytime, Sawyer. I'll see you around."

He nods and leaves my office. When the door opens, the sounds of the gym permeate the small room, grunts, talking, the sounds of gloves hitting flesh or punching bags, trainers shouting over the din so their fighters can hear them. It's been the daily backdrop of my life for several years. Usually, I take comfort in it, the sounds of men, of their incredible displays of strength. The last few days, however, I've kept to my office as much as possible. The anniversary of "the incident" is getting closer, the dreams getting more frequent, the memories becoming more clear with each passing day.

My only respite is the time I spend with Keller. I sit behind my desk and grin at the discomfort that reminds me of last night, of Keller's large hand coming down, raining blows across the tender skin of my backside as he pounded into me until I nearly passed out. I nearly giggle I'm so giddy. Keller gets me. Like *really* gets me and what I need, and he's more than happy to be the one to provide it. Keller is pure alpha domination, both in the ring and in the bedroom, and I love every minute of it. No one makes me feel safe or quiets my mind like Keller Bishop.

Done typing notes into Sawyer's file, I stand up and go to close the door for privacy. As I reach for the knob, a hand smacks against the outside of the door, shoving it open and nearly knocking the thick wood into my head. I stumble back, my heart flying in my chest.

"Max! You almost hit me with the door!"

My god, does he purposely try to hurt me? Is that what's been going on?

His face falls and his eyes go wide. "Oh my god, Britt. I'm so sorry." Max extends a hand to keep me steady and instinctually, I leap back out of his reach. I do not want his hands on me. Something about his touch creeps me out. Max's brow lowers and his eyes narrow at my reaction, the dark color piercing right through me like a shard of ice.

Pissed off, I hold up my hands. "Stop barging in here, Max. You need to start knocking."

"Whoa, Britt. Relax."

That's it. This guy has almost given me a seizure more than once and *I* have to relax?

"No, Max. I'm tired of you sneaking up on me. Either knock before you enter, or stay away!" Before I can slam the door in his face, he slides inside my office. I frown at his refusal to respect my request. "What the hell are you doing?"

"Why can't you just accept my apology, Britt? What's with you lately?" Max comes toward me, forcing me to take another step back. His face crumples into a deep scowl. "It's that asshole, Killer, isn't it? You're fucking him so now you can't be my friend. What, he won't let you?"

"He has—"

"Everything to do with it."

Max and I spin around simultaneously to face the source of the deep, scary growl. Keller is standing in the doorway, filling the entire frame with his enormous body.

Max gapes. "I—"

"Shut the fuck up," Keller snarls, cutting off any excuse Max was about to offer. The fighter steps forward, crowding Max against the exam table.

"Keller…" I start to tell him to back off, to let Max leave. I don't need him fighting my battles for me, but stop. The truth is, I *want* him fighting my battles for me. I want him to protect me, to keep me safe, to eliminate any doubt in my mind that when he's around I have nothing to fear.

Keller is nose to nose with a visibly shaken Max. I don't blame him for being afraid. Not one bit. Keller's liquid silver eyes are cold and hard, like chips of flint. That frightening glare would render anyone incapable of speaking.

"I've already warned you several times to stay the fuck away from Britt. Now I'm going to make sure you listen, you little fucking pervert." The venom in Keller's voice makes the tiny hairs on the back of my neck stand up. Goose bumps sprout on my heated skin.

"Y-You can't hit me," Max says, his eyes darting around the room, searching for an escape that doesn't exist.

"Keller…" I say in a hoarse whisper. "Please don't." The thought of Keller throwing away his career because of me, because of someone like Max, is unthinkable.

Keller's eyes flick over to mine, and the warmth is back for that brief second we share before they return to Max, hard and cold once more. "Get the fuck out of here." He wraps a huge hand around Max's arm and pulls him over to the door. Keller opens the door and shoves Max out, not looking back when Max stumbles and falls to the ground. Keller merely slams the door shut behind him.

"You didn't have to—"

"Yes, I did." I can tell by Keller's rigid posture and tight jaw that there will be no arguing with him. Keller isn't one to mess with, and Max has pushed him to his limits.

Keller stalks over, shirtless and barefoot and so

breathtakingly beautiful. He puts his fingers under my chin, keen eyes roving over my face. Satisfied, Keller steps back, running his hands down my arms and sides, checking to make sure I'm unharmed.

"I'm fine. He didn't touch me." I grab his hand with mine and lift it to my mouth, pressing a kiss on his palm.

"He better not fucking touch you or speak to you like that again," he snarls, his face twisting into a bone-chilling grimace. "I'll kill him."

"You can't hurt him, Keller. You'll lose everything."

The big fighter stares at me, gray eyes shimmering. I suppress a shudder when that strange memory flicks through my mind again as I meet his silvery gaze. It's there, just out of reach as I try to grasp it.

Silver eyes. Huddling with a girl. Boots. Gunpowder.

Unable to make sense of it, I blink away the images to see Keller giving me a look of amazement.

"Britt, the only thing I care about losing, is you."

Keller

"Gabriel, I want that little shit fired." I pace the length of my trainer's office, so furious I'm seeing red. "He tried to put his hands on Britt again."

"Now, Killer, it can't be that bad. Maybe you're, you know, overreacting because of your feelings for Britt." Gabriel sits calmly behind his desk, hands folded, watching me go back and forth as I rant.

"No." I shake my head. "You haven't seen what he does. He fucking sneaks up on her, Gabriel. He watches her without her knowledge. He's spying on her, trying to catch her alone. It's fucked up and I want him gone."

"Listen. I will talk to Britt and Max, *sim?*" I stare at the man, and damn it, if he doesn't so much as flinch. "*Boa, boa…* I'm glad we agree."

It takes a minute of concentrated breathing to pull myself together. Once I'm sure I'm not going to hit something, I put my hands on Gabriel's desk, leaning over it to get in his face. "I. Don't. Trust. Him, Gabriel. I want him gone."

My trainer sits for a minute, thinking it over while making me crazy waiting for him to respond. "Fine." Gabriel gives a sharp nod. "He has been acting strange lately. If this is how you feel and you think he is a threat to Britt,. I will dismiss him and you can have Jerry, *você está feliz?*"

"No, it doesn't make me happy, Gabriel. Firing that douchebag makes me fucking ecstatic." I stalk over to the door, turning to face Gabriel before leaving. "Just know, if he goes near her again, I'll kill him." With those parting words, I storm out.

I quickly clock Max hovering by one of the cages, trying to make it look as though he's not watching for me when I know damn well he is. And he should. If he so much as breathes wrong, he'll find a size fourteen foot wedged up his ass.

The door to Britt's office opens and she breezes past me toward Gabriel's. I nod, but don't stop her. We don't interact at work any more than we have to in a professional nature. The last thing I want is for the other fighters to resent Britt or treat her shitty because she's with me. Unfortunately, that little fucker Max probably spread all the rumors about us already.

God, I could just fucking squeeze the shit right out of him.

I head back to the free weights to do my lifting when Roxie walks over. "Killer, someone is here to see you."

I push back my hood so I can see the front desk. *Holy fuck.* A thick lump forms in my throat and I have to swallow several times in order to grunt a response. "I'll be there in a second."

"Sure." Roxie hurries away, probably freaked out by my facial expression, which is likely a thousand times scarier than just seeing the monster inside.

I sit on a bench for a moment, stunned. Not many people unsettle me—Britt and Gabriel—that's pretty much it. The man in the four-thousand-dollar bespoke suit standing at the front desk? Just the sight of him has my stomach cramping up.

Why the hell is he here?

"Shit." I have no choice but to stand up and walk toward the desk. With each step, my heart hammers harder against my ribs. The man's eyes meet mine and my heart skips a beat. They're identical to mine. Exactly like Kinsey's, an unusual silvery-gray color. Nausea burns in my gut, gnawing a hole the size of Texas through my midsection.

I tilt my head toward the door and the man exits, me close on his heels. Once outside, out of earshot of the rest of the gym, I finally address the unexpected visitor.

"Dad, what the hell are you doing here?"

CHAPTER 10

Britt

I can't believe Keller had Max fired. On one hand, I'm angry at him for doing it. I've known Max for several years and hate the thought of him losing his job.

On the other hand, I love Keller's fierce need to protect me. The fact that he'll go to any length necessary to keep me safe sends a warm, tingly feeling over my skin. And to be honest, ever since Keller arrived at the gym, Max has been acting downright strange to the point of being slightly creepy. Getting rid of him makes sense, but it still hurts my heart that it's come to this.

By the time I leave Gabriel's office, grab my purse and exit the gym, Keller is gone. I send him a quick text to let him know I'm on my way home, and head out.

I stop to get my mail before heading upstairs to my apartment and freeze with the key in the lock when I glimpse the gilded envelope with the SASS return address among the pile of bills and flyers.

Before the panic can take root, I unlock the door and hurry inside, slamming it shut behind me, twisting each bolt into place. Everything in my hand slips to the floor except the thick envelope. I hold it away from my body, pinched between my thumb and forefinger as if it might explode like one of those messages on *Mission*

Impossible. My hand shakes badly, but I manage to throw it on the small kitchen table with the piles of other stuff I ignore on a daily basis. Maybe out of sight, out of mind will work this time, because for some reason, I can't bring myself to throw the letter away.

Great. My nerves are shot and my mind is torn in a bunch of different directions at once. After the scene with Max and Keller, meeting with Gabriel not only about his decision to fire Max but also about Keller's upcoming fight, and now the invite to the upcoming anniversary for "the incident." I'm a complete and total wreck.

Numb, I head into the bedroom, strip off my clothes, and climb under the covers, my phone tucked to my side. Still no response to my text to Keller. It takes so much energy just to keep from falling apart, I pass out from exhaustion a few minutes later.

* * *

By Monday morning, I'm a mess. Keller never responded to any of my texts or calls over the last few days. At first, I was merely pissed off, but with the looming anniversary, and spending the entire weekend alone thinking about it, I'm on the verge of a full-on nervous breakdown and having a difficult time hiding it from everyone.

Exhausted from spending three days tossing and turning and getting almost no sleep, I end up doing something I hardly ever do and drive my car to work. I probably shouldn't, especially after the recent seizure, but it's less than a five minute drive and I don't have to energy to walk.

When I pull into the lot, I swear I spot Max's car in the very back. No, it can't be. Gabriel fired him, I should know. I had the unfortunate luck of watching Max storm out of the gym, shooting daggers at me the entire time, sending chills up my spine.

I hurry inside and notice Keller isn't here yet, which is disappointing. My first instinct is to tell him about possibly seeing Max outside. Then I remember Keller ignored me all weekend and the anger I felt at his callous treatment rises up.

A knock on my office door accompanies the voice. "Britt, you have a minute?"

I turn to see Jackson Wolfe in the doorway, a hesitant look on his face. My shoulders drop and I realize I was hoping, no matter how angry I am, it was Keller.

"Jack, sure. Come in." I wave the big man into the office. "What can I do for you?"

"My shoulder is tight. Can you put some of that icy crap on it?"

He might irritate me sometimes, but today, I thank god for Jackson Wolfe. I laugh at his unique description of my medicated ointment, instantly feeling lighter than I have in days. "Icy crap, Jack?" He grins and I giggle at him. "Get on the table. I need to check the joint before putting it on."

He hops up on the exam table and whips off his shirt. I close the office door so Jack has some privacy. He grimaces when I touch his shoulder.

"Sorry. My hands are freezing."

"It's okay, Britt. I'm hot enough for both of us." He chuckles and once again, Jack makes me laugh.

"If you say so, Jack." After manipulating his shoulder, pushing and palpitating the joint, I dig my finger into the space between his clavicle and his humerus. Jack hisses and gives me a scathing look. "There's no swelling, but if this is tender…" I dig into the spot again and he groans.

"Can you please not do that? It hurts."

"Sorry, Jack." I pat his shoulder and grab the big tub of ointment. As I rub it over the joint, I tell him my thoughts. "You'll need to ice it a few times a day and take some ibuprofen with meals. If it doesn't feel better by Wednesday, we'll have to schedule an appointment with Dr. Watkins to get you a cortisone shot."

"Okay, Britt. Thanks." Jack pulls his shirt on and hops down, but doesn't leave. He stands next to the table, his thumb and forefinger rubbing together.

"Jack?"

The fighter's face is hesitant. Whatever Jack has to say isn't going to be something I want to hear.

"I just… Britt… you know I like you. I mean, I have a lot of respect for you."

"Okay."

"I guess… I want to know… damn. Shit, this sounds so bad." He blows out a breath. "What I'm saying is, just be careful around Killer, Britt. He's… not normal."

I stiffen defensively. "Don't, Jack."

"No, no. I'm not telling you what to do. But come on, you have to see that the man is fucked up. Like seriously."

My jaw tightens. The last thing I want to do is discuss Keller with Jackson Wolfe. "I'll keep that in mind, Jack." I guess Keller and I haven't been keeping our relationship as professional at work as we thought if Jack knows.

"Sorry, Britt. Don't be mad at me." Jack gives me big puppy-dog eyes.

Oh for crying out loud!

"Ugh, Jack! Leave my personal business out of our conversations and I won't be mad."

His mouth turns down, as if he wants to say more. Thankfully, he nods and leaves without pushing any further. If he did, I'd probably get angry and yell, and what good would that do? Keller would still be avoiding me, the anniversary of "the incident" would still be coming up, and on top of everything else, it would then be awkward to be around Jack. It's easier to let his misplaced concern slide. Jack said what he needed to say, now it's done.

Unfortunately, my anxiety hasn't diminished one bit. With Jack mentioning Keller, and the fact that he doesn't want me near him, I'm even more high strung than before. I'm so damn tired of worrying about everything. Of constantly being afraid of nameless, faceless images from a day I don't even remember.

If Keller were here, he'd make it all go away.

Damn him.

Killer

My arms ache, my shoulders are on fire, and my hands are completely numb, but I keep pounding on the heavy bag, over and over, letting the rhythmic smacking sounds lull me into a trance.

Fuck you, Dad. The bastard tracks me down, shows up at the gym out of nowhere, and throws my entire world off its axis, spinning it back into the shit storm I left behind when I ditched this country.

Ten years. It's been almost ten fucking years since I've seen him. A little less than ten years since I got out of jail after serving six months for assault. Nearly a decade since I picked up and left for Thailand, living off my enormous trust fund. And on Friday, the first contact I have with my dad after a decade of silence is for him to give me that goddamn invitation.

Gordon Keller Keating, CEO and founder of Hybrid Technologies, found a minute of free time in his busy schedule to see his only son, the only living member of his family, and it's to give me an envelope inviting me to the tenth anniversary of the day my life ended. The day Keller Keating ceased to exist and became Killer.

I wanted to pound his face in for dropping this shit in my lap. Everything had been going so good with Britt. I actually started feeling things—emotions and crap I haven't felt in a decade. I almost felt… human. Dad managed to destroy all of that in less than five fucking minutes.

"Keller, you look... different."

I shove back my hood and study my father—custom suit, rigid posture, expensive watch. Except for some faint crow's feet and some gray at his temples, he hasn't changed one bit.

"Yeah, well, ten years will do that to a person," I say condescendingly.

Dad nods, clearing his throat and fiddling with one of his shiny cuff links. "I saw you on the television. Your fight. It said you were back in Atlanta, training here." He points at the gym.

I stare at him wordlessly, my arms across my chest. After Kinsey died, Dad worked even more than usual, which meant he was pretty much never home. He knew my mom was in a fragile state after losing my sister. Mom always had issues abusing alcohol and prescription drugs, but the big, important CEO couldn't be bothered to make sure his wife was okay. That left me to be the one to find her dead in our swimming pool.

"So why are you here, Dad?" I snarl.

Not for a single minute do I believe Gordon Keating is here to see me. After Mom died and I lost my shit and went to jail, I never heard from him. No visits, no letters, no contact of any kind. Yeah, he used his money to pay for my fancy lawyer who still couldn't keep me out of jail, but that was the extent of Dad's involvement. He's a cold fucking bastard who left me and Mom when we were at our most vulnerable by burying himself in his goddamn company.

Dad pulls a white envelope with silver embossing out of the inside pocket of his suit jacket. "I received this in the mail for you. They didn't know your address and neither did I. There's an identical one at home for me." He holds it out and hesitantly, I take the thick, heavyweight envelope from him.

"What is—?"

One glance at the silver script is all it takes for me to realize what I hold, what it represents. I stop speaking, my mouth opening silently. Without the protective wall I've built up around me, the one I let Britt tear down, exposing my humanity, the invitation is like a knife plunged directly into my recently repaired heart. I bend over in actual physical pain, squeezing my eyes shut to stop the flood of guilt that threatens to drag me under.

"I'm sponsoring the event. I'd like you to be there, Keller."

I know my dad is talking but I can't listen. The pain is too great. When I try to open my eyes, a wave of nausea swamps me. Gasping for air, I stay hunched over, hands on my knees, head down, as my dad continues shredding what's left of Keller Keating to microscopic pieces, leaving them to scatter in the wind.

"You owe it to your sister, to your mother, to be there. I'll be in touch."

I should stand up, get in his face, yell, scream, do something to let him know exactly what he can do with his goddamn invitation. Instead, I struggle to open my eyes just in time to watch a pair of expensive Italian loafers retreat as my father walks away. Moisture blurs my vision and a sharp stabbing pain digs under my ribs, aiming for the remnants of my blackened soul. The second I hear my dad's car leave the lot, I run, envelope crumpled in my fist, until I'm back to my shitty apartment. Familiar agony rips apart my insides, guilt clawing its way to the surface.

I never should have let Britt in, let down my guard for her. I've become soft, weak, vulnerable. Without my protective, emotionless façade, the agony of the past is too much to bear. I need to put the walls back up, harden into the killer I am. Only Killer can deal with the guilt from Kinsey's death.

I'll have to let Britt go in order to make the pain stop. To become Killer once more.

Only, the thought of losing Britt is almost as painful as the guilt itself.

Exhausted, I snatch my towel and wipe away the sweat dripping off my body. As hard as I've tried to avoid looking in the direction of Britt's office, I can't help myself.

Of course, when I do, that dickbag Jackson Wolfe comes out. Undoubtedly, the ass is smiling and flirting with Britt like a persistent motherfucker. But when Wolfe turns around, I notice he doesn't look happy, not even close. Wolfe's eyes find mine and the man shoots daggers at me, a silent warning of some kind, before stalking over to the cages to speak with a trainer.

What the actual fuck?

Where does Wolfe get off acting like such a self-righteous prick? Like I'm a piece of shit and he's so goddamn great. My eyes flick back to Wolfe, but he's busy talking to one of the trainers. I glance back at Britt's office. The door is already closed, so she's either out or meeting with another fighter.

Shit. The thought of her with someone else, with Wolfe, makes my blood boil. Yet that's the problem, isn't it? I can't have feelings. Keller Keating has feelings. Killer doesn't. Feelings make me weak, open me up to the unbearable agony of my past, my guilt, my never-ending torture. To survive, I have to be strong, a solid wall devoid of emotion. Otherwise, the pain will drag me under.

I take a deep breath and shove everything I've felt since

moving back to Atlanta out of my mind.

Killer is back, and he doesn't give a fuck about anyone or anything except giving and receiving pain. Fighting—it's the only reason I exist.

Britt

By the end of the day, it doesn't take a genius to figure out Keller is actively avoiding me. By avoiding, I mean specifically going out of his way to prevent contact of any kind. My heart hurts from the rejection, but honestly, at this point I'm pretty much just pissed. I don't need a big, drag out your feelings discussion, but a clue as to what changed between us would go a long way. By the next day, I'm halfway to depression.

"Britt." Gabriel's knock is accompanied by him sticking his head into my office.

I look up from where I've been staring at my laptop, not doing any work. "Yes, Gabriel?"

"Meeting in my office in fifteen minutes."

"Wait!" I call out when he goes to leave. The older man turns back, his weathered face open and kind. "What's the meeting about?"

Gabriel laughs, a deep, resounding chuckle that would normally make me smile. Today, I can't seem to find the energy. "About our plan of attack, of course. For Killer's next fight. See you in a few."

The older man closes the door to my office and I sag in my

chair, rubbing my tired eyes. How am I supposed to work with Keller if he won't look at me or talk to me? My heart clenches in my chest. What if Keller wants to get me fired like he did Max?

No. I can't believe Keller would stoop that low. But if he doesn't want me anymore, maybe he could. Can I work with Keller without touching him in moments of passion, feeling the heat of his skin against mine? Without him protecting me and holding me and making me feel alive?

The thought of losing Keller nearly paralyzes me with fear. I finally found someone who can bring me out of my constant misery. Someone who treats me as if I'm strong and capable. Someone damaged like me. Someone who I thought respected me and what I need.

I let out an unamused huff. If Keller respected me, he wouldn't dodge me like I have a contagious disease. Blowing out a long breath, I give myself a pep talk.

"Okay, Britt. Get a hold of yourself. It'll be fine. It's work and you need to be professional."

I've only been at the gym a few hours. There could be a good reason Keller hasn't come to see me yet. Or returned any of my calls over the weekend. There's a good possibility I'm blowing this way out of proportion.

I grab my laptop and decide to treat Keller the same as I do every other day. All I can do is wait and see what happens. If nothing else, I'm certainly not a whining, insecure baby who is going to force a guy into a long, drawn-out fight with tears and begging. Even if every cell in my body wants to cling to Keller and beg him not to leave me.

Better to just go with the flow. My stomach flips anxiously and sweat beads up between my shoulder blades.

Go with the flow. Right. Tell that to my frazzled nerves.

Killer

It's nearly impossible to avoid Britt at the gym, but somehow, I manage. Yeah, I'm an asshole for cutting her off with no explanation, but it's better this way. Talking leads to emotions and emotions lead to messy, human shit. Shit I can't deal with.

Besides, Killer doesn't give a fuck about some girl's feelings.

"Killer, come to my office."

I cut a glance at Gabriel and scowl under my hood. I've been a dick to him as well as Britt, and I can tell by his stilted voice his patience for me is waning. Tough shit. I'm here to fight and train, that's it. They can take their touchy-feely crap and fuck right off. I stalk to his office, head down, and flop down into a chair. It's not until Gabriel speaks to someone else that I realize Britt is in the chair next to mine.

"Britt, have you studied Killer's most recent tapes?"

"I have." The sound of her voice sends vibrations to my dick. *No!*

Gritting my teeth, I will the thoughts of painting Britt's face with my cum right on out of my head. I'm strong. If I can deal with the grief of killing my sister, spending six months in jail, and finding my mother dead in the pool, I can deal with working beside one fucking girl without sporting wood.

"Killer, have you discussed the tapes with Britt?"

Jesus. I can tell Gabriel already knows the answer to his question.

"No. Been too busy," I grunt, still hiding behind my low hood.

"Well, I expect you to do that by the end of today. We only have a week until the fight and you need to make your modifications before then."

"Fine," I reply in an icy voice to let him know I'm pissed.

"Fine," Gabriel responds.

A shuffling sound next to me accompanies Britt's tiny feet passing by my chair. "I'll be in my office waiting, *Killer.*"

Fuck me.

Before I can follow Britt, Gabriel speaks. "I don't know what you did, but fix it."

What the—?"

I shove back my hood, making eye contact with Gabriel for the first time since my dad fucked up my world last week. "Don't start shit you don't know about, Gabriel," I snarl.

"I know enough. You hurt Britt after I warned you. Whatever *problemas* you have in here," he taps the side of his head, "You get them straight and fix what you broke."

I stand up, ready to rip Gabriel apart with my bare hands.

"You have no idea what you're talking about." I step closer, nearly nose to nose with one of the only people to believe in me. "I can't be fixed. Britt will survive."

"Hmmmm," he says, rubbing his fingers on his chin. I pull back, glaring at the man.

"What?"

"Nothing." Gabriel shrugs and turns away, effectively dismissing me.

I curl my fingers into tight fists and storm out of the room. "Fucking people can't stay out of my goddamn business," I mutter to myself. Halfway to the locker room to grab my shit and leave, I remember I have to meet with Britt.

Son of a bitch.

I storm outside to get ahold of myself. I can't meet with Britt while I'm wound up and pissed off. I had no choice but to toss her aside without any explanation, and I'm okay with her thinking I'm a douchebag, but she definitely doesn't deserve me acting like a hostile dickhead right to her face.

I pace in front of the door, clenching and unclenching my hands. An engine starts nearby and I look up, my hood shading my eyes from the bright sun. I catch a glimpse of a beat-up silver car peeling out of the lot and my entire body goes rigid.

That little fucker, Max. What is he doing here?

Before I can chase him down, he's gone.

I growl in frustration. Today just gets better and better. This. This right here is why I don't get involved. This messy, complicated bullshit. Max, Gabriel, Britt... all it does is make my life more difficult.

Except I was happy for the first time in ten years, because of Britt.

I want to punch the little voice inside my head for reminding me of that fact, but when I barge into Britt's office and see those big blue eyes staring up at me with a look of longing, I know the voice is right. I *was* happy. I felt something.

Then I remember my dad and the upcoming anniversary and shut down. I keep it quick and to the point. "Let's watch the tapes."

The hope in Britt's eyes melts away, replaced by sorrow. She swallows, nodding her head, and pushes play on the computer.

If Killer doesn't feel anything, why does the look on Britt's face cause actual physical pain?

I focus on the tiny laptop screen, unwilling to delve any further into my reaction to Britt.

Britt

The fact that Keller's next fight is in Atlanta is both a blessing and a curse. I'm glad we don't have to travel together, share a flight, cars to and from the airport, hotels where we'd see each other around all the time. But with the anniversary less than a week away, getting out of the city would do me a world of good. My nerves are completely frayed.

Plus, my mother won't stop texting and leaving messages on my phone. She's run the gamut from demanding I at least go to the anniversary as a guest and not a speaker, to threatening me that I better show up "or else." With everything else falling to pieces around me, the last thing I need is a guilt trip from my mom. But if there's one thing I can definitively say about Rose Shelton-Reeves, it's that she's a bulldog—she knows what she wants and clamps her strong jaws on it, not letting go without a fight.

Exhausted, I take a deep breath and open the door to Sousa MMA, unprepared for another long day of training with Keller, touching and manipulating his body while pretending it doesn't affect me. Trying not to cringe at the way he ignores me, refusing to make eye contact and hiding under that damn hood of his.

"Britt, you look awful!"

My gaze flicks over to Roxie, standing behind the front desk slash juice bar with her mouth hanging open.

"Thanks a lot," I say, twisting my lips into a pout.

"No, hon. I mean, you look so tired. Are you sleeping at all?"

I give her a small smile, appreciating her concern, but honestly, no one can stop the nightmares and panic attacks.

No one but Keller.

My smile falters and embarrassing tears well up in my eyes when I think of the man who so coldly turned me away without any explanation.

"I'm fine, Roxie." When the tall woman gives me a look of disbelief, I reassure her. "Really, I'm okay. Just a lot of late nights and early mornings. Once this fight is over, I'll get more rest."

And once the anniversary passes.

The gym is fairly quiet, and why wouldn't it be? I'm an hour earlier than usual because the only thing worse than not being able to sleep is sitting awake in my apartment, freaking out. At least here, I feel more safe than I do at home alone. One of our new fighters is chatting with Jack near cage three and there's someone else on one of the cardio machines. Other than that, the place is deserted.

I head to my office and close the door. The last thing I want is to talk to anyone. It hasn't been five minutes when there's a knock on my door.

Ugh. It wouldn't be professional to scream "go the fuck away" like I want to, so instead, I tell them to come in.

"Hi, Britt."

The tall man enters the office, leaving the door partway open as he crosses the room. His brows are pulled low and his eyes reflect concern.

Exactly what I don't need. Pity, worry, questions I can't answer…

"Jack, what can I do for you?" I say, my voice tight and my posture rigid. I just don't want to do this right now.

"Are you…? I mean, Britt, you're not yourself lately. You don't smile anymore—"

"I appreciate your concern, Jack, but I'm fine. Too many long hours is all."

Jack closes his eyes and clenches his jaw. I notice his fists balled up at his sides. When he fixes his gaze back on me, I already know what's coming. Jack's eyes are shining with hatred.

"Did that fucker hurt you, Britt? Huh? Because I swear to

god, if he did—"

This place is worse than a damn soap opera with all the gossip and butting into everyone's business.

"Stop, Jack. I'm fine, and it's none of your concern. Now," I sit behind my desk and pull out my laptop. "Unless you need me for anything medically related, I need to get to work."

I look down at my computer, but can see Jack warring with himself out of the corner of my eye.

Please just go, Jack. Don't do this.

"You might not want to hear it, but I need to say my piece, Britt. Then I'll go." My fingers freeze on the keyboard, but I don't look up at the man as he speaks. "Ever since that, that... creepy motherfucker showed up here, you've changed. You don't smile anymore, you've lost the spark in your eyes. I've watched you shrivel up into a husk of who you were." Jack comes closer, splaying his big hands on my desk to lean over. "He's not worth it, Britt. Something's... not right about him. Don't let that asshole ruin you. You're better than him."

Jack waits another second before turning and leaving my office, gently closing the door as he goes. I slump over my desk, resting my head in my hands.

"Don't let that asshole ruin you."

Jack's words run through my head. They're so similar to what Keller said back in the hotel room in Vegas.

"Things I want to do to you. I can't... I refuse to ruin you."

A single hot tear trickles down my cheek. What neither of the men know, what no one knows, is that I'm already ruined. Ruined by a madman's bullet tearing through my skull. Ruined by a brain that refuses to keep the memories buried, showing them to me one by one, haunting me twenty-four hours a day. Ruined by the pressure from my mother to be someone I'm not. Ruined by my inability to feel safe, to stop the panic attacks, to not lose myself to fear whenever I'm alone.

I bark out a sad laugh. *Ruined.*

Too late. I was ruined long before Keller Bishop came into my life. The only thing he did was show me I could live a different way. Without fear, without being numb, without succumbing to the tidal waves of anxiety. Keller dangled a future in front of me, a future I badly want, only to shatter it into dust.

No, I was always ruined. What I am now, is drained of all hope, and that might actually be worse.

Killer

Fight night. Finally. The need to get into the cage and unleash the monster has grown since the visit from my dad last week. Plus, I swear I saw Max driving past the gym a few times like the creepy pervert he is. The monster is desperate to get free, scraping and clawing at my insides as the anger and violence churn and swirl, growing like a dark cloud, seeping out of every pore in my body.

Killer is back, and ready to do what he does best. Cause pain.

Except for a few sad glances in my direction, Britt hasn't

spoken to me at all outside of professional interactions. I'm not sure why it bothers me so much that she hasn't tried harder to find out why I simply cut her off, but it does. Then I shrug off the idea, knowing it doesn't matter. I can't be who she wants me to be, not if I want to maintain my sanity.

Jerry, the guy who replaced Max on my team, finishes wrapping my hands. I'm so fucking glad that pervy douchebag is gone. Spotting him sitting in his car in the gym parking lot, driving off before I approached, had me furious. It makes me want to find out where he lives and beat him to death.

"There you go, big guy," Jerry says with a pat on my shoulder, snapping me out of my fantasy.

"Time to go." The AFL employee leads us to the ring, through the sold-out crowd at Phillip's Arena in downtown Atlanta.

My heart is beating slow and steady, my mind ready for the fight. I don't get nervous, I don't show fear or hesitation. I get in the cage, and I take down my unlucky opponent. That's what I do. Unfortunately, as I stand ringside, waiting for the officials to clear me, my one weakness shows.

I scan the crowd for Britt.

Our eyes lock and the crowd, the noise, the fight... all of it fades into nothingness. There is only her and me. Even though the monster is inside, begging to be set free, Britt meets my eyes without fear. As the official walks over to do his pat-down, Britt winks and just like my last fight, she mouths, "you got this," before breaking eye contact.

And just like that, she's buried her way back under my skin. No matter how big of an asshole I was, no matter how shitty I treated her, she still believes in me.

"All good. Fighters to the ring."

I step up into the cage, my thoughts still confused and filled with Britt, images of her smiling, laughing, lying beneath me moaning in pleasure. Everything I want, but can't have.

When the ref calls us to the center, I blink and clear my mind. Focus. The anniversary is tomorrow, and Killer needs to purge his demons.

We tap gloves, and I let the monster free.

Britt

Gabriel told me that Keller was fine after the fight and didn't have any concerns. I took that information, and decided to sneak out of the arena before having to come face-to-face with Keller. Cowardly? Maybe, but not any more so than Keller and his inability to flat-out tell me he didn't want to see me anymore. Besides, tomorrow is the anniversary, and I plan to go home, lock my doors, and hide in bed until Monday morning.

Hiding proves more difficult than I thought. When the cab drops me off after the fight, that damn envelope haunts me from its place on the kitchen table. Even buried under a pile of mail, I know it's there and can feel the horror emanating from it.

I check the locks multiple times and finally, after three hours,

I'm satisfied that no one can get in. A microwaved bowl of soup isn't appetizing, but nothing is. I manage a few bites before rinsing the bowl and putting it in the dishwasher.

My phone rings over and over again, every fifteen minutes. There's no point checking it—I know it's my mother. If she had any clue how much worse she makes my anxiety, would she stop? I shake my head. No, she wouldn't. It's about her, not me. It's never about me. Even a bullet to my head wasn't about me. My mother managed to turn that around into a cause, into a career, using her daughter the "survivor" to garner attention and sympathy.

After taking my meds, I climb into bed, pulling the covers up over my head. This is one of those times I wish I could have a drink. Of course, alcohol mixes with my seizure medication so it's out of the question, but I would give anything for the numbness it brings.

The minutes tick by and in the early hours of the morning, I finally fall asleep.

The car squeals to a stop, tires smoking on the hot pavement.

"Britton, run!"

The girl's voice is distorted, as if in slow motion. A hand grabs mine and my body is tugged, floating up a staircase.

"In here!"

The arms of another girl wrap around me and I close my eyes. Without vision, sound becomes magnified. Sobs. Tears. Screaming. Blood. It's too much, so I open my eyes.

And find myself facing down the barrel of a gun.

I shoot up in bed, clutching my head and gasping for breath. My heart is beating so fast it hurts. Air becomes a precious commodity, so I concentrate on sucking it in, blowing out as slowly as I can. Dizziness swamps my head, black spots dancing across my vision. I gulp down breath after breath until the panic recedes. I raise a violently trembling hand to my face and wipe away tears.

The dream comes back to me, slamming into my chest like a freight train.

Oh god. My memory. It's coming back. It's going to destroy what's left of me.

* * *

It took four hours for me to get out of a fetal position and get up, and that's only because my bladder gave me no choice. I check my phone—seven missed calls. Six from my mom, one from Max.

Odd. I haven't spoken to Max since he was fired. In fact, he really freaked me out the last time he was in my apartment. He was… off.

I check the time and sigh in relief. Three in the afternoon. The ceremony is over. Now I can move on with my life.

I snort. Yeah, some life. Horrific dreams, panic attacks, and a man who won't give you the time of day.

Shit, I'm late taking my meds. Quickly, I down the bitter pills that keep my brain from short-circuiting and eat a few crackers to settle my stomach. I pick up my phone and delete my mother's messages. My finger hovers over the delete button for Max's voice mail, but for some reason, I push play instead. His voice is hurried and parts of the message are muffled so I can't tell what it is he wants.

"Britt, it's… ummmm, well…. it's Max. I…. Killer. Anyway…. so maybe…. I can't help……"

I stare at the phone, puzzled. No way do I have the energy to decipher Max's bizarre voice mail right now, and I am *not* calling him back to find out either.

My mind wanders to last night, that moment before Keller stepped into the cage. Something was there between us, I know it. I have no idea why he won't admit that we work, that we need each other, that we both have demons to fight and fight them better together.

Screw it.

I pull my laptop out of my work bag and fire it up, impatiently tapping on the table as I wait. Once it's on, I click through folders until I find the one with Keller's most recent pre-fight physical. It's my job to collect all medical paperwork and submit it to the AFL. On the top, below the name Keller Bishop, is exactly what I was looking for. I jot it down, shove my feet into my shoes, and too impatient to wait for a cab, I grab my keys.

Fifteen minutes later, I pull into the underground garage of one of the newest high-rise buildings in Midtown. All modern design and sleek glass, this luxury condo complex is far from what I expected for a man like Keller Bishop. I blink back my surprise and push the button for the elevator. Seventeen stories later, I'm standing outside of a large gray door.

Taking a deep breath, I lift my hand and knock.

CHAPTER 11

Killer

Knocking. Someone is knocking on my door. No one ever knocks on my door so I ignore it. It gets louder.

Persistent motherfucker.

I haul my sorry carcass to my feet and dump my empty beer bottle in the sink as I walk by. Instead of joining Dad at his celebration of the worst fucking day of my life, I stayed home and drank. Actually, that's not true. I started drinking last night after the fight and just kept going when I woke up. Because I stuck to beer, I'm pleasantly buzzed, not shitfaced like I would be with hard liquor.

The knocking starts again right as I yank the door open. My eyes widen when I see who's standing on my threshold.

Maybe I should have drowned myself in hard liquor.

"Britt?"

My head spins as the small woman who turned my world upside down pushes past me into my home. She stops a few feet in and her pert nose wrinkles, her jaw jutting out defiantly.

"Are you drunk?"

What the—?

I slam the door closed and spin to face my accuser. "What difference does it make if I am? But for your information, no, I'm not drunk. I've *been* drinking, it's not the same thing."

Britt crosses her arms over her chest, her confidence waning. "Oh."

Jesus. Today of all days, pure temptation shows up on my doorstep, literally. The one day of the year, besides Kinsey's birthday, that I allow myself to fall the fuck apart. Frustrated, I thread my hands through my hair, tugging on it.

"Why are you here, Britt?"

Her face colors, those blue eyes shimmer wetly, and I know exactly why she's here. I hurt her. On purpose. Because I'm a selfish fucking bastard.

"I just…" she sighs, her gaze dropping to her feet. "I'm having a really bad day and…" Her lips tremble and she shifts from foot to foot. "And I missed you." Those thick lashes flutter as her eyes flick back up to mine, her bottom lip pulled between her teeth.

Fuck.

I close my eyes and inhale slowly through my nose. I can't do this. I can't let her get close again. Facing reality is too painful for Keller, for the man she needs me to be. Besides, Britt deserves so much more than a walking corpse, someone who goes through the motions of living without feeling any human emotions except anger and violence. And guilt. Lots of goddamn guilt. I dig the heels of my hands into my eyes, concentrating on staying strong. On not pulling her into my arms and kissing her until I rob her of her breath, her kind heart, her very soul, sucking them into my body, leaving her empty.

"Britt…" She takes a step toward me and my pulse kicks up a

notch. "What are you doing?" Without answering, Britt steps forward again, now close enough for me to smell her sweet, citrusy, feminine scent. Close enough to feel the heat radiating off her perfect, unblemished skin. Skin I'd love to mark with my teeth and the tight grip of my fingers on her hips. The thought makes my cock harden and I curse under my breath.

"Keller," she whispers, her soft breath caressing my neck.

"God, Britt. This is such a bad idea." My hands are twitching, aching to reach out and pull that sinful body against mine, to do unspeakable things that would have us both shouting in ecstasy. Sinking into her tight, wet heat would make me forget about today, the anniversary, and all the bullshit that I carry on my shoulders every day. The relief would be euphoric. "I don't want to use you, Britt."

It's a lie. I *do* want to use her. Take her flesh and pound away my guilt into oblivion. But while Killer revels in the thought of holding her down and taking his pleasure, that teeny-tiny human side, the side only Britt can bring out, hates the thought of treating her like another hole to fuck. A release. A way to forget. She's so, so much more than that.

Britt takes the final step, closing the gap between us. She curls her hands around my neck and gazes up at me. I can do nothing but stare back at her, trapped by those stunning blue eyes. I study them, the emotions in their depths, and that's when I finally get it.

Britt needs this as much as I do. Whatever her demons are, they rival mine in their magnitude. The pain and desperation I see in those sapphire eyes reflect what I see in the mirror every single day.

When I finally allow my mind to give in to desire, lust explodes bright white and hot, eclipsing everything else in my overworked brain. I thread my hands into the silky hair at the back of her neck and tilt her head back. "Last chance to say no, Britt," I growl, my fingers tightening on her scalp as my body vibrates with need.

Britt licks her lips and my cock throbs painfully. "Take me, Keller. Make me yours again."

The sound that comes rumbling out of my chest can only be described as primal as my mouth crashes down on hers. The joining is passionate, teeth, tongue, and lips, hot and wet, sliding together in desperation. One of my hands skims down her back to grip her round ass, crushing her soft groin against my rigid length. Britt moans into my mouth and I lose any semblance of restraint.

Tearing my mouth away, I bite down on her lower lip and tug on it before releasing her. "Bedroom, now," I rasp. Britt doesn't move, her eyes hazy with lust. "Right now," I growl, taking her by the shoulders and spinning her to face the bedroom. I land a sharp crack across her firm buttocks, eliciting a squeal as Britt hurries down the hall. She peeks into several open doors before finding the right one.

Following a few steps behind, I pause in the doorway to rein in my urges, Britt standing near the bed. Slowly, she turns to face me. I take in my fill, my eyes slowly roving up and down her perfect body, remembering how every inch tasted, how it felt beneath my hands. Britt inhales and whispers one shaky word. "Keller."

The sound of my name on her lips does something to the

damaged man inside. I haven't been Keller in so long. I haven't *wanted* to be him. But having Britt, gorgeous and willing in my room, seeing the raw emotions in her eyes—desire, adoration, *trust*—makes me long for things I shouldn't. Things I don't deserve. But I'm weak. The chance to feel something again is too tempting. The anniversary, the alcohol, the pain of not being with Britt… the remainder of my walls collapse into a pile of rubble at her feet.

"Britt," I rasp, never needing anything as much as I need her.

I step forward, pulling Britt into my arms, kissing her lips, her throat, across her collarbone. Nose to nose, I grasp the hem of her shirt. She raises her arms, giving herself to me completely. The magnitude of her gift, her trust, makes me breathless. I tug off the fabric, tossing it aside to quickly work off the rest of her clothes.

Once she's naked, Britt reaches out, sliding her fingers along the waistband of my loose athletic pants. The feather-light touch across my abs sends chills up my spine, my skin a riot of sensation. "Fuck." The curse slips free as my head falls back. I stand still, allowing Britt to undress me, allowing her the same level of trust she gave me. Small hands dig under the fabric at my lower back. Britt grabs the firm globes of my ass, kneading and squeezing them, exploring every inch as we grind together.

"I want you. I need you," she murmurs as she licks a path up my throat to my jaw.

"Jesus, Britt. I… I never…" Words fail me. I hardly ever feel emotions let alone put them in words. There *are* no words to describe what Britt does to me.

"Shhhhhh," she whispers, stroking the side of my face. "I know. I feel it too."

I swallow, the lump in my throat making it difficult to speak. My eyes burn as this girl, this amazing woman, makes me feel more with one sentence than I've felt in ten years. Makes me feel… worthy.

Britt pushes my pants down and I kick them to the side. Both of us naked, we spend time standing pressed together, our hands wandering as our mouths and tongues explore. When my body begins to hum with electricity and my balls grow heavy, I gently push her back on the mattress. Britt lies down, pulling me with her.

When I line up and enter her hot depths, our eyes connected, I know without a doubt this single moment is going to change my life. This will either be my salvation or cause my complete destruction.

This will be the first time I've ever made love to another person, and I pray to god I'm strong enough to come through it unscathed.

Britt

When Keller joins his body with mine, everything in my world becomes clear, focused… right. As much as I need the controlling pain-pleasure Keller brings me, somehow, he instinctively knows that today I need to be held. I need to be loved.

Is that what this is? Love?

I look up at Keller. His silver eyes heavy-lidded, his swollen lips parted as he slowly moves in and out of me. He shows me with his body what he holds in his heart and to me, it feels like love. I respond in kind, my back arching under his touch, my hands caressing the rippling muscles of his arms and shoulders, my hips lifting to meet each one of his long, deep thrusts. Keller leans on his elbows, his hands gently framing my face. He stares down at me, his expression filled with such wonder, tears spring up in my eyes unbidden. Unashamed, I let them flow down my cheeks to be absorbed by the sheets and gasp as the intensity of Keller opening his emotions takes me to the edge.

My heart stutters and my breath catches. I'm in love. In love with this dangerous, tortured, violent man. This man who is also kind, protective, loyal, and gets me like no one else does.

"Britt... I...." Keller's eyes flutter closed and he increases the pace, his hips snapping faster, harder, his breathing becoming more labored. His cries are raw, real, emotional as he clings to me as if I'm the only thing keeping him grounded.

"Keller..." I moan, sparks exploding into fiery heat as his cock rubs a spot deep in my pussy, growing into a powerful orgasm.

Keller grabs my hands, bringing them over my head and threading our fingers together. "I'm so close, Britt. Tell me you are too." His voice is strained but his rhythm never falters, his beautiful, muscular body undulating over mine.

"Yes. I-I... *ohgod*, Keller!" My breath is cut off as my body tightens, sensation overwhelming me. It tips me right over the edge.

Keller shouts as I contract tight around his cock, pulsing around him. I arch back, my head pressing into the bed as my orgasm rips through me, liquid fire running up and down my body, hitting every nerve ending, and making my toes curl. Spots flash behind my eyes as I shudder and moan.

"Fuuuuck, goddamn, Britt!" Keller fucks me through my release, causing me to scream and thrash as the pleasure becomes almost unbearable. He lets go of my hands and pushes into a kneeling position between my thighs. Grabbing my hips, Keller pounds in once, twice more, shouting as he comes deep inside me. I stare in wonder at this stunning man, his muscles tight, tattooed skin shimmering with sweat, his head thrown back in ecstasy.

It's the most beautiful thing I've ever seen in my life.

When he's finally drained, Keller collapses on top of me, careful to keep most of his weight to the side so he doesn't crush me. I wrap my arms and legs around him, burying my nose in the crook of his neck. I never want to lose this feeling, never want to separate from this man.

I'm in love with Keller Bishop and I've never been happier.

After a nap and a shower, Keller brought out his dominant side, forcing me to kneel on the wet tiles to suck his cock before yanking me up, spinning me around, and fucking me into the shower wall until I became limp in his arms. Eventually, we ended up in the kitchen, starving and thirsty after our activities.

Now Keller is bent over, peering into his fridge, gorgeous

round ass on full display.

"Britt?"

I blink. Keller is staring at me, holding two bottles in his hands.

"Huh?"

He smirks. "You didn't hear a word I said, did you? You were staring at my ass, weren't you?" My face heats up, but I don't deny it. I simply shrug. I mean, how can I not stare at such perfection? "I asked if you want coconut water or sweet tea?"

I shake my head. "Whatever you're having is fine." Seated on a barstool at the island, I lean on my elbows, chin propped on my hands, and watch as Keller pours us each a glass of sweet tea.

"Here." He pushes one toward me while draining his own.

"Thanks." I take a few sips, but prefer to watch Keller, shirtless and leaning against the countertop, his throat rippling as he swallows his drink.

"Britt." I blink again, lifting my gaze to find shining gray eyes. Keller looks amused. "Maybe I should put a shirt on?"

This time, my face flames up. Apparently, I can't go two seconds without ogling the man. But really, he's stunning, and at work I can't get caught openly staring at him or I'd be drooling all over the gym, so I'm going to get my fill when I can.

"Sorry." I divert my attention to spin the stool around, taking in his condo. "This is really nice, Keller."

I hear him place his glass in the sink, and not gently. "Thanks."

I glance over my shoulder to see Keller all tense, his mouth pressed into a tight line. Okaaay. Note, don't talk about his condo.

Keller circles the island and presses a kiss to the top of my head. "Let me throw on a shirt and we can… I mean, if you want… I guess watch a movie or something?"

The look on his face makes me burst with laughter. "You have no idea what to do with me when we're not having sex, do you?"

"Ummmmm, is it bad to say no?" Keller scratches his head and his cheeks pink up. It's adorable.

"Don't worry. We'll figure something out." I wink, getting the serious man to smile. I nearly choke on my drink. He's so beautiful when he smiles, positively breathtaking. It's so rare I've only seen it a handful of times.

Keller walks down the hall, disappearing into his bedroom. I slide off the stool and wander over to the tall windows on the other end of the room by the couches and television. The view is spectacular. It's not quite dusk, so the blue sky is streaked with brilliant shades of yellow fading to tangerine along the horizon. I turn and check out the rest of the living area and frown. No art on the walls, no pictures, no personal items. It's almost as if Keller moved into a staged home, cold and impersonal. This is a pretty expensive home for a rookie fighter. Just one more of a million things I don't know about Keller.

On a small table next to the door is a pile of papers and bills. I don't mean for it to happen, but one of them catches my eye, an embossed corner peeking out from under a larger envelope. I step closer and my heart slams against my ribcage. I shiver, a cold sweat breaking out across my skin as I approach the table.

It can't be.

As if watching myself on TV, my hand reaches out, going through the motions without being aware of it. With one finger, I nudge the larger envelope to the side, exposing the one underneath.

Panic grips my throat, sucking the breath from my lungs, and my vision shimmers. Unable to make sense of anything, I bend over the table and read the silver embossing.

Keller Bishop Keating

My head spins, the room suddenly too hot, the floor tilting back and forth beneath my wobbly legs. I read the return address, already knowing what it says, because I have the very same envelope sitting at home, buried under my own thick stack of mail.

Students Against School Shootings

I stare at the invitation to the tenth anniversary of "the incident," pain and confusion shattering my reality.

Why? Why is this here? Why is his name Keller Bishop... Keating?

I jerk back as if slapped, hundreds of images assaulting me at once—the dark-haired girl, the boy with the guns, huddling under the countertop... I cry out and press my palms into my temples. The memories are so real, so fresh, I can smell the gunpowder, the blood, the feel of the trembling girl in my arms.

And that's what they are. Memories. Not images. Not dreams. Memories. They're coming back.

Oh god.

"Britt? What's going on?"

I try to focus though blurry, tear-filled eyes. Somehow, the envelope is in my hands, dotted with moisture as it drips from my cheeks.

"How—?" I whisper, the envelope crumpling as my fingers tighten around it.

When Keller doesn't respond, I look up and stop breathing.

His eyes. My world spins off its axis, hurtling me straight into hell.

Silver eyes. Staring into mine as a bullet rips through her skull. I watch as the life drains out of the beautiful eyes of the girl in my arms. Then, a fraction of a second of fiery agony and... nothing.

I drop the envelope like a hot coal and clutch my head. "Britt? Why are you acting like this? Are you okay, baby?"

Keller's sweet endearment goes unnoticed. He steps forward to comfort me and I let out a primal scream, thrusting my arms out, palms up. "Stay away! Don't touch me!"

The memories keep coming, one after another. Now that the vault locked and buried deep in my mind has opened, they crash over me in a bone-chilling surge of death and darkness.

The parking lot. A girl with a crush looking for a cute boy. Disappointment when he isn't there. Approached by a smiling girl with... silver eyes.

Silver eyes just like Keller's.

"Britt." Keller holds out his arms, as if trying to calm a frightened animal.

"Don't!" I sob hoarsely, cries ripping from my chest one after another as the long-suppressed memories fracture my mind, Britt on one side and Britton Reeves, victim, on the other. "I can't... I can't be here right now." Air becomes a precious commodity and I suck in one ragged breath after another.

"Britt, baby, don't do this. Tell me what's going on!" Keller sounds frightened and confused, but I can't worry about him when my psyche is literally splitting in two.

"Just leave me alone!" I cry, flinging open the door and running for the elevator. Keller steps out of his condo, intent on chasing me. "Stay the fuck away!" I scream as loud as possible, my voice choked with tears.

Keller flinches, his expression devastated. He watches with those damn silver eyes, the same ones I stared into as a life was snuffed out.

I can't. It's too much. The elevator doors open and I step in, my heart breaking as they close, cutting me off from the only man I've ever loved and throwing me into the shadow of my past.

CHAPTER 12

Keller

"Fuck! Fuck! Fuck!"

I punch and kick at a section of wall next to the front door of my condo until it's pretty much pulverized into scraps of dusty drywall and battered studs. My hands are torn to shreds and my feet swollen and bruised, like I give a shit. Physical pain is something I can deal with. The gaping hole in my chest is another matter altogether.

I forgot how much it hurts—caring about someone. Watching helplessly as Britt cried and screamed, her eyes wild with terror… terror from looking at me. The agony is almost equal to what I felt when I lost Kinsey, guilt from her death rearing its ugly head as well. Whatever made Britt lose it was my fault somehow, just like Kinsey's death.

Crumpled on the floor, exhausted and bleeding, I see a flash of white out of the corner of my eye. Ignoring the shooting pains in my limbs, I crawl a few feet and retrieve the object from under one of the barstools and turn it over. My hands clench around the thick paper, sending fresh streaks of pain through my busted knuckles.

The invitation. Britt was holding it when she flipped out. Is this what caused the strong woman I know to fall to pieces in front of me? Why?

Not knowing is driving me insane.

Hours later, my head is throbbing. I'm sitting on my couch in the middle of the night—*or is it early morning?*—feeling confused and sorry for myself. I managed to clean up my hands and am pretty sure one knuckle might be broken, but could care less. The invitation sits on the glass and chrome coffee table in front of me, unopened. Taunting me with its secrets.

Why would this letter frighten Britt? My mind churns through the possibilities. Maybe she recognized my name from the papers? Maybe she knows I'm the asshole that killed his little sister.

No. The reasons behind Kinsey being at the school that late were never released. Dad, me, and Logan. We're the only ones who know. We never told the police my role in Kinsey's death.

I flinch when another thought crosses my mind and force myself to go to the desk wedged in a far corner of the room to boot up my laptop. By the time the browser comes up, I'm in a cold sweat.

Blood thumps against my eardrums as I type.

North Atlanta Prep Shooting

Fuck. I take a deep breath and steady my hand.

Enter

Hundreds of results come up, the most recent being news covering the ten-year anniversary of Atlanta's biggest tragedy. My fucking father's brilliant idea.

Nausea and rage eat away at my insides. The fact that my dad thinks he can make up for missing Kinsey's entire life by throwing some sick, pointless party and erecting a memorial at the school makes me want to rip out his throat with my bare hands.

Further down the screen, I click a link for a news report from ten years ago. After the page loads, I have to close my eyes and swallow several times to keep from throwing up. Photos of the victims line the top of the article, including one of my beautiful little sister, smiling and happy and full of life.

Tears prick my eyes when I open them back up, the moisture blurring my vision. I dash them away with my bruised hands, determined to see this through no matter what it costs me emotionally. I need to know Britt's involvement in the shooting, if any. I need to make things right. I need her.

The beginning of the article covers facts I already know, so I skim quickly. A decade ago, these same facts were repeated on the news over and over and over until they became a low hum in the background of my guilt and selfishness. The principal, vice-principal, school secretary, football coach who happened to stop by the office to pick up some forms, the clerk, school nurse, seven other students who were part of an after school club, and my sister were all pronounced dead at the scene of multiple gunshot wounds along with the shooter, who killed himself. Shaking, I read further and stop, blinking in disbelief.

One survivor, an unnamed student with traumatic brain

injuries from a bullet to the head.

One survivor.

Student.

Head injury.

How did I forget there was a survivor? Probably because I was a complete, near suicidal mess at the time, drinking myself into oblivion every day.

The image of Britt lying on the cold concrete in the Nevada Arena, her entire body rocking with violent tremors as a seizure took hold, enters my mind. Britt hit her head pretty hard, but is it possible that wasn't the only reason for the seizure? Is Britt the lone survivor of the crime that took my sister's life?

Out of my chair and flying down the hall, I make it as far as the bathroom sink before retching, the contents of my stomach forced from my body. It takes forever to stop heaving, my guts clenching again and again until I'm empty and my sweaty shirt is sticking to my chest.

On autopilot, I brush my teeth and change clothes. Further online searches yield no results. The name of the survivor was never released to the public.

I'm not scared of much. Hell, I'm not scared of anything. Except this. The past. Facing my actions and admitting my role in the tragedy. No matter the cost to me, I need to make things right with Britt. Without thinking, I shove my feet into a pair of sneakers and grab my keys, leaving the condo without looking back.

I'm coming, baby. No fucking way am I going to let you

down the way I did my little sister and my mother. You're not running away from me. We'll face this shit together.

Britt

My head feels as if it's wrapped in gauze and weighs a thousand pounds. That thought causes a moment of déjà vu. When I realize why, fear stabs into me like a dagger to the heart. This is exactly how I felt after waking up from the coma—head heavy, mind foggy, disconnected body. Am I back in the hospital?

When I try to look around, my eyelids refuse to cooperate, staying closed despite my efforts to open them. My limbs feel like lead and testing each one, I can't get a single one to move. The only part of me responding to the situation is my heart, which is now pounding erratically as my body holds me prisoner.

"Still out, huh?" The voice is distorted through the murky sludge in my brain, but it's familiar. "Just sleep." A cold hand caresses my face, brushing my hair back. I want to slap the hand away. It feels wrong, creepy. With chills rippling across my skin, I slip back into darkness.

The next time I wake up, my eyelids open on command. I'm in a dark room. Specifically, on a bed in a dark room. A hint of light peeks through a crack along the curtains, but isn't enough to give me a clue as to what time of day it is. I try to lick my lips but my mouth is too dry, my tongue sticky and swollen. The muggy air is tinged with a chemical scent. When I try to sit I tense up and freeze.

Some sort of fibrous rope is cutting into my wrists. My hands are tied together. I test my feet only to find those bound as well. Panic rises quickly, gripping me in its tight fist. Breathing becomes difficult as my lungs squeeze the air out and refuse to let more in. My pulse rockets sky-high, and I have to fight the urge to scream.

My hands and feet are bound. Oh my god. I'm tied up. Have I been kidnapped?

Freaking out, I curl into a ball. Apparently, I'm tied up, but only hand to hand and foot to foot, not to the bed I'm lying in.

Breathe, Britt.

I focus on staying calm so I can get the hell out of here. After a few moments of deep breathing, I clench my abs to swing both feet over the edge of the bed and *can't…* because of the arm wrapped around my waist.

I'm not alone. The realization sends me over the edge.

Unable to contain the hoarse cry that rips from my constricted lungs, I scream until I wake whoever is in bed with me. I shout over and over and over, not caring that my voice eventually becomes ragged and sound no longer comes out. Hands grab my shoulders, holding me down on the mattress. I keep screaming silently, now struggling to get out of my assailant's grip. But I'm weak and dehydrated, my head filled with cotton balls. It doesn't take long for me to realize the futility of my actions, so I let my body go limp and slam my lips together.

"What's wrong, Britt? I've got you. You're okay."

The man pulls me into his arms, holding me on his lap while rocking back and forth. My rapidly clearing mind is spinning with questions, none of them making any sense. I break down and ask the most important one, my voice no more than a soft whisper.

"Max? What am I doing here?"

"Shhhhhh," he continues swaying back and forth on the bed with me in his arms, using one hand to caress my hair.

Using as much strength as I can manage, I place my bound hands on his chest and shove, falling off of his lap and onto the mattress. Before Max can react, I scramble to my hands and knees and scurry back on the bed.

"What is going on, Max? Why am I tied up and why are you in bed with me?"

Max lifts a hand and I let out a gravelly cry, swinging at him with my bound fists. Max's expression of tenderness and concern turns into one of fury. I stop cold, terror slithering around my spine. The look on Max's face is so frightening it chills me down to the marrow.

"It's that bastard, Killer. He's turned you against me, Britt. But that's all in the past. Here, we're free of him. We can be together now." His disturbing mask slips away. Max is now smiling warmly, gazing at me like an old lover.

In shock, I stare at him, a man I worked with for *two* years. A man I accepted rides from, who has been in my apartment. A man I thought I knew and now don't recognize at all. Keller was right all along in thinking something was off about Max. Nobody else noticed a thing. He fooled everyone.

"Max," I say, trying to sound calm even though my hoarse voice wavers. "We're not together. We were never together. You can't tie me up and keep me here."

"Shut up!" he shouts, smacking his hands down on the bed. Max jumps to the floor, standing over me as I cower away from him. "You were almost there, Britt. You were almost mine! Two years I worked on getting you to be with me and as soon as that... that... disgusting Killer shows up, you go and forget all about me!"

Max grabs my shoulders, strong fingers digging painfully into my flesh. He might not be a fighter, but he's a trainer, and not weak by any means. Especially against a small, bound female.

"M-Max..." I struggle to ignore the pain of his fingers digging into my arms and stare into his eyes. They're predatory, cold, like empty glass orbs placed into two holes in his face.

"You're mine!" he roars. I squeeze my eyes shut and duck my head to avoid looking at that lifeless stare. "I don't care how long it takes. You *will* come around, Britt." He tosses me back like a rag doll. I bounce on the bed helplessly and curl up into a tight ball.

Between the loud hammering of my heart and only having one functional ear, I don't hear Max move around the room. I certainly don't hear him prepare the cloth. When Max's hand slides around my mouth and nose, his other hand holds the back of my head, keeping me in place.

"Shhhhhh, it's okay, Britt. It's for your own good."

Max's words don't affect me because a sweet, medicinal scent stings my nostrils with each ragged inhale. I know now I'm in bigger trouble than I ever imagined. I can't fight, I can't move, all I can do is breathe in the chemicals until my world fades to black.

Keller

"Britt! Open the goddamn door!" I pound my fists on the door to her apartment. "Britt! Fuck!" I thread my hands through my hair as I pace back and forth on her front step. Spinning on my heel, I slam my hands into the thick slab of wood again. "Britt! Open up! Now, goddamn it!"

Multiple calls and texts have gone unanswered, and now she won't come to the door. The need to speak to her about the invitation, the shooting, has me at the edge of coming completely unhinged.

Several of Britt's neighbors peek out of their own apartments to see who is making such a loud disturbance. No one challenges me or tells me to fuck off, and who would? I must look insane. Wearing loose shorts and tight T-shirt, covered in tattoos, with an expression on my face that likely screams of violence and danger.

I contemplate kicking her door down. It wouldn't be too difficult, despite the outrageous number of deadbolts Britt has in place. A dozen strategically placed kicks is all it would take, but I can't chance getting arrested. Hell, someone probably already called the cops.

Shit. I have to leave. Not only would an arrest get me kicked out of the AFL, but being locked up would keep me from finding Britt, and that's something that I can't allow to happen.

More frustrated than I've ever been in my life, I slam my hands into the door one last time and stalk back to my car. Pounding on the steering wheel doesn't help lessen my agitation either. I breathe slowly to calm down, having absolutely no idea what to do next. The car is stifling, so I turn on the engine and lean back on the leather seat, letting the air conditioning cool my sweat-slicked skin.

While I wait for my temperature and blood pressure to return to normal, I notice the lot is only half full. It's not surprising, being a Sunday afternoon and not a workday for most people. This time, I scan the lot with a purpose and realize Britt's red BMW is nowhere to be seen.

"Son of a bitch!"

If I had just paid more attention I would have known Britt wasn't here. She doesn't use her car very often, usually walking to and from work just the same as I jog every day. Traffic is a bitch around here and taking a car makes very little sense. So Britt went somewhere a little further than the gym. Where would she go?

Fuck. I don't really know jack shit about her. Not really. How can a person get so completely under my skin and invade my soul without me knowing such simple things as her favorite restaurant, or hobbies, or even if she has any family? Because I'm a selfish prick, that's why. Wait…

Family.

With a new plan in place, I jerk the car into gear and head for the gym.

"Come on, Roxie. You helped me before. Why can't you help me again?" I lean on the front counter where the tall woman is manning the juice bar, blending up a shake for another fighter.

"Killer," she says as she pours the thick pink liquid into a tall cup and hands it to the guy at the other end of the bar. "It doesn't feel right to invade Britt's privacy like that. Besides, it could get me fired."

I growl, slamming a fist down on the counter hard enough to rattle the glassware. "Fuck privacy! I need to talk to her. It's urgent!"

Roxie frowns, looking at me but not *looking* at me. Not at my eyes anyway. She's staring somewhere around chest level so she won't have to see the monster. But the monster is gone. At least for now. The monster wouldn't give a shit about Britt or the shooting or anything. Keller does.

"Roxie, look at me." She flinches, hesitant to do as I ask. "Please?"

Roxie bites her lip and reluctantly flicks her eyes up to mine. For once, she doesn't look away. I don't see the fear that transpires when people look into my eyes. No, Roxie's expression softens. She looks... sympathetic.

"Killer. Get Gabriel's permission and I'll give you what you want. Okay? That's the best I can do." Roxie reaches out and pats my hand before turning to the sink to wash out the blender.

Gabriel isn't here on Sundays unless a fight is coming up, so I whip out my cell phone, find his contact, and hit send. It rings so many times, I'm about to give up when the call connects.

"*Fala.*"

I nearly sink to my knees in relief.

"Gabriel, it's Killer. I need your help," I rattle in rapid-fire Portuguese.

"Killer? What is the matter? Are you okay?" The man sounds genuinely concerned for me, something I haven't heard from another person in over ten years.

"No," I say, my throat closing up as I think about Britt. "It's… it's Britt. I screwed up, Gabriel. I need to see her. It's very important."

"So go see her," he says simply.

"She's not home," I explain. "And she won't answer her phone."

"I see."

"I need… I need you to allow Roxie to show me her emergency contact." I swallow nervously, praying Gabriel understands the importance of the situation. "I think something really bad is going on with her." My voice cracks and I rub my forehead. "She saw something at my place, something… personal. It shouldn't have meant anything to her, but she freaked out and left. Gabriel, it scared the shit out of me."

"You? You are scared? *Meu Dios.* Nothing scares you."

"Gabriel…" I'm becoming desperate, which makes me angry. It's impossible to keep him from hearing the hostility.

"Tell Roxie to give you whatever you need," he says and I let out a long breath.

"She'll want to hear it from you. Hold on." I catch Roxie's attention and hand her the phone. Roxie nods and keeps saying "okay" over and over.

"Here." She hands me back my phone. "Let me get the employee binder."

Five minutes later, I'm clutching a scrap of paper with the address for Britt's parents. It takes about twenty minutes to get there. If it were a weekday it would be more like forty-five and I'd be frothing at the mouth by the time I arrived.

I pull into a long curving drive and stop out front. Gaping, I stare at the enormous structure. Britt is so quiet and understated, the house isn't at all what I was expecting. In fact, it reminds me of the house I grew up in. One of those huge, cold mansions filled with expensive things and showy displays of wealth but containing no love or warmth. Nothing to make it an actual *home*. I don't see Britt's shiny red BMW. She's not here.

"Jesus," I mutter, looking down at my shorts and shirt. I'm woefully underdressed to approach anyone who lives inside this house, let alone ask questions about their daughter. Money is all about appearance. That's what my mom lived and preached. Fat lot of fucking good it did her.

Fuck it. I climb out of the car and scale the stone stairs leading to the front door. The doorbell is loud and pretentious, once more bringing me back to my own childhood home. I guess if you know one rich asshole you know them all.

The door opens, revealing a tiny woman wearing black slacks and a white blouse. Her eyes bulge and she closes the door some, blocking my view of the inside.

"Yes?" she asks, her voice tinged with the hint of an accent.

If Britt's mother is anything like mine was, she doesn't want her employees sounding foreign and likely forced the woman to modulate her speech. Can't be caught mingling with riffraff, can we? Even if they are just the hired help.

And right now, this woman is looking at me like *I'm* the riffraff, which I am.

"I need to speak to Mr. or Mrs. Reeves. It's urgent."

The tiny woman closes the door a little more, ready to slam it in my face.

"They are occupied," she says. Before she can shut the door completely, I throw out an arm, slapping my palm on the wood to keep it open.

"Please. It's about their daughter." I give what I hope is a desperate look, and not a frightening one. I know with the tats and the clothes and the frantic way I'm twitching that I look like I'm crazy, but I have to talk to them. "Please," I say again when it appears the woman is about to dismiss me.

"One minute." She steps back and closes the door, leaving me on the front step to freak out. I pull at my hair and pace back and forth for what feels like hours. The door opens again and instead of the tiny housekeeper, I'm facing a tall, well-groomed man of about fifty.

Britt's father. He has her eyes, blue and shimmering. The sight nearly knocks the wind out of me.

"Who are you?" he asks, his voice even but in that no-bullshit tone I recognize from dealing with adults like him my entire life. He's rich, powerful, and used to getting whatever he wants.

"I'm Keller Bishop, I work with Britt. Your… daughter?" I ask, hoping I'm right.

"Yes, she's my daughter. What is it I can do for you, Keller?" The man's eyes drift up and down my body, taking in my rough appearance. He's too polite to grimace, but I'm sure he wants to.

"Please. If I could just talk to you for a moment. Britt kind of… ummmm, freaked out last night and I can't find her. I was hoping…"

"What did you do to my daughter?" he snarls, stepping out of the house to get into my space.

This guy has balls the size of coconuts. Not many people will challenge me so boldly. I'm glad Britt has him on her side.

"I didn't do anything, sir. She saw something and I don't understand… Please, this isn't a conversation to have out here. I only need a minute."

The man assesses me, calculating my sincerity, I'm sure. He gives me a sharp nod. "Follow me."

The man leads me into a grand foyer, taking an immediate right into a huge office. It's exactly like the ones I've seen in all of my high school friends' houses, including my own. Dark wood, dark walls, shelves of old books that are only for show. A bunch of pretentious art hangs on the walls and an enormous desk rich men like him use to measure their dicks. Like the bigger the desk the more important you are.

"Sit," he says, pointing at a leather chair. He takes the seat behind the desk, giving me the typical rich-CEO stare. Too bad years around my dad made me immune to it. "Tell me about Britton. All of it."

"This is uncomfortable for me to say, sir," I admit. Just the thought of bringing up the shooting has my stomach churning. Britt's father narrows his eyes, indicating I should get the fuck on with it. Fine. "Did Britt go to North Atlanta Prep?"

The man's mouth falls open and his all-business exterior vanishes. He slumps back in his chair and suddenly looks years older.

"What are you really asking?" he asks, his voice wary.

"I… my sister…" Breathing through my nostrils, I force out the rest of the words. "My sister died in the shooting, sir. Britt saw my invitation to the anniversary. I mean, there was a ten-year anniversary Saturday, and—"

"I know. My wife and I went." The man drags his hands down his face. When he makes eye contact with me, this time he looks less CEO and more human. Like a man worried about his daughter. "Yes, Britton was there. She was the only survivor."

Even though I suspected as much, hearing it confirmed is like someone reaching into my chest and pulverizing my heart.

Gasping, I bend over, putting my head between my legs.

Long-suppressed tears overflow, dripping all over the fancy Persian rug. "Fuck," I whisper. Pain like I've never felt lances every inch of my body, like a hundred thousand stab wounds opening at once.

Britt was there. With Kinsey.

"She doesn't remember it," the man says. I wipe my face the best I can and sit up, still overcome with the agony of the truth. "Britton suffered a gunshot wound to her head." Her father closes his eyes and swallows. "She lost all hearing in her left ear, and suffered cognitive trauma—forgetting how to do the simple things. She was quite the little fighter though, and figured most of it out pretty quick, eating, tying her shoes, stuff like that… but it took months of therapy for her to walk again."

"Oh my god," I whisper. What Britt went through. It's so horrific, I can't even imagine. She's not just strong, she's stronger than anyone I know. "I can't find her. She started screaming when she saw the invitation. She… she took off. She's not at her apartment and neither is her car. I was hoping she'd be here."

"She's not here," her father says, his voice mirroring the despair in mine.

"Could she be with a friend?" I ask, desperate for any lead I can get.

He shakes his head. "Britton isn't the same girl she was before the incident." I grimace, but he continues. "She doesn't trust easily. She's scared all the time. She doesn't have any friends I know of." Her father sighs and stares out the large window that overlooks the front drive. "I'm proud of how far she's come. Most people would have given up a long time ago, but Britt still has a long way to go."

"I should leave," I say, pulling up to my feet. "Thank you, sir." I extend my hand, waiting to see what he'll do.

He clasps it firmly. "Thank you for coming here. For caring about my daughter." I turn to leave, but he stops me, handing me a card with his cell phone on it. "Luke." I stare at the man, not sure what he means. "My name is Lucas Reeves, but you can call me Luke."

Unable to manage a smile, I nod. "Thank you for your time, Luke."

Back behind the wheel of my car, my mind is going a mile a minute as I weave through light traffic on my way back to my condo. I probably shouldn't be driving as distracted as I am. I hate feeling helpless. I hate knowing what Britt went through. I hate that I can't see her, hold her, tell her I'm here for her no matter what. If I could take all of her demons and add them to my own, I'd do it in a heartbeat. No one as good and sweet as Britt should have to suffer so much.

I pull into the parking garage beneath my condo, lean over the steering wheel, and allow myself to feel. And fuck, does it hurt.

CHAPTER 13

Britt

Even though I'm lying down, my head is spinning. I know what's happening to me. There's no clock but I know it's been at least twenty-four hours since I've had my seizure medication, possibly longer. I'm going through withdrawal.

"Max, please?" I beg for the hundredth time, too tired to even feel a sense of panic. My voice is raspy and ragged, too soft for him to hear. Max locked me in his bedroom while he's doing god knows what out there. I don't even know how long I've been here or where "here" is.

Has it been one day? Two? A week? Whenever Max puts the rag over my face, which I've decided is some sort of chloroform or ether, I wake up wrapped in his arms wanting to scream. The daylight showing through the curtain is fading. Time means nothing anymore. Max just keeps telling me I'll eventually love him. Right now, I'm grateful he hasn't touched me, sexually that is. I'm pretty sure even if he knocked me out, I'd wake up and know if something happened. The thought sends a dark ripple of fear across my skin.

The lock on the door turns and I tense up. I'm not sure if I'm better off alone or when Max comes in to chat with me. When he visits, he leaves the door unlocked, giving me a chance to escape. But I'm not stupid. How can I outrun him with my feet bound together?

The knots in the natural fiber rope are too tight to work free and the room is stripped bare of anything I could use to cut through them. I can't even chew through them—I've tried. Besides, my head feels odd, spacey—probably from all the chemicals Max makes me inhale.

"Time to eat," Max says as if it were just any old day and we were a couple, about to enjoy a normal meal together.

"Max, you have to let me go. I need my medicine."

Max puts the tray down on the bed and stares. He studies me for so long with those cold, almost reptilian eyes that goose bumps prick my skin.

"What medicine?" he asks.

I swallow down my fear. "I have seizures, Max. I can't skip my medication. I don't even know how long I've been here."

"You had one seizure, Britt. At the fight in Vegas." Those empty eyes narrow and another chill goes through me.

"No, Max. I had a brain injury, when I was fourteen. If I hit my head hard enough or skip my meds, I can have seizures. If it's a big enough seizure, I can end up a vegetable or brain dead." As strong as I'm trying to be, my hoarse voice trembles.

Max continues assessing me, unblinking. "How do I know you're not bullshitting me?"

"Check behind my left ear." I tilt my head for him. "There's a scar where I had brain surgery." Max glances at the door and back. Fear jolts through me when I realize what he's thinking. "You don't need the cloth, Max. It might cause a seizure. Just look at me. I promise I'll stay still."

He approaches slowly, his gaze predatory. It takes all my willpower not to scream or flinch when his cold hands sift through my hair, parting it to see my scalp. I feel his fingers slide along the twisted tissue where the doctors removed the bullet. After an eternity, he sits back.

"I believe you." I exhale in relief. Max moves back, standing over me. "I was whispering in your ear the entire time I was looking at your scar and you didn't hear a word I said, did you?"

I shake my head, too frightened to respond. He's too close and his touch makes my skin crawl. With a sharp nod of his head, Max leaves the room, coming back a few seconds later with the cloth in his hand.

"No, please!" I scramble back, pressing against the headboard, the sheets twisted up beneath my feet.

"It's for your own good, Britt. Until you love me back, it's really the best way. If you want me to get your medication, you won't fight me." Max grips my head firmly and presses the cloth over my face. No matter how many times he does it, I still struggle against the pull of the fumes.

At least one good thing comes from it. When I'm sucked into the blackness, I'm not afraid anymore.

Keller

I wipe my face with the hem of my shirt. Here I am, big badass Killer, sitting in my car bawling my eyes out like a fucking baby. But the thought of something happening to Britt… the realization that something *did* happen to Britt ten years ago… it's too much to not let it hurt. Even for a cold bastard like me.

With unfocused eyes, I stare out the windshield at the concrete wall of the garage, wanting Killer to make an appearance, wishing for the numbness I use to keep everyone out and emotions suppressed. Just a fraction of that strength could end the agony that plunges a fist into my heart, squeezing the organ in its icy grip until I can hardly breathe.

Just as quickly as I wish for Killer to return, I change my mind. If I didn't feel this way—feel the searing pain in my chest, know that I have an actual heart to break—it would mean I don't have Britt in my life. And above everything else, I want her in my life. The thought of losing Britt, the possibility of already having lost her, cuts me down at the knees.

My once dead heart falters at the thought. I can't lose her. I love her.

Fuck. I love her. How did I let that happen?

It doesn't matter. Right now, I can't do a goddamn thing to find her and fix whatever she's going through. It makes me want to tear something or someone to shreds. To break bones and shatter objects and throw a violent, rage-infused tantrum. The only thing that stops me is knowing it won't help Britt. I take a deep breath and get out of the car. All I can do is wait for her to come to me, and I despise the feeling of helplessness.

Mentally drained, I head for the elevator, my head so full of "feelings" I don't notice the cherry red coupe until I've passed it by. Doing a double take, I spin around and hurry to its side. Granted, it could be anyone's car, but a beacon of hope sparks like a flicker of light in a dark ocean. There are hundreds of red BMWs in Atlanta, possibly thousands. Yet, somehow, I know this one is Britt's. Circling the car, I cup my hands and look through the window. It's immaculate, except for a glint of metal on the front floorboard.

I scan the garage for something I can use to break the window. Finding nothing, I pull off my shirt and wrap it around my hand. One hard strike and the glass shatters into a million tiny pieces. I reach in and pull out a silver chain with a purple crystal pendant.

I've seen this before. Hanging around Britt's neck.

I know Britt was here, at my condo. It seems she drove, which she doesn't do often. But she had a complete meltdown and left. So why is her car still parked in my garage? I circle the car again, this time looking underneath and all around on the surrounding pavement. Nothing.

Britt wouldn't leave her car here, no matter how upset she was. I live on a very busy midtown street with no sidewalks for several blocks. Unfurling my hand, I study the delicate chain. The tiny silver clasp is broken, as if the necklace were yanked off her neck, perhaps during a struggle. *Fuck!* I open the doors to the red BMW and climb inside, thoroughly searching the floors, seats, and every crack and crevice in between. When my hand closes around a set of keys with a BMW fob and a Souza MMA keychain, my newly awoken heart stops.

Is she upstairs waiting for me? But the necklace…

A car pulls into the garage, interrupting my thoughts. Not wanting to be seen, I duck behind Britt's car. With the smashed window and me standing shirtless with the fabric still balled around my hand, it wouldn't take a genius to put two and two together. The engine cuts a few spaces away and someone gets out, whistling as they walk my way.

Shit. I glance around, desperate for an escape. Maybe the person won't notice the glass on the ground. That thought dies when shoes crunch on pieces of the broken driver's side window and the whistling stops dead.

"What the—?"

The sound of that voice makes the hairs on the back of my neck stand on end. Adrenaline floods my veins, pushing liquid fury to every cell in my body. I step out from behind the car, shirt around one hand, Britt's keys and necklace clenched in the other. My eyes lock on to my prey, currently half inside the car with his upper body through the open window. The pure, instinctual violence inside me, Killer rises, shoving all other emotions to the side. He's primed and ready to strike.

The intruder doesn't notice until I drop the shirt and clamp a hand on the back of his neck, yanking him out of the car.

"What the hell?"

The man stumbles, but my hold is too tight. I spin him around and slam him bodily into the frame of the small coupe, my palm pressed against his chest. He recovers his balance and I see the moment he realizes exactly how much danger he's in. His eyes widen and his jaw drops. It gives me immense satisfaction to feel his body trembling under my hand.

"Max," I growl, leaning in until our noses nearly touch.

"W-what are you doing?" he stutters.

I move my hand to his throat and squeeze. His hands immediately go to his neck, scrabbling to remove the pressure of my tight grip.

"What did you do with her, you sick fuck?"

His eyes bulge and his face turns a dark shade of red. Wheezing, he answers. "I don't know what you mean."

I clamp down harder, now able to feel the rapid beat of his pulse through his jugular as well as the flexible cartilage of his windpipe.

"Don't fuck with me, Max. Tell me where Britt is or I'll crush your goddamn throat with my bare hands."

Max fights hard, but tires quickly with no air pulling into his lungs. He pushes at my face and I catch a sweet, chemical odor on his fingers. That smell makes me snap. I let go of his neck and before he can recover from the lack of oxygen, I land a punch to his solar plexus, preventing him from taking in a deep breath. When he collapses to the ground, his skin taking on a white pallor, I kick him in the ribs, feeling immense satisfaction at the cracking sound that accompanies my shoe landing on his side.

Killer raises his violent head, begging to unleash on this bastard. I allow one more punch to his face, the crunch of his nose and accompanying scream making the monster in me very, very happy. As much as I desperately want to continue hurting Max, making him suffer, causing him pain beyond anything he could imagine, I stop. It takes more willpower than I've summoned in my life to not beat Max to death. The only thing that stops it is the need to get to Britt.

Max is on the ground, nearly unconscious. I roll him over roughly, not giving a shit about the bits of broken glass digging into his flesh. Once I have his wallet out of his pants, I read his address and throw his shit on the ground next to his bloody face. I'm far from perfect, so I bend over and grab a hunk of hair, yanking his head back.

"You're lucky I didn't fucking kill you, but you better listen good. If I don't find Britt or if she's in any way harmed, I promise, I will finish you."

I let go, his head hitting the ground with a thump. I'm in my car, phone in hand, calling the police to direct them to pick up Max's carcass in the parking garage while speeding toward Britt.

I take the stairs three at a time, sprinting down the hall to number three fifty-five. I don't give a shit anymore if I get arrested and can't fight professionally. All I care about is Britt. Holding her, protecting her, *loving* her.

Without bothering to knock, I raise one leg and begin to kick down the door. It's such a piece of shit it gives after three hard blows, the frame splintering to pieces.

"Britt! Britt! Baby, are you here?" I hurry past the broken doorframe. Close to losing it I mutter to myself. "She better be alive you piece of shit motherfucker!"

I check a tiny kitchen and empty living room without finding a thing. The bathroom is next, also empty, which only leaves one door. When I grip the knob, it turns but doesn't open. I glance down. *The lock is on the outside?* Son of a bitch. It's a padlock. This door is even flimsier than the other and it splits with one kick.

Patting the wall, I find the switch and flip it, illuminating the dark room. Every scorching bit of adrenaline and rage still boiling in my veins frosts over into pure, unadulterated fear. I hurry to the side of the bed in the center of the room, my feet heavier than blocks of lead. Britt is here all right. Her hands and feet are tied together and she's in the middle of something I hoped I'd never have to witness again—a violent, bed-shaking, limb-twitching seizure.

"Oh my god!" I dial nine-one-one, spit out the address, and climb up on the bed, pulling Britt's head onto my lap. Once again, I'm struck completely and absolutely helpless. "Britt, please come back to me," I whisper, stroking her cheeks as her small body thrashes on the mattress, her eyes rolled back in her head. I wrap my arms around as much of her as I can, trying to keep Britt from injuring herself. "Come on, baby. You're strong." More damn tears fall from my eyes, but I hardly notice. My only concern is the woman in my arms. The woman I know I can't live without. "You're stronger than anyone I know, baby. Way stronger than me. Please, Britt. I need you." My sobs grow louder, the sounds ripping from my chest almost inhuman. "I love you! Don't leave me."

Commotion outside catches my attention. Two large paramedics enter the room, bags slung on their shoulders. They begin talking in abbreviations and terms I don't understand, pulling out various syringes and jabbing Britt's pale skin.

"Sir, please let her go. We need to get her to the hospital immediately." I nod woodenly, watching as they load Britt up, looking so tiny on the gurney, and roll her out. It feels like they took my heart with them, placing it on top of Britt on the stretcher. Fitting, since she holds my heart in her hands.

"Are you coming?" one of them shouts at me.

I snap out of my daze and hurry to follow. "Yes."

As I climb into the back of the ambulance, Britt is still convulsing, her frail body twitching in the moonlight. It's complete chaos as the medics continue shooting drugs into her system through an IV in her arm. One of the paramedics keeps giving me strange looks. That's when I realize I'm still shirtless from punching out the car window and probably have streaks of Max's blood on my hands.

Like I give a fuck right now.

I know I'd never leave Britt's side, but a small part of me wants to go back to the parking garage. Take pleasure in hammering Max's face with my fists over and over until it becomes unrecognizable. I know if I did, I'd literally kill him, and I can't take the chance. All I can hope is the police got to him before he was able to get up. Britt needs me right now, and if I go to jail, I can't be there for her.

I need to be there for Britt. Hell, I need her to be there for me. Like I said, Britt literally owns my heart. I'm not strong enough to lose someone else I love.

Britt

My throat is as dry as the cracked brown earth stretching across Death Valley. I swallow, attempting to create some sort of moisture, but all I manage to do is stick my tongue to the roof of my mouth.

Confused, I glance around the bright hospital room and find my mother asleep on one of the recliners.

Why do I keep waking up in hospitals?

Then I remember.

Keller. The invitation. The memories that came back. Max. The cloth.

Was any of it real?

I hold my arms out and see raw red and purple rings circling my wrists. Oh god. It really happened. All of it. My eyes burn, but I'm too dehydrated to create any tears.

"Mom," I croak. She doesn't move. Straining my parched throat, I try louder. "Mom!"

My mother's eyes open slowly, blinking back sleep. When she realizes I'm awake, she jolts upright and rushes to my side, taking my hand.

"Britton? Thank god!" Her lip trembles and her eyes shine

with moisture. "They weren't sure of the extent of the damage from…" She pauses. "It's not important. Let me get the doctor."

Before she can leave, I grab her hand. "Mom?"

She tilts her head in curiosity. I can tell she's itching to get out of here and fetch the doctor. "Britton?"

"Keller? Where is he?"

"Who, darling?" My mother's guilty eyes dart to the side and I know she's aware of exactly who I'm talking about.

"Keller. Fighter. Tattoos. Big." I lick my dry lips in another attempt to wet my mouth. "Where is he?"

My mother grabs a large container with a straw and puts it between my lips. "Drink, darling. They said the medications would dehydrate you. They'll hang another bag of fluids to help."

I suck in gulp after gulp of cool water, letting it soothe my ragged throat. "Thanks," I say when I'm done. "Now. Where. Is. Keller?"

"Let me get the doctor, darling. She needs to know you're awake."

"Mother!" I shout, my voice more clear now that I've had some water. I know my mother's weak spot, and I'm not afraid to use it against her. She will not manipulate me like she did ten years ago. "Tell me where he is right now or I'll inform the hospital staff to keep you out of my room."

Her eyes go wide. "You wouldn't."

Mine narrow. "Try me."

With a huff, Rose Shelton-Reeves flicks her hand through her shoulder-length, blonde hair, tossing it back. "If you must know, that... *man*, is in the waiting room. He's been quite rude and very disruptive." She grimaces.

"Send him in."

"Britton, darling, you can't—"

"It's your choice, Mother. Send him in, or I'll call the nurse, have you removed, and then they will fetch him for me. I'm over eighteen years old and not a child. *I* decide who visits, not you."

My mother gasps, probably remembering how she kept all of my friends from visiting me in the hospital after "the incident." Either out of a misplaced sense of protecting me or because she wanted all of the sympathy for herself, I'm not sure. It doesn't matter, because I'm not allowing her to run roughshod over me again.

"Fine," she says, her lips pressed in a tight line. "I'll get your *friend* and the doctor."

"Great," I respond, lying back and closing my eyes. I have so many questions for Keller, I don't know where to begin.

There's no time to gather my thoughts because Keller barges into the room, his expression one of exhaustion combined with aggravation, probably from my mother keeping him at arm's length.

"Britt! Oh thank god." He rushes to my side and collapses to his knees, throwing his arms around my waist and laying his head in my lap. "I didn't know if you'd wake up. Jesus, I've never been so scared."

My hands find their way to his head, threading through his

messy dark hair. "I'm okay," I say, a lump in my throat forming.

Keller's entire body shakes and I realize he's having some strong emotions of his own. This beautiful man lifts his head, our eyes meeting. I suppress a shiver, remembering the silver eyes of the girl as she died in my arms. Keller opens his mouth to speak.

"Miss Reeves!" the doctor interrupts, gliding into the room, electronic tablet in hand, skimming through what I assume is my chart. "Good to see you awake." She gives me a kind smile and nods at Keller as he climbs to his feet. The doctor turns to Keller. "I see you finally got to see her."

"I did. Thank you, Doctor." Keller takes my hand and stays at my side. I notice he's wearing a blue scrub shirt with his shorts.

"Well, I'm very sorry I couldn't let you in. Next of kin has final say."

"What?" I nearly shout. Two heads turn in my direction and four eyes widen at my outburst. "Are you saying my mother wouldn't let you see me at all? How long have I been here?"

"Only twelve hours," the doctor responds. "But you were missing for almost sixty."

Oh god. Sixty hours with Max. My stomach heaves at the thought.

"Britt," Keller whispers, noticing my distress. "We'll talk later."

I nod, swallowing back the nausea. The doctor steps up and does her exam, flashing a light in my eyes, checking printouts, flipping through screens on the tablet.

"What do you remember, Miss Reeves?"

"Ummmmm." I glance at Keller for help. He merely uses his chin to say *go on and tell her*. "I was going to my car." I leave out the part where I remembered everything about "the incident" and how I freaked out in Keller's condo and was mid-panic attack when I reached the parking garage. "Then I woke tied up." My breath hitches as I think about Max and the horrible time I spent with him. "How did I get here?"

"Mr. Bishop found you in the middle of a cluster of grand mal seizures. It's my opinion that the chloroform used to sedate you plus the lack of your seizure meds are what caused the episode. Thankfully, Mr. Bishop called the paramedics, who administered medication. You haven't had any more seizures and we're monitoring you while we fine-tune your blood levels."

"You found me?" I ask, squeezing Keller's hand.

"Later," he says, squeezing back.

The doctor finishes her notes, informs me that the police will be by later to take my statement in regards to the kidnapping, and breezes out of the room.

"Did... did they catch him? Max, I mean?" My heart hammers so hard I wouldn't be surprised if Keller could hear it.

His face darkens, his eyes turning lethal. "Yes. I found him by your car in my parking garage."

"He-he was getting the keys to my apartment." Keller's brows furrow. "To get my medications for me. I had to tell him about, you know..." My face heats up. I needed my meds."

"Fuck. He's lucky I didn't do more damage to his pathetic ass…" Keller closes his eyes, struggling to remain calm. "Let's just say it's better all around that the police have him in custody."

"I don't want to talk about Max."

"Me either." Keller sits on the edge of the bed, using one hand to brush my hair back, tucking it behind my ear. "Before you say whatever it is you're dying to say, I need to tell you something."

I tense up, wondering if Keller is about to volunteer information about the invitation. Then his eyes go soft and his hand gently caresses my cheek.

"Britt, I-I figured out some stuff while you were… *gone*." He hisses the word *gone* as if it were laced with poison. "Bear with me, I've never done this before." For a brief second, Keller looks uncomfortable, but it doesn't last. His expression returns to soft and kind… and something else on his handsome face I don't recognize. "I realized I love you, Britt. I never thought I'd find love. I definitely don't deserve love, let alone from someone as sweet as you. But I can't help it. I love you."

My mouth falls open in shock. Keller *loves* me? This time, when the tears well up in my eyes, there's enough moisture for them to fall.

"I love you too, Keller. Sometimes I'm strong, but when I'm not, you make the darkness go away. You make me feel safe." I glance down at my lap. "It sounds stupid."

"No," he says, putting a finger under my chin to lift my face back to his. Keller leans forward and presses a chaste kiss to my lips.

"It's not stupid. Nothing about you is stupid."

"Keller…" I take a deep breath, knowing I might be about to ruin everything, destroy the budding love we have for each other. But I have to know about the invitation and Keller deserves to know about me. *No more secrets.* "I freaked out when I saw your invitation."

I hear his sharp inhale and his face goes a little pale. "Yes."

"I have one too. I-I was there, Keller. At the school. I was the only one who…" My voice cracks and the tears flow faster. I sniff and grab a tissue from the bedside table to wipe my nose.

"I know," Keller says.

"What?" My head jerks up.

"I know you're the survivor. The one they never named."

"How? How long have you known?"

Keller trails his fingers down my cheek, swiping away tears with his thumb. "I kind of suspected it after you freaked out, but I didn't know for sure until…" He tapers off.

"I went to your parents' house when I couldn't find you. I spoke with your father."

"Where is my dad?"

"He went to get food for your mother."

I snort and roll my eyes. "My mother doesn't want him here because it takes attention away from her." Keller lurches back at my scathing words. "Oh, please. Tell me you didn't notice that *everything* is about Rose Shelton-Reeves, even when her daughter is unconscious in a hospital bed it's about how much sympathy she can get from the nurses, the staff, whoever happens to be around."

Keller's cheeks turn red and he looks away. "Yeah, I noticed. I wanted to tell her off, but I knew if I did, I'd never get in to see you."

"She'd never have let you in no matter what you did, Keller. That's just how she is." I reach up and this time, I pull Keller's chin until he's looking at me.

"Now," I say. "I need to tell you what happened in your condo."

He nods, so I begin.

Keller

I don't know if I should have stopped her and mentioned my sister died in the shooting, but once Britt begins telling her story, I don't want to interrupt and blurt a bunch of shit out. So I remain silent.

"I was shot in the head, behind my left ear. I got lucky. It wasn't a direct hit. It… it went through…" Her voice cracks. "another person before hitting me so the bullet was slowed down enough that the bullet didn't go in deep." She stops and shudders. "I didn't remember anything from that day. None of it. Or any of the days leading up to the shooting. The doctors said the memories might come back eventually, but I was glad I couldn't remember. I didn't *want* to remember. Who would?"

Britt shudders and all I want to do is pull her into my lap and tell her everything will be okay. But I can't. I don't know if it will be okay or how she feels. Besides, she needs to say this out loud. She needs me to hold her and listen.

"After they took out the bullet, I had to relearn how to do a lot of stuff. They said I could do it physically, but I couldn't remember how. I had to learn to walk again. That was the hardest part." My heart breaks for Britt, for the struggle she went through to regain her independence and make a life for herself after going through so much physical trauma. "I'm deaf in this ear." Britt taps the left side of her head.

"I'm so sorry, Britt."

She scowls. "I don't want pity, Keller. That's why I don't tell anyone. My life isn't about being a victim or a survivor. I just want to put it all behind me and be Britt. I'm not broken."

"I can understand that, and you're not broken, Britt. It might have broken a weaker person, but not you. Never you. I'm in awe of your strength." I understand where she's coming from. I would give anything to put my past behind me. I've created an entire other persona to pretend the past doesn't exist.

"But not remembering didn't mean I wasn't traumatized. I have random panic attacks, bad ones." I remember how she hid under Gabriel's desk when the door banged against the wall. How shaky she was after being in the crowd backstage at the fight. "I never feel safe at home." Her big blue eyes meet mine. "That's why I work at a gym filled with strong, muscled men. The fighters, *you*, make me feel safe. Protected. Anyone who comes through the door to hurt me would never get to me."

"No," I say. "They wouldn't."

"That's one of the things I love about you, Keller. You make me feel safe. It's something about you specifically, being in your arms."

I nod, speechless. She does the same for me. Makes me feel human, that is.

"Anyway, the memories have been trying to come back for a while. I have dreams where I see little bits and pieces here and there. But you…" Britt studies my face. "Your eyes," she whispers, raising a hand to touch the thin circle of skin just below my right eye. "They were so familiar, but I didn't know why."

No. My body tenses, liquid ice drips down my spine.

"I saw your invitation and I knew. Somehow I knew."

"My sister," I rasp, amazed I can make any sound at all.

"Yes. I-I held her, Keller. We…" Britt chokes on a cry. "We held each other. I saw… I watched her die. Her eyes. How they lost their life. It's the last thing I saw before…" Britt reaches back and touches her scar. "I'm so sorry, Keller." Britt is openly sobbing, her tiny frame shaking as she lets out a decade of misery. "She saved me… her body was between me and the… the…"

Stunned by her revelation, I try to stand, to get a minute to put myself together, but Britt has a death grip on my hand.

"Keller! Don't leave me!" Britt's eyes are wide with panic. "I'm sorry. I didn't know. I didn't remember!"

"Just…just give me a second." I tug my hand free and run it through my hair and over the stubble that grew overnight.

Britt held Kinsey as she died. Britt was shot in the head. They were together. My sister's body saved Britt from certain death.

Everything crashes over me at once, the tsunami of emotions I've held back breaks through the dam, washing away the last vestiges of Killer, leaving Keller Keating alone and vulnerable to deal with the fallout. After ten years of hiding behind anger and violence, I have no choice but to face my grief. As my shields erode, guilt rises to the surface, exposed and raw as my divided soul repairs itself.

I turn to Britt, my vision blurred with tears. "I killed her, Britt. I was supposed to pick her up after school and forgot. It was my fault my little sister died."

"No! Keller, that's not true."

"It is. I was so selfish, Britt. I forgot about Kinsey because I wanted to party and she died." My legs nearly give out from the sheer weight of my sister's death pressing down.

"Keller, please. Come hold me."

Britt's voice is like a beacon in the fog, pulling me in.

"Your sister saved my life, Keller. I'll never forget that."

Britt lowers the side of the bed and I climb in, pulling her warmth against my chest, heating my frigid skin. We stay wrapped up like that, holding, caressing, comforting each other through our shared pain. Eventually, Britt pulls back, brushing her lips over mine.

"Maybe we can find our way out of the darkness together," she says.

"Maybe."

Britt lays her head back on my chest and I bury my nose in her hair. For a brief moment, I allow myself the luxury of believing everything will turn out all right. Just this one time, maybe it can.

CHAPTER 14

Epilogue

Ten years later.

Britt

"Honestly, Marco. If you don't stay off of it, you won't be able to fight next month." I look over my laptop and shoot the young fighter a serious look.

"I'm sorry. I didn't plan on injuring it again."

Shaking my head, I finish typing my notes and walk over to the exam table.

"I don't say things I don't mean, Marco. If I tell you to elevate your ankle and keep weight off of it, I'm not secretly saying 'go jogging then jump rope for an hour.' Understand?"

The young man nods, properly chagrined.

"Okay. You're all wrapped up and iced. Go home and keep it up, I want you here in two days so I can look at it again." I tap his leg gently and step back, knowing he won't want help getting down from the table. They never do.

"Thanks, Britt." Marco gives me a crooked smile and heads for the office door.

"Oh, and Marco?" He stops and glances over his shoulder.

"You get to tell the boss what happened."

The fighter's eyes nearly bulge from his head. "No, no, no. You need to do it for me. Please? Oh my god, he'll kill me." Marco's olive skin is significantly paler than a minute ago.

"For Pete's sake, he won't kill you."

"Oh yes he will." Marco shakes his head. "He's scary as hell. I don't know how you do it."

I laugh and pat the young man's shoulder. "He's really not that scary, Marco. Just… ummmm," I have to concentrate to keep from smiling. "Just don't look in his eyes when you tell him. That'll help." I push the reluctant fighter out of my office and close the door, managing to last until it clicks in place before I burst out in a fit of the giggles.

I clean up the table, spraying it with disinfectant, and toss the open wrappers. My conscious gets the better of me. With a sigh, I go to my desk and pick up the phone.

"Hello, my love."

"Keller." I grin even though he can't see it.

"To what do I owe this pleasure?"

Boy, he's laying it on thick today, not that I mind. Not one bit. "Marco is coming to see you. Can you go easy on him?"

"Britt," Keller warns.

"I know, I know. I'm too soft on the fighters. You've told me. Just, don't make him pee his pants."

Keller's laugh lights up my insides, filling me with warmth and love. Laughs were rare our first few years together. Between Max's trial in which he was sentenced to twenty-five years in jail, my therapy for PTSD, and Keller dealing with his sister's death, neither of us had much to laugh about. Then our life completely changed and the good times began to outweigh the bad.

"I won't make him pee his pants, I promise," Keller says when he finally stops laughing. I hear a soft knock on his door though the receiver. "I believe I have a visitor."

"Be nice," I warn.

"I'm always nice," he drawls in his sexy voice. The one that after ten years together still gets me hot and bothered in less than three seconds flat.

"Love you."

"Love you too." The phone clicks off and I grin, a silly, stupid, lovestruck grin. Why wouldn't I? I have everything.

Keller

I shut down my computer and head into the main area of the gym.

"Bye!" I look up to see Roxie heading out the front door.

"See you Monday, Roxie." I wave as she leaves.

Left alone in the huge space, I put a few things back where they belong and turn off a few lights. When Gabriel retired a few years ago, he asked if I wanted to take his place as head trainer. After five years of fighting and winning three AFL Championships, I was ready to spend more time at home and less time training and traveling to fights.

The door to the gym opens and footsteps pound on the cement floor, echoing in the warehouse-like space.

"Daddy!"

Two colorful blurs dash across the mats and leap on top of me. I pretend to be knocked over and fall to the padded ground. "Oh no, you took me down!"

"That's because my takedowns are the best, Daddy."

"Nuh-uh! Mine are. Besides, my arm bar is better than yours!"

The two boys begin bickering so I hold up my hands. Instantly, two sets of eyes focus on me and the noise stops.

"You're both excellent fighters, okay?"

They seem to think that over for a minute.

"Okay, Daddy," says Gabriel, my oldest, who is almost eight.

Not only is my son named after the only man to ever believe in me, a man who has become a father to me, but my little Gabriel really is an angel like his namesake. Britt and I were both having a hard time working through our pasts when we found out she was unexpectedly pregnant almost two years after we met, pushing me into finally getting the courage to give Britt the diamond ring I had stashed in my dock drawer for several months.

Something about creating a new life, being parents, sparked our determination to move on from our pain. To live how Kinsey would have wanted. I can't bring my sister back. I can only accept the gift she gave me by saving Britt, honor her by being a good man. A good husband. A good father. Everything our parents weren't.

"I don't know. I still say I'm better than Gabe," Lucas pipes in. At five, he doesn't understand the concept of losing or good sportsmanship, but I'm working on it.

"No you're not!" Gabe shouts.

"Lucas, you are both very talented and I'm proud of you." I get up and haul them with me, one in each arm so they don't start grappling right then and there.

"Hey! You guys coming?"

Britt is leaning in the doorway, trying to hold on to the wiggling pink bundle in her arms.

"We're coming." I put the boys down so they can race each other to the car and shake my head. Everything is a competition with those two. Literally everything. Who can eat faster, who can jump higher, who knows more superhero trivia. It never ends.

I flip off the final lights and crowd Britt against the doorframe, giving her a sweet but lingering kiss. "And how is my gorgeous wife?"

"Ready to eat," she says, giving me a wink that lets me know she's not thinking about food.

"Daddy!" Two chubby hands reach out for me. Backing away from Britt, I sweep our daughter into my arms, making loud raspberries against her soft neck. She squeals in delight, the sound going straight to my heart.

"How's my little Kinsey? What did you do at preschool today?"

"We made puppets and mine had a lot of glitter and it spilled everywhere, but Miss Martinez said it was okay." My adorable little girl goes on and on about the trials and tribulations of being three years old while I lock the front door of Sousa MMA.

By the time Britt and I make it to the car, the boys are loudly arguing over which one of them runs faster. The whole time, Kinsey is still giving a play-by-play commentary on crafting puppets. Britt breaks up the fight while I strap Kinsey in her seat. Britt and I have to tag team Gabe and Luke, wrestling them into their car seats before we drop, exhausted, into our own seats.

I start the car and look over at my wife, my love, my soul mate. The woman who pulled me from darkness and showed me beauty in the light. She threads our fingers together and smiles while the three kids battle over which superhero is the best, Superman, Batman, or Wonder Woman. It's chaos and love. Arguments and hugs. Boo-boos and sweet kisses.

It's absolute perfection.

* * *

AUTHOR'S NOTE

Some of you may be wondering about the shooter. Why did he do what he did? Who was he? What were his motivations that brought him to commit such a heinous crime?

My answer? It doesn't matter. *Killer* is a story about the victims and how they stumble through life after such a traumatic event. The shooter's motivation doesn't make one bit of difference in Keller or Britt's journey in healing.

There is no excuse for what the shooter did. What does it matter what he was thinking? Nothing is reason enough to walk into a school and fire a weapon at staff and students. Nothing.

Do Britt and Keller know the shooter's reasons? Possibly. If they needed it for closure, maybe his reason was known and I just didn't feel the need to include it in their story. Maybe the shooter didn't leave a note. Maybe his reasons weren't clear. Maybe everyone is left wondering.

This book is not about the shooter. It is about the journey of the victims. I hope you enjoyed it.

Thank you for reading.

Heather C. Leigh

BOOKS

As Heather C. Leigh- M/F Romance

Killer (a dark romance

The Famous Series

Relatively Famous

Absolutely Famous

Extremely Famous

Already Famous (Drew's POV)

Suddenly Famous (a novella)

Reluctantly Famous (a novella)

Sphere of Irony (a rock star series)

Incite — Adam

Strike — Dax

Resist — Gavin

Wreck — Hawke

Ricochet— Military Romantic Suspense

Locked & Loaded

Friendly Fire

Extraction Point

As Leigh Carman- M/M Romance

Sports of the Seasons -by Dreamspinner Press 2016

Match Point- Volleyball (Summer)

Fair Catch- Football (Fall)

Power Play- Hockey (Winter)

Full Count- Baseball (Spring)